Andrew Ogden had a career in broadcasting before forming his own media company. He has four children, a dog called Dave, and lives in Norfolk.

To my late grandmother, who could reach back through dementia and tell vivid stories of her childhood.

Andrew Ogden

FINDING ALFIE: A SANDRINGHAM MYSTERY

AUSTIN MACAULEY PUBLISHERS

LONDON * CAMBRIDGE * NEW YORK * SHARJAH

Copyright © Andrew Ogden 2024

The right of Andrew Ogden to be identified as the author of this work has been asserted by the author in accordance with sections 77 and 78 of the Copyright, Designs and Patents Act 1988.

All rights reserved. No part of this publication may be reproduced, stored in a retrieval system, or transmitted in any form or by any means, electronic, mechanical, photocopying, recording, or otherwise, without the prior permission of the publishers.

Any person who commits any unauthorised act in relation to this publication may be liable to criminal prosecution and civil claims for damages.

This is a work of fiction. Names, characters, businesses, places, events, locales, and incidents are either the products of the author's imagination or used in a fictitious manner. Any resemblance to actual persons, living or dead, or actual events is purely coincidental.

A CIP catalogue record for this title is available from the British Library.

ISBN 9781035871094 (Paperback)
ISBN 9781035871100 (Hardback)
ISBN 9781035871117 (ePub e-book)

www.austinmacauley.com

First Published 2024
Austin Macauley Publishers Ltd®
1 Canada Square
Canary Wharf
London
E14 5AA

Thanks to David Stilgoe for the first draft proofreading and period rural affairs corrections.

Table of Contents

Chapter 1: Norfolk, Present Day — 11

Chapter 2: Norfolk, Present Day — 15

Chapter 3: Norfolk, Present Day — 19

Chapter 4: Norfolk, Present Day — 23

Chapter 5: Norfolk, Present Day — 28

Chapter 6: Norfolk, Present Day — 33

Chapter 7: Norfolk, Present Day — 37

Chapter 8: Norfolk, Present Day — 41

Chapter 9: Norfolk, 1933 — 47

Chapter 10: Norfolk, 1933 — 53

Chapter 11: Norfolk, Present Day — 59

Chapter 12: Norfolk, Present Day — 65

Chapter 13: Norfolk, Present Day — 70

Chapter 14: Norfolk, 1933 — 75

Chapter 15: Norfolk, 1933 — 80

Chapter 16: Norfolk, Present Day — 85

Chapter 17: Norfolk, Present Day — 89

Chapter 18: Norfolk, Present Day — 93

Chapter 19: Lincolnshire, 1933 — 97

Chapter 20: Norfolk, Present Day — 102

Chapter 21: Liverpool, 1933	107
Chapter 22: Norfolk, Present Day	112
Chapter 23: Belfast, 1933	116
Chapter 24: Irish Free State, 1933	121
Chapter 25: Norfolk, Present Day	125
Chapter 26: Norfolk, Present Day	129
Chapter 27: Irish Free State, 1933	133
Chapter 28: Irish Free State, 1933	136
Chapter 29: Irish Free State, 1933	140
Chapter 30: Irish Free State, 1933	146
Chapter 31: Irish Free State, 1933	151
Chapter 32: Norfolk, Present Day	157
Chapter 33: Irish Free State, 1933	161
Chapter 34: Norfolk, Present Day	166
Chapter 35: Irish Free State, 1933	170
Chapter 36: Norfolk, Present Day	175
Chapter 37: Norfolk, Present Day	180
Chapter 38: Norfolk, Present Day	185
Chapter 39: Norfolk, Present Day	189
Chapter 40: Ireland, 1954 Onwards	193
Chapter 41: Norfolk, Present Day	196
Chapter 42: Donegal Town, Present Day	200
Chapter 43: Donegal Town, Present Day	204
Chapter 44: Donegal Town, Present Day	208
Chapter 45: Norfolk, Present Day	218
Chapter 46: Norfolk, Present Day	222
Chapter 47: Morecambe, Lancashire, Present Day	224

Chapter 1
Norfolk, Present Day

When Simon Jones was killed, no one saw it happen.

It's not as if there weren't plenty of people around.

Dersingham may not be the busiest village in Norfolk, but it's not the quietest either, and while just after eight in the morning could not by any stretch be described as a 'rush' hour, it is, perhaps, fair to describe it as a 'bustle' hour.

Children were being ferried to school, builders' vans were setting off to sites along the coast, postie was on his rounds and the handful of shops along the main drag were opening up for another day's trade.

Simon Jones had just been to one such shop. The florist. And he wasn't happy.

He'd described in some detail the bouquet he wanted and he'd wanted it bang on opening time. He didn't want to wait while a still morning groggy Debbie Jones painstakingly added red rose to white chrysanthemum again and again until the masterpiece was complete. Or was it?

"Bit of gyp and some fern to finish it off?" she asked.

"Did I put that in the email?" said Simon Jones.

Missing the sarcasm by some distance, she checked the printed-off email on the counter in front of her.

"No," she said.

"Then put a bow on it and give it to me." Humour, as in good, and humour, as in ha ha ha, were not Simon Jones' strong suits.

Still, it wouldn't matter much longer.

Yes, Dersingham was bustling that morning. Pavement traffic was lighter than street traffic, but still, plenty of people were on their morning manoeuvres.

Funny that not one of them saw Simon Jones killed a minute or so after leaving the florist shop.

But there again, not many people have ever seen a car crash.

They think they have.

They'll rush home and tell mothers and fathers, brothers and sisters, friends, barmen, shopkeepers and strangers all about it.

Sometimes for weeks afterwards.

But, in truth, not many people have actually seen a car crash.

This is a problem for all sorts of people because, when there's a car crash, it's important to know—exactly—what really happened.

Blue police signs advertise for people who think they've seen a car crash.

Fatal accident here. Did you see it? Call this number.

And plenty of people will call that number. And they will talk at length about an accident which, in reality, they didn't actually see.

No, a car crash isn't just a single, final, metal-bending event. That's the interesting bit. That's the final scene. But there's much, much more to a car crash than just that.

The police know all about these things. They need to establish car number 1, where it came from and where it was going. They need to know who was driving and who was on board. They need to know the make, the model, the speed and the state of repair.

Car number 2 leaves from a different point, usually, is probably differently sized and powered, maybe a different colour, although grey and shades of grey seem to make up an absurdly large proportion of cars these days.

Anyway, car number 2 is likely to be a different make and model. It must be very rare indeed for two cars of exactly the same make, model, age, repair and colour to crash into each other.

So the clear differences between car number 1 and car number 2 would, you'd think, make it much easier for those people who say they've seen a car crash to make those differential points. For the contrast in vehicles to make it plain to all those who claim to have seen the accident and to give precise and consistent accounts.

But, in reality, they don't.

When the police number was called and those who saw the crash gave their accounts, car number 1, let's call this Simon Jones' car, could have been driving anywhere between 30 and 50 miles an hour, in a straight line or weaving on the road both pre and post-impact and so much more. There could have been brakes applied, or not. Car number 2 could have been across the white lines, or not. There was a swerve to avoid a big/small brown/black dog. Or cat. Or not.

Time, so much the constant dimension, so precise a measurement, bends hopelessly. It was anywhere between five and ten past the hour. For car number 1 to enter the crash scene took anywhere between 5 seconds and half a minute, and it was anywhere between a minute and three minutes before the first help arrived, in the shape of a man, or two men, who ran out of the Caffe Nero coffee shop, Sue Ryder shop, or from round a corner.

No, not many people have actually seen a car crash.

What they can say with much more accuracy is what they themselves were doing. Where they place themselves in this scene. What part, active or passive, did they play in this event?

They were walking, with the dog, to get the morning paper. They were coming back from a visit to the doctor's, from checking on an elderly relative, looking over the shoulder of a delivery driver. They can identify themselves in the dramatis personae. But they can't describe the scene with any real authority or accuracy. They are players of a part in a scene which has been improvised, not rehearsed.

Feelings, well, they are very real. They can say how they feel about it. It was terrifying. It was horrific. It was such a terrible shame. It was a great pity, wasn't it, that car number 2 didn't see what was coming the other way.

The actual event is a mirage but the emotions are real.

One person who did, actually, see the car crash was Dr Simon Jones.

Or rather Mr Simon Jones, consultant dermatologist at West Norfolk Hospitals NHS Foundation Trust, or St Margaret's as everyone still called it.

Mr Jones had left home that morning as he always did, at 0730, just after the sports news on the *Today* programme on the BBC. He got into his car, a Range Rover, diesel, 4-litre turbo, 5 years old, Westminster pack, Pennine Grey. He drove steadily from Westfield Farm House along the winding county lanes of Norfolk until Heacham where he pulled into the BP garage, filled up with diesel and bought a bottle of water.

Avoiding the tailbacks of traffic on the by-pass, he made his way via roundabouts and traffic lights through to Dersingham where he stopped at exactly opening time to pick up his bouquet and then pressed on down the main street and that's where he saw the car crash.

Coming out of a side road, between the playground and the next line of little houses and occasional shops which ran like ribbons of brick and flint along both sides of the road, came a VW Golf, GTi, Tornado Red, just about maintained, 89,000 miles, not very quickly but possibly a little too wide.

That's when Mr Simon Jones saw his car crash.

Mark Elwin didn't see a car crash that day.

He'd just come downstairs from the flat over his photography shop, had picked up the mail and was contemplating the brown official-looking items with indifference.

No, Mark Elwin didn't see a car crash that day, but he heard one. A very short howl of brakes, an even shorter thump and scrape, a woman's scream, a child crying, a shout of "call an ambulance."

Simon Jones saw the crash all right. But he saw nothing after that.

Mark Elwin heard the crash and looking at the clock on his shop wall registered the time as 0811. He heard the crash and noted the exact time that Simon Jones died. He heard the very moment that Ellen Jones became a widow at the age of just 38. He heard the exact moment when 6-year-old twins Sam and Gemma Jones became fatherless.

But he didn't see the car crash that day. Apart from Simon Jones, no one did.

Chapter 2
Norfolk, Present Day

Mark Elwin looked at the scene unravelling on the road and the pavement directly in front of him.

After looking at the clock he picked up his Canon EOS 350 DSLR camera and started firing off shots through the shop window.

It wasn't his best camera but it was his nearest, a relatively inexpensive workhorse already laid out ready to take shot after shot after shot of pug-faced boys and girls in all classes of St Who-really-cares infant school later that day.

After a quick digital blast through the window, he took the two strides to the door, stepped outside and started taking more pictures.

First, as wide as he could, both cars.

Then still on wide, action around the Tornado Red VW, where a man in, a brown jacket, about 30, was trying to wrench open the driver's door.

Quickly, action around the Pennine Grey Range Rover, where a woman stood, small child by her side, her hands to her mouth, her pale blue eyes wide open registering something between horror and disgust. The date and time information embedded in the camera's SD memory card showed that this picture was taken at 0812.

The next images captured the woman turning away from the car, head and shoulders down, protecting the child from seeing anything. More accurately, she was protecting the child from seeing anything more. 0813.

From wide to medium close-ups of short tyre scorch marks on the road behind the Range Rover, the damage to the front passenger side wing where evasive action had proved too little, too late. The V-shaped caving in of the passenger side wing and door of the VW shows it sharing the road, almost head-on.

0814 and here's a shot of the man in the brown jacket taking a metal milk bottle holder produced, from who knows where, by an elderly woman in slippers and a house coat.

He smashes the window of the Tornado Red VW, reaches inside the car, releases the door and starts to pull a woman from the car.

Close-ups now, of her face, half screaming, half crying, her legs flopping around underneath her like a badly managed marionette, the man in the brown jacket carrying her, no dragging her towards the pavement. By now a second man stops being a spectator and joins the cast, chunky knit sweater, jeans, fashionable tearing at the knees and helps the woman sit down on the pavement edge. Still only 0814.

Three steps to one side and close-ups now of Mr Simon Jones, head deep in the billowing airbag, face very slightly turned to one side.

By 0816 Mark Elwin was two steps forward, very close up. Click whirr. One eye is visible. Click whirr. One eye open. Click whirr. Dead.

The man in the brown jacket pushes him hard.

"Fuck off man, what are you doing taking pictures," and, finger out, pointing straight at Mark Elwin, he takes an aggressive step forwards.

"He's dead, nothing you can do." And the man in the brown jacket looks back and his face registers the truth of what he'd just been told.

Mark Elwin then retreated, backwards, six, eight steps, to the doorway of his shop. Sirens could now be heard, police from the east from Hunstanton, ambulances from the west, from the West Norfolk Hospitals NHS Foundation Trust.

He fired off a few more shots but only really from some residual professional instinct to complete the narrative. By now, bystanders numbered twenty people or more and the crowd was growing all the time. Budgen's, 'Your Local Supermarket' was emptying and elderly shoppers with paniers on wheeled push frames joined at the back and asked veterans of the crowd what had happened.

Mechanics from AFC Motors wandered up the lane past the allotments to see what was going on, but not wanting to get too close they were perching up on tiptoes to see as much as they could, but from a distance.

The crowd was mostly quiet. Occasionally people turned to stranger-neighbours and whispered a hushed word or two.

The police and ambulance arrived, with noise and energy and shouting directions to each other and everyone on the road.

Most of those in the crowd under 70 years old were taking footage on their iPhones, Samsungs, or whatever brand they favoured this month.

There was a time, thought Mark Elwin, that his photographs, professional photographs, by a recognised freelance news photographer, would have fetched £50 from the *King's Lynn News*.

There was a time, about the time when the baby was young there was no money, that the few remaining occasional freelance shifts for the local press brought in much-needed extra funds: a charity event featuring the great and good of the county; various Royals down for Christmas at Sandringham; the first day of the partridge shooting season; morning mists sneaking over the marshes at Titchwell. Easy money.

Now everyone was a freelance photographer. Mark watched as a couple of dozen phones were held aloft.

"Thanks, iPhone," he said to himself and turned into the shop. It was time for another brew.

In the road, it was a matter of official process and procedure. Fire crews arrived but by then Mr Simon Jones had been pulled out, laid out, stretchered out and was being taken away at needlessly high speed to the accompanying sound of retreating sirens and flashing lights. There was no rush really.

Minutes of action turned into minutes of procedure, the tape was reeled out, official photographs were taken, the road closed in both directions, cars parked inside the cordon ushered out, diversions put in place, and names and addresses and mobile phone numbers taken of all those who stepped forwards to say that they had, definitely, seen the car crash.

Mark Elwin closed the shop door and left the sign on the door as "Sorry, closed." There'd be no passing trade for a while. He called Trish, his assistant. There'd been an accident, he said, the road was closed. She couldn't get to work and anyway, he'd closed the shop. She might as well just meet him at the school for the pug-faced kids photo session this afternoon. He'd bring the kit. Trish had already laid it out by the back door of the shop, ready.

By noon the recovery vehicles had been, wrecked cars winched into piggyback positions and taken away to the police car pound for further forensic tests, if required.

The road was open again, a fact relayed to the waiting public of West Norfolk and Wisbech by the local radio station playing at volume four from the back of the shop.

Only fragments of glass from the smashed VW and the indicator lights of the Range Rover remained in the gutters of the road. Litter was the only evidence that a life had ended there, that day.

Apart from on the pavements in both directions, at distances of two hundred and a hundred metres or so, police signs.

Fatal accident here. Did you see it? Call this number.

Mark Elwin hadn't seen the accident. But he had got a couple of hundred images of what happened next.

They might be useful, he thought. His lightweight aluminium flight cases were packed and loaded with lights, screens, cameras, batteries and all the kit he needed to capture the images of the pug-faced children for adoring mums and dads, aunties and uncles, nans and grandads. The more the merrier at £5 a copy.

Before loading his car, he called the number.

"So you saw the fatal accident today then did you, Sir?"

"No," he said.

Chapter 3
Norfolk, Present Day

Emma McMillan was diagnosed with multiple sclerosis when she was 26 and the baby wasn't quite two.

On the scale of 'manageable' to 'life-altering', she was relieved to be reassured it was down at the 'manageable' end.

Her husband left her a couple of weeks later, maybe three. It was a while ago but the emotional turmoil of the diagnosis, being abandoned and having to pull herself together for the sake of Daisy meant she had put away all of the swirling emotions of that time in her life. Locked them away and hadn't let them out since.

She was now 36 and Daisy was 12.

These were better times. Daisy was a good girl and she was doing well at school. She had asked to join the after-school reading club and she loved playing football on Saturday mornings for the Docking Devils.

Mother and Daughter had their term time routine. Every day after dropping her off at school Emma drove the short distance to her favourite sandwich shop to select a baguette for her lunch before going on to Hunstanton and the offices of Scammell and Partners, Chartered Accountants and Tax Advisors.

She was the office assistant manager.

The job was ideal. The part-time hours allowed her to take and pick up Daisy from school, there were nice colleagues, everyone was in smart office suits, the kitchen had a decent coffee machine and the money was okay. There was even 'working from home' if there was childhood sickness in their little cottage. The money, a little help from the government and lots of help from her mum and dad and life was very much okay. Better times indeed.

The MS did turn out to be mercifully mild. She was occasionally a little unsteady walking and the numbness and tingling down her legs could drive her insane some days. Her blurred vision was helped by some new, rather chic she thought, glasses.

On the bad days, and there were bad days, she was just very, very, very tired. The cannabis helped.

None of that psychedelic skunk stuff. No. Just a gentle little joint of old-fashioned California grass sourced from a nice Lithuanian chap in King's Lynn and mixed with dried purple clover from a local health shop. Emma McMillan couldn't stand smoking. Emma McMillan couldn't stand rudeness, swearing, poor time keeping and clothes that weren't ironed. She was, what her father called, quite proper.

But she did smoke cannabis.

She knew she shouldn't really drive and at first, years ago, it did bother her, guilt every trip. But that was years and years ago. Now she had convinced herself it actually made her a better driver. No wobbly legs drove very carefully and always within the speed limit.

"Oh, come on Mum!" was the most common start to a car-based conversation with Daisy.

There's a backseat driver in the making, Emma thought. She will make a husband very cross one day, and the thought made her smile. Always.

"It's not funny!" Daisy would say with petulance which only hinted at the potential teenage anger years looming in the near future. "We're going to be late for school/the party/ballet/anything/everything."

"The speed limit is 30. I'm doing 29," Emma said. "Now 28. Back to 29. So I'm what you call, Daisy McMillan, a good driver."

It didn't look that way today.

After dropping off Daisy at the school gates with all the other school-run mums, and they were all mums, she went to get lunch. Another day, same routine. Today she had selected a brie and cranberry baguette for lunch with a small pot of olives and a bottle of SmartWater. She got into her treasured VW Golf GTI and edged out onto the main road.

Mr Simon Jones must have been very surprised indeed to see the Tornado Red VW Golf GTI present itself immediately before him, but no one would ever really know.

Emma McMillan certainly did not see a car crash that day. It appeared out of nowhere. She was sneaking a quick look the other way when boom! And for her, it was lights out.

When her head cleared a couple of moments later, she was staring at the sky. Why?

She was aware she was moving but couldn't feel her feet on the ground, but that was not entirely unusual.

A man in a brown jacket said "It's all right love, you've been in a car accident. Are you all right?"

No, she thought. I've been in a car accident.

And as she thought she did a full mental body scan. Nothing really, really hurt. Maybe her shoulder, a little. She couldn't really tell. She tried to stand up into the arms of the man in the brown jacket but he had another idea.

"Here you go love, just sit on the pavement here and wait for the ambulance," and he shouted 'Ambulance' and louder still, "Has anyone called an ambulance?" He started to reach for his mobile phone.

And from the crowd, as if as an offstage cry during a Shakespearean battle, someone shouted back "Yes, they're on their way." He put his phone back in his pocket.

"Wait here love, the ambulance is on its way."

"Why is that man taking pictures?" was her reply, pointing to the man directly in front of them. And then Mark Elwin was gone and her view was opened up but without her glasses, all she could see were colours and mist and shapes and movement.

"Where are my glasses? I can't see without my glasses," she said. But the man in the brown jacket was gone.

A couple of minutes ahead of the ambulance in Dersingham, that day was PC Ian Adams.

Parking up, blocking the road, lights flashing on his police car he went first to the Range Rover.

The dead take no time to triage. He just ordered everyone away from the Range Rover and in his mind, he left that one for the paramedics.

He went to Emma McMillan.

"Hello. Have you been in this accident? Is that your car there? The red VW? Are you ok? There's an ambulance on its way. Are you okay sitting there and waiting for the ambulance?"

"Yes," she said.

"What's your name?"

"Emma McMillan," she said.

"Are you ok?" asked PC Ian Adams, again.

"Yes," she said.

And so he asked his other questions and she told him her name, her address, where she'd been, where she was going and PC Ian Adams wrote it all down in his notebook.

He kept looking over his shoulder at the Range Rover and at one point shouted to a young man in jeans and a hoody "You…yes you, get away from that car and back onto the pavement. Now!"

He turned back to Emma McMillan.

"Are you sure you're ok?" he asked again.

"I'm okay," she said.

And then she said, "I've been smoking cannabis."

"Say again," said the policeman.

"I've smoked cannabis. This morning before taking my daughter to school. I'm on my way to work."

Within twenty minutes she'd be seen by a paramedic, who asked again if she was alright, again she said she was fine, the paramedic looked at PC Adams and shrugged and nodded and Emma McMillan was eased into the back of another police car and was taken to King's Lynn police station.

Chapter 4
Norfolk, Present Day

Lower Farm Care Home hadn't been close to farmland for the best part of 60 years as the ugly post-war sprawl of homes for heroes crept up the road from King's Lynn towards what was once the village of South Wootton.

It was hard to tell which end of that particular journey these days was the least attractive.

Lauretta Harrison had left school at 14 like everyone else in from her class at Sandringham School. From lessons in Arithmetic and English under the tree in the school field that hot, hot summer of 1940, in her pretty uniform with her friends, she went straight to E H Abbott Ltd. (Fish Wholesaler) working alongside the whelk men, cockle men, fish wives, porters, packers, ice house men and van drivers, slicing, gutting, boiling and despatching stone after stone of fish and shellfish from the E.H. Abbott sheds just back from one of the main jetties at King's Lynn port.

Fishing was a restricted trade in the war and so a lot of the men were young and strong and rough and they, along with old man Abbott himself, were having a pretty good war.

Churchill had famously refused to ration fish and chips as being bad for the morale of the nation and the E.H. Abbott vans waited in turn with despatch notes and stacks of iced fish, the good stuff ready for the tables and the chip shop newspaper of Norwich and Cambridge, sea bass, oysters and lobsters for the grand tables of London.

It was hard and filthy work. At just 14 years old she was given few concessions, certainly not from the language of the men, and even though some of the women sometimes chipped in 'mind your language, young girl here' or to Lauretta herself 'take no notice lovely' nothing stopped them. Lauretta's jobs covered everything from being the char lady for the managers at 11 in the morning and 3 in the afternoon, which was the easy part, to being the general dogsbody. The worst job was pushing crate loads of guts out into the back yard where men with horses and carts would take them away either to be used as bait on the next ship out or to be strewn over farmland as fertiliser. Nothing was wasted.

By the time she was 30, she had risen, if that's the right word, to being the E.H. Abbott Housekeeper, the duties for which still included being char lady for the managers but also included being the office cleaner and, worst of all, at the start of every working day, cleaning and mopping out the two vast asbestos workers' toilet blocks, one for the men, one for the women. It was hard to tell which of the two was generally the filthiest. At nine o'clock each morning, she put up a 'Cleaning in Progress' sign on the main door handle of each block and after bowls had been scraped clean and the stale urine mopped off the floors, she declared the toilets once again fit for use.

Lauretta was affectionately known to the hundred or so porters, processors, drivers and fishwives at E.H. Abbott as the Chief Petty Officer, partly because of the seagoing nature of the business, but mostly because, well, mostly because she cleaned the toilets.

The place stank of fish, of course it did, as did Lauretta a lot of the time, the stink sticking to the clothes and hair of everyone who worked there. Guts sloshed across the floor and were hosed down into gullies. Whelks and cockles were dragged out of the Wash, boiled and the shells chucked into big bins for taking away to be buried in worked-out quarries and gravel pits along the coast.

Sometimes the work was frantic. When the vast seasonal shoals of herring and cod, bass and mackerel made their way steadily down the coast from Scotland to the North Norfolk beaches the fishing boats could go out for two and three days until their holds were full of fish ready to be sold on the port side market and taken off to E. H. Abbott and others for processing.

In 1950, a fresh-faced 24-year-old Lauretta Harrison met a gentle-faced boilerman called Jack Carey at a Saturday night dance 'down Lynn'. They married six months later when she was two months late and Jean was born and brought home to live with Mum and Dad in one of the new 'temporary' pre-fab bungalows. Lauretta and Jack put their names down with the council and waited for a proper house. There were no more children.

Lauretta Carey would have been around 35 when her future care home was slowly being circled by ugliness, the marshland drained and ancient tracks to the

Wash turned into row after row of semi-detached uniformity. Ugliness and uniformity which remained.

By the side of her bed at Lower Farm Care Home was a wooden carriage clock with 'Tempus Fugit' engraved on a little brass plate. Underneath it said 'To Lauretta Carey on your retirement. From the Directors of E.H. Abbott' and she had cried, when she was presented with it. She was 60. That was 35 years ago.

It didn't keep time. It might have done, had she wound it up. But it was one of the many, very many, mundane aspects of everyday life which now, at 95, completely passed her by.

Two years after she retired to the council house, they'd waited ten years for, Jack died from a stroke, following an unremarkable career as a boilerman and a quiet life of devotion to King's Lynn football club. The sight of a nearly brand-new Vauxhall outside the house testament to the fact this wasn't expected. Jean died six years after that, from cigarettes. It didn't stop Lauretta from smoking.

E.H. Abbott was still there. It was smaller, but it was still there.

Most of the fishing fleet and the chaos of King's Lynn fish port from the decades either side of the War were all but gone. The fish were still taken from the North Sea but these days by foreign trawlers, and vast fishing factories, allowed there under some deal, some quota rules, some last-minute trade stitch up with Europe that still rankled in King's Lynn two generations later.

Just a few boats were hanging on in King's Lynn and Brancaster Staithe and Wells-next-the-Sea to supply E.H. Abbott and in turn the new gastropubs feeding the Chelsea boys and girls up on the trendy Norfolk coast for second homes and hols. Gentrification had almost finished creeping over the old fishermen's cottages. They were not for locals now. The once rowdy, ramshackle pubs, The Jolly Sailors, The Hero and The Ship now sanitised so that each pub proclaimed Eat, Drink, Rest and all sported new coats of Farrow and Ball paint.

'Come on Lauretta, it's time for some lovely dinner' said the sturdy woman in a blue sort of nurse's uniform after she knocked on the bedroom door and bundled herself into the little space between the single bed and the window, where Lauretta, in her wheelchair, was looking out at the car park.

The car park was a vast tarmac expanse with white lines and sections marked 'Staff' and 'Visitors' and, more ominously, 'Emergency Vehicles'. It was a car park which once would have been the Lower Farm farmyard full of chickens scratting around, terriers just being angry and men setting off for a day in the fields, perhaps with a horse or two to help. If you went back far enough, that is. Back to when Lauretta Harrison might have been 6, or 7, or 8.

Lauretta Carey stared out of the window from her wheelchair for 12 hours a day. That was when she wasn't asleep in her wheelchair. Or when she was staring at the TV, the complex plot of the latest detective story far too much for her to comprehend.

But it was 'company' she said.

"Come on let's take you through," said the sturdy woman. Wheeling Lauretta round they set off for the Lower Farm Care Home dining room.

'I'll sit you next to Irene Thompson. You like chatting to her, don't you, Lauretta?'

'Oh yes', said Lauretta, a very tiny old lady indeed and even in the wheelchair she was hunched over, thin legs propped up on the footrests, skinny, bandy legs testimony to the rickets and starvation of an inter-war, fatherless childhood.

She had no idea who Irene Thompson was but the woman pushing her seemed confident she did and Lauretta had throughout her life always aimed to please. It was easier that way, she had found.

The sturdy woman eased Lauretta into the space at the communal table next to Irene who was a relatively young woman, for Lower Farm Care Home. Perhaps 80. Perhaps 85. It was hard to tell.

There were maybe thirty around the table, mostly women.

"Hello Lauretta," said Irene. "It's fish and chip Friday. You like fish and chips don't you."

"Oh yes," said Lauretta.

"Do you want me to help you cut it up?"

"Oh no, I can manage," said Lauretta. Who did this woman think she was?

Dinner progressed, as it usually did, in near silence. Further sturdy women and a couple of noticeably fresh-faced blonde teenagers from the large and thriving East European community in King's Lynn swept in and out bringing fish and chips, taking away plates and emerging with something sweet. Very sweet.

Thousands of men had been drawn to King's Lynn from Poland, Estonia, Latvia and Lithuania for jobs in the fields, in the food processing plants and as builders, plumbers and electricians. Their women followed the men and secured easy jobs in the gastropubs and the care homes. Even women who carried degrees in chemistry, engineering and business studies worked in care homes and gastropubs. The money was better than no work back at home and they were only working with the old people of King's Lynn for a short while. Until something in business, engineering or chemistry turned up.

Mark Elwin pulled into one of the bays in the car park marked 'Visitors' and as he went into Lower Farm Care Home he was, once again and as always, hit by the heat.

The sturdy woman in the near-nurse's outfit spotted him straight away.

"Oh, hello Mr Elwin. She's just finishing her sweet. Come on, I'll take you through. Do you want to go into the residents' lounge or to her room?"

"Oh, the lounge I think." More to look at, he thought.

And they made their way to the dining room.

"Here you are, Lauretta. You've got a visitor! Isn't he a handsome young man? Who is he then? Who is this handsome young man come to see you?"

"Wouldn't you like to know?" said Lauretta Carey.

Chapter 5
Norfolk, Present Day

Mark quickly tired of the residents' lounge. The age and the decrepitude of the company made him scared for his own future. He grasped the handles of the wheelchair and with a "Come on then, let's get you back to your room," they were off.

She didn't agree or disagree. People pushed her here and there all day long. She never said anything.

Once they were both seated Mark began the word game, the name game, the memory game, whatever he called it whenever he was talking to doctors, or nurses, or the nursing home assistants. It was the game that they played every Friday at around 7 o'clock or occasionally a little later depending on the time it took to eat dinner.

It was a game played by many of the visitors to Lower Farm Care Home. The result was nearly always the same.

Lauretta looked at Mark with the same innocent eyes she had done for the last 18 months or possibly even two years. And the game began.

"So," he started, keeping his voice calm and low. "You know when you were asked who I was, this handsome man," and you replied, "wouldn't you like to know? Well, tell me, who am I?"

She looked at him. Then she said, matter-of-factly, with a smile: "Oh, you're a nice man," she said. "A nice young man."

Mark Elwin urged patience on himself. It didn't always come naturally to him. It increasingly came very rarely to him, certainly not easily here with his grandmother, certainly not at the shop with the irritating men who came in and looked at every camera on the shelves, then wrote down some serial numbers and left to buy it online from bloody Amazon, never with the pug-faced kids sitting in the portrait set, in fact increasingly not with anyone. His assistant Trish was excepted.

"Yes," he said 'but who am I' and he paused and gently pointed a finger at her "who am I, to you?"

A frown formed on her face pushing a little closer together the many lines on her forehead and around her eyes.

She thought.

And looked hard at him.

"Do you work here?" she said, her eyebrows, plucked and then drawn on in pencil liner since the 1940s, lifting with hope rather than expectation.

"Gran, it's me. Mark. I'm your grandson," he said, as he had done almost every Friday for the past however long it actually was. Patience, he urged upon himself, again.

Five years ago, when the skinny, bandy, rickety legs had finally given up trying to support her tiny frame she was still sharp, quick-witted, full of questions about her great-grandchildren and when they were going to come to visit, tales of comings and goings in the car park, complaints about her dreadful luck at the weekly bingo, squeals of happiness at her success at the weekly bingo, tales of the woman in the next room.

"Dreadful snorer," she said in a very loud fake whisper, "dreadful noise it is. It was quieter when they came to bomb the airfields," and she would rock back with laughter.

And Lauretta was full of tales of intrigue about the staff.

"She's nice," she would say, pointing as Mark wheeled her about the home or into the garden on warm summer days.

"I think she's sweet on the gardener."

Or… "Don't like her. Bossy," she'd say. "She's a trouble causer. She likes causing bother she does. Enjoys it."

"See her, she's away with the fairies that one. A bit like your mother in many ways!" and she'd chuckle with fondness at the memory of her daughter, Mark's mother, her only child, long dead from a short lifetime of cigarettes.

But slowly, at first, and then with pitiful speed the names of those dear to her, those who'd once been dear to her, friends, fellow residents, members of staff, favourite TV detectives, they all began to drift away as friends from a party until there was only one party-goer left in the room.

"Gran it's me, Mark…look, there on your dressing table. My picture."

"Oh, yes. That's lovely Mark. Who are those children?"

"Gran. That's Beth and Tim. Your great-grandchildren."

"Oh," she said. "Who's that woman?"

"That's their mother," said Mark, the last man at the party.

"I don't recognise her," she said.

"No Gran, you only met her a few times. The wedding. Beth and Tim's Christenings. Mum's funeral."

"Who are Beth and Tim?" she said.

"These here, in the photograph. Your great-grandchildren. I've just told you."

"Oh," she said. "Are they your children?"

And so the game always went on. And on.

And then finally and all of a sudden, one Friday visiting day, one summer or early autumn, she stopped recognising him as well. And the game changed.

It was a shock the first time. The word game, the name game, and the memory game were that evening played with urgency as if to lose it would be to lose the world. Her world.

"But Gran it's me, Mark. Your Grandson. Look, there on your dressing table the photograph…"

"Who are you?" she asked, gently.

"Mark. Your grandson. Please try to remember. Your grandson…look," he said, holding the photograph up next to his face.

He hadn't realised it but his voice had got steadily louder and there was now a woman dressed in a real nurse's uniform in the doorway to the bedroom of Lauretta Carey.

"Mr Elwin, I don't think volume is going to make any difference, do you?" she said, smiling.

He turned and saw the Lower Farm Care Home Chief Nurse.

"Of course, Mrs Jenkins, of course. I know."

There was no point. The word game, the name game, and the memory game would never be played with any success, ever again.

But it was played.

Every Friday evening, about 7 o'clock.

And this evening when the game was over, and it was lost, as it always would be now and until the inevitable day, he said "Gran, can you just let me have your handbag…just for a minute?"

"What for?" she said and pushed it a little deeper between her leg and the arm of the wheelchair.

"Just for a minute," he said calmly, smiling.

She let him take it. He opened it and removed a neatly folded napkin inside which was a small piece of fried fish. There were never any leftovers on Lauretta's plate.

"How did that get there?" she asked. "I didn't put it there."

"Gran you don't need to hide food. There's plenty of food. Here's your handbag."

This was a recent development.

Last Friday morning Lower Farm Care Home staff under the supervision of Mrs Jenkins, had found fish, rashers of bacon, half a sandwich—all kinds of salvaged food hidden in her wardrobe. She'd been stashing it for at least a week and eventually, the pong led to a search.

It was brilliantly hidden in an old hat box at the bottom of her wardrobe, behind her shoes. The box contained not just her one hat but also a fox fur stole given to her by a woman, Mrs Front, whom she used to run errands for during the war. After the war, it became out of fashion and Mrs Front, keen to hit the fashion high notes once again, gave it to Lauretta. Sixty years later it was still her pride. Her one item of luxury. An ancient fox fur stole.

There was just enough room in there also for sachets of sugar from the bowls on the dining table, little ketchup tubs, mustard, brown sauce—not HP but the cheap generic catering stuff—and tartare sauce. Dozens of sachets, pots and tubs.

"But Gran," he had said when Mrs Jenkins presented them both with the stache, "you don't even like tartare sauce. Looks like something left by a seagull you used to say," said Mark.

"It wasn't me," she had claimed. Nonchalantly. A shake of the head. "I don't know how that got there."

And she didn't. She didn't remember taking and hiding the food. But somewhere, right at the back of her mind, somewhere way, way back she did remember always being very, very hungry.

"Nothing left on your plate Lauretta," the voice said, from way, way back. "Nothing left on your plate."

This evening he asked her, "Then if you didn't take food and hide it in your handbag who did?" thinking this simple logic would register with her and she'd be forced to admit, forced to concede.

"Alfie Sidebottom," she said at once.

"Gran, really...?" he said.

"Yes. He's very naughty."

Fair enough, thought Mark, and when that visit was over and Mark was making his way back to the car park, by the door, he was spotted and "you whoo'd," by Mrs Jenkins.

"I hope you don't mind us occasionally searching her room," she said. "I hope you don't mind if we do it every now and then. Just for food?"

"That's all right," said Mark, a smile. Resignation. And they both smiled.

Just as he was leaving, he turned.

"Oh, Mrs Jenkins, just to let you know she says it's Mr Sidebottom who's doing it," and he gave an easy laugh at the absurdity of it.

"But we don't have a Mr Sidebottom," said Mrs Jenkins.

Chapter 6
Norfolk, Present Day

There's no easy way to tell someone the man they waved off to work that morning had died in a car crash.

There's no easy way to tell someone the man they waved off to work that morning and who had died in a car crash wasn't, actually, on his way to work.

PC Ian Adams had been the first police officer on the scene of this morning's crash.

He identified Mr Simon Jones through his car registration number first, and his wallet second.

He identified his place of work through the West Norfolk Hospitals NHS Foundation Trust designated car park pass stuck to the windscreen.

And it had made sense to telephone the hospital to let them know that one of their own was dead and on his way in an ambulance. Killed, no doubt, on his way to work so patients and his team might need to be alerted.

But no, they said. Mr Simon Jones was not due for work that day.

It was Norfolk Constabulary protocol that when informing a female relative of the death of a loved one there should be two officers present and one should be female. So it was that PC Ian Adams collected WPC Davina Clements from Hunstanton Police Station.

"Okay, how are we going to play this one Davy?" said PC Adams.

"Well, if there's anyone in, you get her inside and break it, I'll hover beside you and offer consoling advice if she needs it."

"Done." And so they set off, in silence.

The village of Stanhoe was once a thriving farming community as almost every North Norfolk village was. Farming and everything that went with it from blacksmiths back in the day to tractor showrooms, servicing and repairs, agricultural haulage, food processing, seed merchants, vets and so many more people and professions to keep the food production going.

Now Stanhoe was an enclave for the affluent London set, their second homes, the holiday lets and the excellent gastropub to keep them fed. For the few remaining locals a fine medieval church, a Methodist chapel, a duck pond and the village hall or the Reading Rooms as they were called.

The Reading Rooms were dedicated to the memory of a long-forgotten woman of the local gentry whose mausoleum lay in near ruins in the churchyard.

The Reading Rooms were home to various clubs, Knitter Natter, Friday Film Club, Women's Institute—of course—and available to hire for parties and events.

PC Adams' police satnav took him past the Reading Rooms and on towards Westfield Farm House.

They drove down a private road opposite the mighty All Saints church, a testament to the wealth of the Hervey family in the 13th century and then down an even longer and even more private driveway to the huge house with its manicured lawns, full gravel turning circle and imposing double front door.

"Not short of a bob or two then," said PC Adams.

"Not sure that's going to be much consolation," said WPC Clements.

A 'his and her's' Range Rover was parked on the drive.

"Looks like she's home then," said PC Adams. He'd done the 'death knock' many times but he always took a minute just to settle himself before getting out to walk the three paces to the doorbell.

The doorbell sounded far too cheerful.

The door opened.

"Mrs Jones?"

"Yes, what is it? Is it the fly-tipping?" said Ellen Jones with repressed, but only just repressed, irritation. "We called about it last week. Last week, I said. What took you?"

"No Mrs Jones. I'm afraid it's not about the fly-tipping. I'm PC Adams. This is my colleague, WPC Clements. Can we come in?"

"What is it?" she said, settling squarely in the doorway, defending her territory against unwelcome visitors, as a bouncer might at a particularly exclusive nightclub.

"I'd rather we came inside if that's all right."

Norfolk Constabulary protocol demands on these occasions that the next of kin should be clearly identified, questions asked if there were any children present—there were not, it was a school day—and that they should be seated.

Then they must be told directly and succinctly. In plain language. The fashion for people 'passing' holds no sway in police matters. Dead at the scene leaves no one in any doubt.

"I have some very bad news for you Mrs Jones, please sit down," said PC Adams. And she did. They always did, the next of kin. By this point, they, the victim's relative, were also way ahead of the scene being played out. They just needed confirmation.

"I'm afraid your husband was in a road traffic collision this morning and he was killed. He died at the scene. Instantly, we believe," said PC Adams.

'Instantly' was the closest word of comfort Ellen Jones would get that day.

"Oh, I see. Where? How?" she said. No shock response. Measured. Possibly even detached. But not shocked.

The officers were relieved. A response of shock was a medical emergency requiring the attendance of an ambulance. So not a shock response. But not entirely composed either. Then Ellen Jones simply crumpled. Her right hand was on the arm of the sofa she had chosen to receive the news in, as if for balance if it was required even though she was sitting. Her left hand was in her lap, palm up, as if it was about to be raised as an act of supplication.

"In Dersingham. Outside the 'Visionary' photographer's shop if you know it."

"Yes, yes I do," and her brain started putting together the scene like Google StreetView.

"Are you okay Mrs Jones?" said WPC Clements. "Would you like a glass of water?" These were the lines of the supporting actor in this scene.

"No, no thank you," said Ellen Jones, and her mind moved into practical mode, domestic organisational overdrive.

"I'll need to tell his mother," she said.

"I'll need to tell my mother for that matter," she added. "I need to pick up the children from school."

"Might be best to leave them there for now," said the WPC. "Pick them up after school perhaps. As usual. Give you a little bit of time, you know?"

"Yes, yes. But the hospital. I'll need to let St Margaret's know," said Ellen Jones.

"I've already told them. They've been informed," said PC Adams.

"But what about his patients? He had a huge list today?" she said, urgently.

PC Adams looked at his colleague who right then, at that moment, was pleased to be the supporting actor in the scene about to come.

"Mrs Jones," said PC Adams, then very slowly and as gently as he could, "Mrs Jones. Mrs Jones your husband wasn't due in work today. I spoke to the hospital's deputy chief executive. He had no patients today."

"Then where was he going?" asked the widow, Mrs Jones.

"We rather hoped you would be able to tell us that," said PC Adams.

What followed was a sob so long and deep and sad that when she finally came to draw back the air it might have been that there was no air left for anyone else.

Then there was silence. For quite a while.

"Calm yourself Mrs Jones," said WPC Clements, "Would you like some water?"

Eventually, "Yes, please."

And when she was calm PC Ian Adams asked her again. He had to. It was his job.

"So, do you know where your husband was going this morning?"

"Does it matter?"

"Well, it might."

"Why? He's dead. What difference does a destination make?"

"This is a criminal investigation, Mrs Jones."

"Really? Why? Why is it a criminal investigation?"

"It is possible that the person driving the other car was under the influence of drugs at the time of the collision."

"Oh no," and then a sob. A mini sob compared to the one earlier, but the sob of a woman whose life, she knew, was being cracked open and exposed. "Some drugged-up bloody youth does this. Does this! Does bloody this."

"No actually, Mrs Jones, not a drugged-up youth."

"Then who?"

"I'm afraid I can't tell you that at this stage of our enquiries."

"Then I'm not telling you anything either," she said. And she didn't.

Chapter 7
Norfolk, Present Day

The name game was over for another Friday evening and a carefully wrapped piece of fried cod, three sachets of tartare sauce, four of ketchup, five of brown sauce and a dozen or so packets of sugar each containing two cubes had been retrieved from his Gran's handbag and handed over to a startlingly blonde and pretty, previously unseen, Lower Farm Care Home assistant.

"Well, Gran. What have you been up to?" said Mark.

Lauretta looked first at him, straight at him, not staring at him but examining him, and then she slowly turned to look back out of the window to the car park.

He picked up the photograph from her dressing table.

"Who are these Gran? Who are these people in this photograph on your dressing table?" he asked.

She looked.

"Well, that's you," she said, as if he was an idiot and pointing "That's you, there." And as if she had solved his riddle, turned again to the car park.

"Gran," he said. It always got her attention however briefly. She never challenged it or acknowledged the assumption. But she never accepted it either. And she turned away again.

"Lauretta Carey," he said. And she turned.

"Yes?"

"Lauretta Carey. That is you, isn't it?"

"Yes of course. Are you an idiot?" she said. "What do you want young man?"

Wow, he thought, this is more active interaction than he'd had since, well, a long time. How to keep this going?

"Where did you used to work?"

She looked at him as she did and he could see in her face the clouds that were passing once again across her memory. She turned away again.

"Lauretta. Lauretta Carey. Grandma!"

"What is it?" said the old lady, not with irritation but as if she had something far more important to do, somewhere, perhaps in the past.

"What did you have for your dinner?"

"Ask one of them," she said waving towards the door. "They're in charge."

"What are looking for in the car park?"

No reply.

"Lauretta?"

"What is it?" she said, again not sharply, not irritated, but for the first time firmly. With spirit.

"Lauretta…who is Alfie Sidebottom?"

She paused. The old woman looked at him but she wasn't examining his face. She was turning something over in her mind.

A small smile and then a frown of irritation passed over her face.

She shifted in her wheelchair. She looked again at Mark and even leaned slightly forward in her wheelchair.

"Oh, Alfie Sidebottom," she said with a vigour that took Mark by surprise. "I'll tell you who Alfie Sidebottom is. Alfie Sidebottom is a very naughty boy. A very, very naughty boy," and it was as if she had stepped out of the shadows and was back into the world.

"What did he do Lauretta?" asked Mark, astonished at what was possibly going to be a real, actual, conversation.

"He got me into trouble he did."

Tread carefully Mark, he thought.

"How? How did he get you into trouble?"

"Well, he was always talking that boy. Never stopped talking. I never talked. Not in class," she wagged her finger from side to side. "No talking in class I was a good girl. But Alfie Sidebottom…natter natter natter. Whispering to his mate, oh, you know, blonde-haired he was. Anyway, I used to tell him to keep his mouth shut or we'll all get into trouble but did he listen? No, he didn't!"

Wow, thought Mark. More words in 15 seconds than in 15 weeks.

"When was this, Lauretta?"

"In school of course! Where do you think?"

School? School? Quick, think Mark. That must have been in the 1930s. Maybe even the late 1920s.

"When was that then Lauretta?"

"When I was in school. I just told you!"

"No but when? What year?"

"When I was eight. Alfie Sidebottom used to sit in the row next to me. Mrs Cartwright—ooh she was a right old tarter, she was, used to keep a yard rule on her desk so you knew what you'd get if you crossed her. That Alfie Sidebottom he was always getting it. I never did. I was a good girl," and she wagged her finger from side to side again.

"I always did as I was told. Always. Anyway, one day Alfie and his mate are chit-chatting away when Mrs Cartwright is writing on the blackboard. And I go shush to him. Well," and with that she folded her arms and leaned back in her wheelchair and looked at Mark.

She looked at him, but not in the vacant, empty-eyed way she always did. She looked at him with fire in her eyes, her thin plucked eyebrows drawn in and now arched upwards challenging him to ask the question.

"So what happened then?"

Perfect.

"Well, Mrs Cartwright she turns round all mad and angry and she says 'Who is shushing me?' and everyone in the class sits tight and says nothing. 'Who is shushing me in this class? She goes on again. Was it you Alfie Sidebottom?' and Alfie says no it wasn't, Miss. 'Then who was it, or you'll be getting the stick, you'll be getting the stick' and Alfie Sidebottom says straight off—it was Lauretta Harrison, Miss." And back she sat again, arms folded, begging the next question.

"So what did you say?"

Perfect.

"I said I was shushing Alfie Sidebottom Miss, 'cause the boys were all talking Miss and I couldn't hear what you were saying, Miss." And she said, "Well all I could hear was you shushing so loud I could barely hear myself speak."

And back she rocked again.

"And what happened then?"

Perfect.

"Come to the front of the class, Lauretta Harrison," she said. "Come up here now." And everyone in the class was quiet. They knew what was going to happen. And I knew what was going to happen. And I walked up to the front of the class and she said, "Hold your hand out." And I did. You had to. You had to do what you were told in them days. And she said, "And don't try to pull it away or you'll only make it worse for your'sen. Hold still now." And she gave me three of the best right across the palm of my hand. Three times. And it hurt like billy 'eck. And there was a big red mark in my hand and she said, "Now go back to your seat and let that be a lesson to you." And I went back to my seat and Alfie Sidebottom had this big grin on his face. But I didn't cry. I didn't cry at all. And I thought, *"Alfie Sidebottom, I will get you back for that, I really will."*

And with that, she sat back and looked at him as if to say, "So what do you think of that?"

"And did you?"

"Did I what?" she said.

"Did you get him back?"

"Well I didn't get the chance, did I?"

"Why not Lauretta?"

"Well," she said, "the next day was the day his uncle was found shot dead and he and his dad disappeared. My word, there was such a fuss at the time. But we never saw him again."

And with that, the lights in her eyes slowly faded and no amount of 'Lauretta' questions could turn them back on.

And she turned and looked at the car park.

Mark Elwin left Lower Farm Care Home with his head full of questions which he was certain his grandmother would never provide the answers to.

As he made his way to his car, he could see her in her bedroom window looking out.

He waved to her.

She didn't wave back.

She didn't wave to strangers.

Chapter 8
Norfolk, Present Day

The online archive of the *Eastern Daily Press* is all very well and good but it's nowhere near as good as having someone on the inside.

Dave Wheeler was the Picture Editor at the *EDP* and Mark and Dave had known each other since the early noughties when Mark was a freelance photographer with ambitions of international scoops and Dave was a junior photographer with the *EDP* with high hopes of Fleet Street.

Back in the day, Dave had thrown Mark a few jobs, court room stakeouts, Norwich Christmas lights turn on by local pop star Cathy Dennis, the kind of jobs that old-time staff snappers didn't want to do. Hours waiting for one decent shot or out of 9 to 5 hours jobs when the pub had already beckoned. Mark gobbled up the work and the experience.

These days one of them was a local paper lifer and the other took wedding photographs and cheesy snaps of cats and dogs and kids at school. It was not easy for either of them to say whose career had been the bigger disappointment.

Anyway, a phone call was made and after a two-hour wait the email from Dave Wheeler pinged into Mark's computer in the Visionary office at the back of the shop.

There it was, headline news, June 14 1933, with a photograph of Keeper's Cottage, Sandringham, and a policeman standing to attention in front.

Murder Hunt
For Royal
Gamekeeper

Norfolk Constabulary has launched a major manhunt for a gamekeeper on the King's estate at Sandringham House after the discovery of a man's body.

Mr Clement Sidebottom, 30, an estate labourer, was found dead from shotgun wounds yesterday afternoon by his sister-in-law Mrs Nika Sidebottom, 28, at her home, Keeper's Cottage on the Sandringham Estate.

It's been revealed that the man police wish to trace is Mr Sidebottom's brother Mr Montgomery Sidebottom, a gamekeeper on the Sandringham Estate.

Police have appealed to anyone who knows the whereabouts of Mr Montgomery Sidebottom to get in touch with them but not to approach him as he may be armed and dangerous.

A neighbour, farm labourer Mr Eric Tinkler, 64, told this newspaper 'My wife says Nika came back to the house yesterday about teatime and found her brother-in-law dead on the floor. She hasn't seen her husband since, according to my wife.'

It is not believed that His Majesty King George V is in residence at Sandringham House at this time.

There was some Sandringham Estate background filler material but that was about it. It was probably a late-breaking story ahead of an old-fashioned print deadline because the following day's edition had much more.

EDP June 15 1933.
Sandringham Murder
Search For Royal Gamekeeper
And Son Continues

The search is continuing for a gamekeeper from the King's Sandringham Estate who has gone missing following the death from shotgun wounds of his brother.

The body of 30-year-old Mr Clement Sidebottom, a labourer, of Apple Tree Cottage, Sandringham was discovered the day before yesterday in the early evening by his sister-in-law Mrs Nika Sidebottom, 28, at her home, Keeper's Cottage at Sandringham. According to police stationed at King's Lynn, he had been shot with a 12-gauge shotgun which was found at the scene.

Mrs Sidebottom's husband, Mr Montgomery Sidebottom, 32, known locally as Monty, is now believed to be on the run and is the chief suspect in what the police are treating as a murder investigation. Also missing is their 8-year-old son, Alfred.

"At this time, we are searching the woods on both the Sandringham House Estate and the adjoining Houghton Hall Estate," said Detective Inspector Raymond Linsey of Norfolk Constabulary.

"Because of the nature of his profession, Mr Monty Sidebottom knows these estates very well indeed but I have had every available officer searching from first light."

Local enquiries by this newspaper suggest Mrs Sidebottom had been taking food to her mother in nearby West Newton. When she returned home, she found the body of her husband's brother.

We understand that neighbouring cottages were mostly empty at the time as the farm workers were out in the fields.

"No shot was heard but the county coroner has initially put the time of death at around 11 o'clock in the morning. Mr Sidebottom died from a single shotgun wound to the back from close range," said DI Linsey.

And then more filler material.

Wow, Mark thought.

"Wow," he thought again and this time he said it out loud.

"Husband shoots his brother in his own home then scarpers with Lauretta's naughty boy Alfie Sidebottom. And all on the King's Sandringham Estate. No wonder it caused a fuss," he continued out loud and then as if it hadn't occurred to him already, a final "Wow."

Now that Mark had a date for the murder, several names and plenty of peripheral details he quickly put together a comprehensive set of keywords and shovelled them into the 'great Google search engine in the sky' as he called it.

Instantly a list of search results filled his screen.

The story had been covered comprehensively in *The Times*, *The Daily Mail* and the *Manchester Guardian*. Even Dundee local papers, with their huge Royal connection at Balmoral, gave it a few paragraphs and *The Scotsman* ran a decent length story making it their page 5 lead, the editorial team in Edinburgh probably wished it had happened on the Balmoral estate instead of at Sandringham.

But then the story started to fall away. The *EDP* was different. On the third day covering the story, they printed a photograph of the Sidebottom family, Nika and Monty and a baby, Alfie, credited to A J Pugh of Hunstanton. Typical of the time it showed the couple rather stiffly in what was undoubtedly their Sunday best in a studio, Nika sitting on a sturdy chair with baby Alfie cradled in her arms, and Monty standing behind, masterful and proud. A crafty few shillings earned there Mr A J Pugh of Hunstanton thought Mark.

For a while in his own career, when there was a big story locally, Mark would rifle through his computer records just in case he had tucked away somewhere a photograph of any of the people involved. A wedding photo perhaps, or the child at school, ready to be offered to the local newspaper for a small fee. But everyone's a photographer these days, Facebook can be raided at will and the occasional little bonus payday for him was a thing of the past.

Back in 1933, it seemed the search continued and it continued to be reported daily for a while. One day there was a photograph of two police officers at King's Lynn station peering in through carriage windows. Another day a report of the dragging of a lake on the Holkham Estate 15 miles away. Someone had reported to the police that they had seen a man with a boy on its bank. The police had ordered it to be dragged and the Earl of Leicester had 'lent his full support to the police operation' by ordering the lake to have a dragnet put through it. A photograph in the *EDP* showed a dozen burly estate workers pulling the net across the lake but according to the report, there was nothing in it except a lot of carp.

After that it was just the anniversaries to report, a month, six months, a year—any excuse really for the *EDP* to revive what it by then liked to call *The Sandringham Murder Mystery.*

The story then just faded into history. It was by now a very, very cold case indeed.

But Mark had nothing much better to do.

All the routine office pre-job planning and post-job processing was handled by Trish. Mark drummed up new clients, and new fancy home owners, and kept the big school clients happy, especially if a new person was appointed in charge of contracts and he shmoozed the guys running the big corporate game shooting days.

But generally speaking, he had time on his hands, he was definitely bored and he was certainly intrigued by The Sandringham Mystery. Especially as his own grandmother knew the son of the chief suspect. He briefly thought 'Wait until I tell her' but quickly knew there probably wasn't any point.

He decided to look up UK National Census material to see whether Clement Sidebottom and Montgomery Sidebottom had any other family.

Once more to 'the great Google search engine in the sky' and instant access to the treasure trove of information and insight he hoped would be in the online census records.

The great Google delivered him a resounding blank. He went to the fridge and considered a Corona beer and a slice of lime. For a change this time, he opted for tea and he put on the kettle.

Back to the computer and down into research rabbit holes. It turned out the relevant and closest census to the murder in 1933 was for 1931 but that he soon discovered had been destroyed by a fire in the war, in 1942.

The next census was the National Registration programme ahead of the war. That was carried out in 1939 and this time there was something of interest. It showed that Clement's old home, Apple Tree Cottage was by 1939 at the latest occupied by the Ledger family, George, 28 years old, the head of the household and himself a farm labourer, with Kathleen, who was also 28, and no fewer than five children under the age of 10.

"Wow. A mother of five before you are 30. Seven of you in a tiny worker's cottage I bet that was a bit of a squeeze," Mark said to himself.

He turned and scrolled up and down the screen until he found Keeper's Cottage.

Now there was something of even more interest.

In 1939, at Keeper's Cottage, Sandringham remained Nika Sidebottom, now 33, listed as a widow. Listed as a widow. She would have supplied that information but, wondered Mark, had Monty's body been found? If it had, surely there would have been more articles in the *EDP* at the time. And if Monty was dead, where was little Alfie? Also listed as living at Keeper's Cottage was Zither Malone, 67, presumably Nika's mother.

But it was the final listing that was by far the most interesting.

With Mummy and Granny was Charles Sidebottom aged 6. Date of birth December 13th 1933.

Mark pushed the computer keyboard away from him a little on the table and took it all in.

"Well, well, well, Nika Sidebottom," he said out loud.

"Well, well, well. Naughty, naughty. Pregnant, were you? At the time of the murder, eh? No mention of that in the *EDP*," he said out loud again. "I'd say old Norfolk Constabulary would have been very interested in that…except I very much doubt you mentioned it, did you girl?"

He printed off the census pages and added them to the printouts of all the newspaper reports. It was starting to be quite a pile.

Time to start a file, he thought. And time to start a beer.

Chapter 9
Norfolk, 1933

June 1933 was flaming.

There was day after day after day of pure sunshine and for days at a time in a small meadow next to the little school in Sandringham village, in the shade of a huge and ancient sycamore tree, lessons were routinely being taken.

As it turned out, there were to be no lessons at all that day.

Just after register had been taken and every pupil accounted for and marked as present, Mrs Cartwright decided the pain in her back was just too much to bear.

She scolded herself for not seeing the doctor often enough or more recently but it was expensive and whatever it was he was giving her it wasn't shifting the almost constant pain in her back and sides.

As it was, and for this morning only she told herself, firmly, for this morning only there was nothing else to do.

"Children," she said, with little response.

Then more sharply "Class!" she said and whacked her wooden yard rule with its thin brass edge hard down on her desktop. There was instant silence and instant attention as the dozen or so pairs of eyes stared forwards.

"Class," she repeated, "there will be no lessons today. Go home. Go straight home. Apologise to your mothers and say school will be back tomorrow."

She sank slowly down making sure not to wince in front of her pupils.

"Now off you go, girls first."

It was Mrs Cartwright's way. The school was not big enough for boys' and girls' separate entrances but she would not have them leaving, all mixed up together.

Little Lauretta Harrison put on her satchel and led out the seven girls quietly and in good order. They said their goodbyes to each other, broke formation and headed off to their respective homes.

The boys were already pushing and shoving each other with the first footfall outside the door. A couple of them were soon giddy with plans to seize this free holiday and go fishing in the big pond at West Newton while there was still plenty of water in it.

Alfie Sidebottom waved to his school friends over his shoulder and set off. The journey home was no more than 20 minutes of walking, and much less if it was raining and he would run.

Today, it was already hot and he lazily took his time, kicking a stone here and there, stopping to make a mental note of a small covey of English partridge when they flushed over him chirruping as they went. His father would be interested in that.

On and on he wandered. His mother would be surprised to see him. He thought of a fishing trip too, or perhaps go up to Hanging Wood where he knew his father was working that morning. In the end, he just wandered slowly homewards.

When he was nearly there, turning at a crossroads in the footpaths and then down a gentle slope between two hawthorn hedges hiding fields of wheat not yet ripe, he first heard raised voices coming from inside his home.

He couldn't make out what was being said but he could easily make out a man's voice and a woman's voice. He slowed to a stop. It would be his mother and father arguing again. There was a lot of that these days.

He briefly thought he could just go off to join the fishing party but instead, he decided to go home but to stay out of sight until he could judge how the land was lying inside the house.

When he got to Keeper's Cottage, he cut down the side, climbed over a low fence that marked out the garden and the backyard and edged his way to the back door which was wide open. If his mother had been baking bread, as she nearly always did in the morning, then on a hot day like this she opened the back door to let in some air.

He put down his school satchel by the back door and listened. It was his mother alright, sharp and short, but the man's voice wasn't his father's but his Uncle Clem's. What was he doing here? he wondered. And what was the shouting about?

Staying just outside the back door but leaning as far forwards as he dared, he tried to listen in but the chickens behind him in the yard were making their usual racket and he could only catch fragments of what was being said.

The first thing he heard clearly was "It's my baby and I will have it," from his Uncle Clem. Alfie had no idea what that was about. Uncle Clem wasn't married.

"You'll not tell anyone. There'll be a scandal. You tell no one, Clem Sidebottom. This ends now," said his mother and Alfie could tell she was crying. "You tell no one or we'll all be ruined."

Alfie had no idea what any of this meant.

He missed the next bit as he went to softly shoo away chickens that had advanced on him thinking feeding time had come early. They moved away, clucking in disappointment.

Alfie made his way to the back door again. It wasn't easy for him to hear what was being said as the door between the kitchen and the front room was only half open. But when Uncle Clem raised his voice again Alfie heard "We'll go to London, Nika love," and then he heard "Start again, make a new life for us."

Now it was time for his mother to raise her voice and he glimpsed her shape walk across the gap in the door between the kitchen and the front room. He guessed she was going towards where his Uncle Clem must be standing, somewhere near the front door.

"No! What about little Alfie?" said his mother.

What about me? thought Alfie. What's all this got to do with me?

"He's his father's son. Let his father have him You belong with me Nika," his uncle now screaming. Alfie knew this was very serious indeed. But he didn't know why it was serious. And it was odd hearing his mother called by her name. His parents always referred to each other as Mother and Father.

Alfie turned back to look across the small yard, the vegetable garden, the chicken coop and the gently rising estate fields beyond. There was no one else in sight. He turned to listen again as the words became louder. This was clearly a bad row he thought and anger now replaced the frantic desperation in his mother's voice.

Then things happened quickly, tumbling over each other before he could take things in and try to make sense of what was happening.

"No!" his mother screamed out loud, but why she was now screaming? Then he briefly saw her arms flash past the gap in the doorway.

Then he heard clearly.

"No, no, no Clem it's not right! Don't do it."

Don't do what?

Then his mother screaming and crying at the same time.

It was a terrible noise.

Alfie had never heard that noise before, even when his parents were fighting at their worst. It was a noise he'd remember for the rest of his life.

And then there was another noise he'd remember for the rest of his life.

A single, loud gunshot. A shotgun. He knew that sound but he'd only heard it outside, when the bang was taken on the wind. Inside a house, the sound of a shotgun being fired was a terrible, dark noise.

Then he heard the crash of something heavy, something very heavy hitting something else first and then the floor.

And then his mother cried.

And then "Oh my God. Clem! Clem...?"

And with that Alfie was running, running as fast as any eight-year-old boy could run, running away from something terrible he didn't understand, something he certainly didn't want to see, and he was running towards safety, running towards the safety of his father.

Monty Sidebottom didn't yet know it but that was to be the last morning of peace he would have for some time.

The day had started well, a golden dawn, more sunshine, a day he planned to spend up at one of his favourite places on the whole of Sandringham Estate, in the whole of the world that he knew.

"I'm going up to Hanging Wood today, Alfie," his father told him as he was standing up after his morning cups of tea. His father was up early and home late in the summer and the autumn. "I'm going to put down some feed and water up there. There's plenty of partridge in the hedgerows."

Monty always gave his boy the agenda for the day and often, after school and always in the school holidays, Alfie would meet up with his father and learn firsthand the craft of a gamekeeper. He learned how to trap and how to shoot foxes. He watched his father shoot squirrels, rabbits, jays when the songbirds were nesting, feral cats, in fact, anything which threatened the health of the estate in general and the precious game birds in particular.

In the winter, if there was a Saturday shoot and Alfie wasn't at school, he would walk the line with his father's team of beaters. His father ran shoots with precision and a success that made him admired among his fellow keepers. Alfie had been following in his father's footsteps, often literally, since he was five.

Monty knew he needed to be up at Hanging Wood that day to replenish piles of food in the feed hoppers and troughs of water for the partridge. His Majesty liked to call his Sandringham shoot 'the finest shoot in England' and by that, he meant he needed to be shooting by far the greatest numbers of birds on any given day, anywhere in Norfolk.

Monty also knew that come September the King would have his friends up from London, down from Scotland and some of the local Norfolk worthies over for grand shooting parties.

After breakfast in the Sandringham House dining room, the men would gather at the house and then be taken by gun cart out into the fields for their day's sport.

His Majesty expected to shoot plenty of birds, hoping even for a thousand birds in a single day. If the King didn't get what he wanted, for himself and his guests, well, it didn't matter how lavish the evening dinner with the ladies was, how excellent the food, how wonderful the entertainment and how splendid the dancing, this was a shooting party and if His Majesty and his guests had not had their day in the field then the King could have a fearsome temper and the gamekeepers took both barrels of it.

So Monty and the other keepers quietly went about establishing feeding stations all over the estate. Monty had Hanging Wood, the Dumble, Hun's Edge and other named drives, as did the other keepers.

Come September Monty knew that his line of beaters needed to slap and flap their way through this wood to push out dozens and dozens of partridge up and over the line of guns in the Royal party lined up just in front of a hedge and a line of beech trees below.

And as the birds rose higher and higher, and the guns blasted away, birds crumpled in the air and fell dead behind the guns. Into action would go the pickers-up, men with the labradors and spaniels, working away to find and retrieve the dead partridge, despatching the wounded ones with a knock to the head with their sticks and loading up the dead birds on the game wagon, paired up, a brace at a time hung over the wooden dowel.

As he worked away that beautiful June morning Monty was thinking about making sure the King and his guests got exactly what they wanted. For one thing, it was his job. For another thing, big numbers of shot birds meant healthy tips from the King's guests. Monty has a tin at the cottage slowly filling up with tips and he had a mind to buy himself a horse and a cart with it. One more good season and he'd be just about there.

It was when he stopped to stretch his back that he first spotted Alfie running up the hill towards Hanging Wood. Monty knew at once something wasn't right. For a start, the boy should be in school. For another thing he was running and shouting at the same time.

"Father, Father," screamed Alfie, still fifty yards short of his father. Instinctively Monty picked up his gun slip and threw it around his back.

"Father, Father come quick. Something's happened!"

Chapter 10
Norfolk, 1933

Monty ran a few yards forward and met his son coming up the rise.

"What boy?" he said, and then taking his son by the shoulder to make him breathe a little more evenly, "Quick Alfie, what is it?"

"Mother," said Alfie between gulps of air and wiping sweat off his face with the back of his arm, "Mother. And Uncle Clem."

Monty stared at his son and then after the briefest moment's thought, picked up his knapsack, threw it over the shoulder without the gun slip and set off down the sloping path away from Hanging Wood.

"Walk with me now Alfie…quickly mind," said his father, "Now tell me Alfie, what about Mother and Uncle Clem? Tell me, Son. Tell me."

"I don't know," said Alfie. The boy had heard some things, seen almost nothing. He just started saying the words as they'd come out of the front room to him by the back door.

"Something about a baby, I think. And London," said Alfie. "Then me and you. That was Uncle Clem. And Mother. Something about scandal or ruin, or maybe both. I can't really remember. I was by the back door."

"What else?" urged his father and the pace quickened. "What else?"

"Then the shotgun went off," said Alfie, and the two of them started running as fast as they could towards Keeper's Cottage.

Hot, sweating and out of breath Monty reached the front door of Keeper's Cottage in less than ten minutes. Alfie was lagging behind, which was a good thing, thought Monty, as he leaned into the front door.

It wouldn't budge.

"Nika let me in now!" he shouted and banged his fist on the door.

"Back door," he heard her say through loud sobs and huge, involuntary intakes of breath.

He charged to the side and round the back of the cottage catching a glimpse of Alfie slowing down as he reached home. Alfie was not certain he wanted to be there.

When Monty finally came stamping through the kitchen and into the tiny front room, he could see immediately why he couldn't move the door. His brother Clem was bent, collapsed double as if he was about to do a somersault against the front door. There was a hole in his back and right side the size of five men's fists. There was blood everywhere, on the door, the floor, the walls and splattered across the ceiling. Remarkably there was none on his wife that he could see. The force of the shot was directly forwards and that's where the blood had travelled. His brother's ribs were sticking out of his body like a leaf rake.

"Oh Holy Christ," Monty said.

"I didn't mean it, Monty! I'm sorry Monty. I just picked it up and it went off. I just wanted him to stop," words were rushing out of her like an incoming rip tide.

"Wanted to stop him what?" he asked.

She fell silent her brain scrambling for words.

"Stop him what? Stop him what?" Monty was inches away from his wife and the words were literally spat out.

"Just..." she started.

"Ah, shut up you whore," said Monty just as Alfie came into the room. Shut your mouth, Monty, he said to himself. Think of the boy.

"I didn't mean to," she said again. "I never meant to. It just went off."

"Sit down and shut up," he said, and he pointed to a wooden ladder-back chair by the small table he had made himself from wood off the estate.

He turned to the boy.

"Alfie get out. Go and get changed into your camping-out clothes."

Alfie looked at his father. What could he mean?

"Camping-out clothes?"

"Just do it. Now!" his father left no margin for error. It was an order. His father rarely gave orders.

When Alfie left the room and they could hear his footsteps beating up the bare wooden stairs Monty turned to his wife, seated, head up, looking at her husband.

"You'll hang for this woman," he said, and he saw the fear come into her eyes. "You'll hang for sure," he said, determined to feed that fear.

"But I didn't mean to do it!"

"Who cares, eh?" he said, pointing his finger at her. "Who cares? They won't care. They'll hang you anyway once they know you're carrying his bastard child. You'll hang for sure!"

Nika's head collapsed. She knew that he knew. About the child. About everything.

"How?" she asked meekly. "How?"

"The boy. He heard the words baby and then the gunshot. You'll hang. For certain." The last two words were like punches landing in her gut.

"It might be yours?" she offered, but it was weak. The words of a frightened, cornered woman.

"Get away with you woman. You're not showing. And you've not come to me since before Christmas. It's his alright."

Nika Sidebottom was down and out. She looked to Monty.

"What are you going to do?" she pleaded with him. "Monty? What's going to happen?"

"For a start, they'll hang you. After you've had your bastard, I imagine too. But your stink, the stink of your shame and your crime, that stink will smear all over me and the boy. The estate won't stand for it. The King can't have bastard children on the estate. They'll turf me and the boy out for sure. That's me finished. No one will take me on. No one will take me on…anywhere. They'll say…oh yes, Monty Sidebottom, the man whose wife was hanged for murdering his brother, her lover, carrying on behind his back, whose bastard she was carrying." He was angry now and shouting.

Alfie appeared. Monty stood in the boy's line of sight so he couldn't see again his Uncle Clem's blasted insides.

"Alfie. Go upstairs. Get yourself two pairs of underpants, two clean shirts and a sweater. Get the same for me. And my big haversack, the one hanging behind the cellar door…and empty all your stuff out of your satchel. Do it now boy and do it quickly," he said. Measured but firm.

"Yes Father," said Alfie and he was off again.

"You can't leave me?" said Nika.

"I can if you want to live," he said.

The word 'live'…

"I don't understand?" she said.

"You'll hang for this. You'll hang and I'll be finished. And, what's more, the boy will carry the stain of your sin forever. The boy whose mother was hanged for murder. The boy whose mother was hanged for murder," he repeated jabbing his right index finger to within six inches of her face repeated, "Do you understand?"

"No, Monty. What's going to happen?"

"We're off. Me and the boy…"

"You can't take Alfie from me…"

"You should have thought of that eh? Eh? You told me it was over woman. Over you said. Never happen again you said. Please Monty you said. You. Are. A. Lying. Whore. I gave you your chance. More fool me. You promised me it was over Nika."

"I'm so sorry, Monty." She began crying. Soft tears of a broken woman. Tears of defeat not desperation.

Monty was not to be held up any longer. The time was for action and not a debate. For decision, not recrimination. His time at Keeper's Cottage was up and it was up right now.

"Too late. Too late now. But I tell you this woman, and you listen well, listen to me now woman like you've never listened to me before, I won't have my life destroyed because my slattern wife killed my treacherous brother. And I won't let Alfie's life be ruined. Do you understand? "

"But you can't just run away? They'll think it was you?"

"They might think that. They might. But…and listen to me very carefully," he said as her eyes started to look over to the body by the door, "Look at me! You will not tell them that. Do you hear me? You will not tell them that. If you tell them that and tell them where we went to…and they find us, we'll tell them the truth. Me and the boy. Do you want that? Do you understand me?"

She understood.

"Do you understand me?" he repeated. "If they find us, me and the boy will tell them the truth and you will force your own son to give the evidence that sends his mother to the gallows. I won't have that for the boy. I won't have it. You won't do it. So you listen. Listen to me well. Listen! It's not even noon. You stay here."

Alfie appeared.

"Alfie get my canteen and yours, fill them with water. Get what's left of the ham and cheese and wrap it in greaseproof paper. Get today's loaf. Do it now, boy. Put them in the haversack and your canteen and your clothes in your satchel." Alfie went off on his next mission.

"And get the matches by the stove," he shouted to the boy's back and Alfie put his hand up to show that he'd heard.

Monty turned once more to his wife.

"You do not raise the alarm until tea time. Do you hear? Half past five. Say you've been at your mother's. I assume she'll lie for you. She's been lying for you while you've been out whoring with my brother, hasn't she?"

Nika Sidebottom said nothing.

"Just say you came home and found him dead. Don't touch the gun. Leave everything exactly where it is. Don't go out. Let no one see you between now and raising the police. That'll give me and the boy nearly seven hours start and by the time they get a search party together it'll be nearly dark," he said.

"They'll catch you, Monty, they'll catch you."

"Let's hope for your sake that they don't, eh?" There was to be no mercy now from Monty. He needed his wife to listen, to do exactly as instructed, for fear of her life. "Or you will hang."

"Where will you go?"

"Into the woods for a start. Here, Houghton, Holkham. I know them like the back of my hand. Those King's Lynn coppers are fat old townies. They'll never find us in there."

"But you can't stay there forever? What about Alfie?"

"It's a bit late to start thinking about others now, isn't it? Isn't it!" he was angry but now he was getting himself under control. He needed to be under control and ready to run.

"I'm so sorry Monty," she was looking down at her feet, not at him.

"You weren't sorry when you were out with him, were you?" he said pointing at the body of his brother, but she wasn't looking at him. Just down at her feet.

Alfie was back.

"Alright boy, in the kitchen. Let's see how good you are at packing," and he ushered him out of the front room away from the stink of blood, and of death and shame.

The haversack was packed. Monty took his shotgun out of its slip, stripped it apart, wrapped it in an oilcloth and put it in his haversack. It was an old William Evans 12-gauge side-by-side bought from a retiring keeper. It was old but it was reliable, true and it was the tool of his trade. He threw in a couple of handfuls of cartridges.

"Right Alfie, wait there," he said pointing to the back door.

Monty turned and went back into the living room, opened the door of a small cabinet and took out a biscuit tin.

"I'm taking all the money," he said. "All of it."

And she nodded.

"I'll come and say goodbye to Alfie," she said, crying.

"You won't," he said. "You can stay there with the father of your bastard child."

She let out the longest sob. And another and another and another as she realised that she might never see either of them again.

And sitting in the room, head down, for the first time, but not the last, she hoped she never would.

Chapter 11
Norfolk, Present Day

If you were to ask Mark Elwin to describe himself, he would probably say he was a reasonably successful failure.

By that, he would mean he was both reasonably successful. And a failure.

As a boy, Mark Elwin was enthused, energised and excited by photography.

Every Saturday morning he spent 3 hours back at Smithdon School in Hunstanton at what was called Camera Club. He loved it. It was run by an old, retired chemistry teacher called Brian Bilson whose enthusiasm and skill as a photographer coupled with his ability to teach meant Mark could not wait to go back to school for an extra half a day each week.

Every Saturday during term time Mark turned up at the cricket pavilion along with a handful of others, all boys. Many of the others weren't there by choice. They were there because their parents, or in many cases parent in the singular, worked and needed free child care. Or were simply not wanted at home.

Mark was different. He devoured the basics of lenses, depths of fields, lighting, F-stops and more. He really did love it and he was Mr Bilson's star pupil.

His parents encouraged it. Mostly just for its own sake. They admired creativity in anyone and at any standard. Some of their friends were amongst the worst types of amateur potters, painters and craft jewellery makers and the family home was full of their best efforts.

They also encouraged it because it suited them too. Mark's mum and dad were card-carrying, signed-up, pledge badge-wearing children of the 60s and could be found wheeling in behind many a cause.

Remarkably the boy Mark Elwin was spiritually unscathed in the 90s, despite long nights upstairs in his bedroom listening to hours and hours of the Allman Brothers, the Doobie Brothers and the Brothers Johnson drifting up from under the floorboards.

His parents were also early adopters of the Friends of the Earth movement. They became vegetarian. The boy Mark was only an at-home vegetarian. Uncommitted to the vegetarian cause he ate meat of the greyest kind and poorest quality at school. And with relish. Fish and chips from the local Tropical Fish and Chips shop a regular treat. His parents both knew and didn't mind. They had never forced a view on anyone in their lives.

At some point, the family car had been traded for bicycles, which Mark had wholeheartedly supported much to his parents' surprise. Mark realised that no car meant the end of Sundays driving out to Cambridgeshire and Lincolnshire for a bleak hike across miles of flat fenland, and that suited him just fine.

Mark's parents were the sort who went on retreats. There were occasions when they truly believed that there wasn't a problem known to any grown human that couldn't be solved—or eased—by the judicious application of crystals, yoga, ensemble folk singing, marijuana or a combination of all four.

Mark's father was a gardener for the local council who still sported a ponytail even though he was completely bald on top. Mark's mother was a teaching assistant and wore tie-dye maxi skirts and muslin linen blouses, embarrassingly braless.

When Mark entered sixth form his parents discovered Car Boot Sales. Every Saturday morning they set up shop—or, more accurately, a trestle table—at the car boot sale on the cricket field in a nearby village. They would load up two trailers for the bikes which had been made by his father out of aluminium tubes and old pram wheels and they would cycle off, loaded with stuff to save the world a pound at a time.

They were purveyors of all things vaguely hippy, vaguely ecologically sound, vaguely right-on crystals, CDs of Peruvian Pan Pipe music, Fair Trade carved wooden lizards, recycled scented candles 'Pine Fresh' 'Tiger Balm' and "Ocean Spray," garden planters made by his father out of old forklift pallets, incense holders, tobacco tins decorated with marijuana leaves, images of Bob Marley, the CND logo and the like and, of course, the classic range of Vietnamese wooden wind chimes to hang in trees.

Their trestle table and any bigger items such as the planters went with Gary, another bald man with a ponytail and, crucially, the ubiquitous plumber's white van.

When the car boot sale was done and the cricketers wanted their outfield back for the afternoon match Mark's parents and their fellow boot-mongers decamped to the adjacent Rose and Crown pub and drank most of the takings with all their like-minded hippy, tree-hugging, car boot sale chums.

The Elwin marriage was completely bombproof and Mark led an entirely placid, single-child, domestic existence. Too placid. He was bored.

So, when Mark asked if would they mind if he went to Camera Club every Saturday morning, well, that was just fine.

And he did love it.

Mr Bilson introduced him in particular to the photography of news and events. The history of the great photographic agencies such as Magnum with the legendary Henri Cartier-Bresson, the author of the great Second World War Times Square kiss photo. Mr Bilson was also a huge fan of the work of the UK Press Association, images of grim industrial landscapes, or bleak Scottish moors, of striking miners, world-conquering pop singers and terrible terrorist attacks. Mr Bilson's tastes extended to the photographic journalism of the Vietnam War in *Paris Match* right up to the September 11 attacks on the World Trade Centre in New York. Mark hoovered it up, romanced about it and wanted it. He wanted the thrill of it, he wanted to be part of the recording of history and he wanted to be part of the history of news photography.

At eighteen he passed his A levels, mostly only just, but with an A in English he was offered, and he could have taken up, a place at the University of East Anglia for a BA Honours degree in Photography and Journalism.

Instead, he declared himself and his selection of Canon bodies and lenses open for business as an actual freelance photographer. His parents had urged him towards the bright lights of Norwich and the UEA but to Mark's thinking that was just three years of reading about doing things. He wanted to get on with doing things right now. His parents cleared the spare room and let him have it for his kit, his computer and his printers. It was his first studio.

It got off to an excellent start.

A school friend's father was the chief sub-editor on the *Eastern Daily Press* in Norwich, one of the great remaining regional newspapers. He 'put in a word' and got Mark four weeks' work experience, unpaid.

He got a lift to the newsroom every day with his friend's father who gave him little pep talks on what made a great news photograph, what made a great news story and, usually, his own part in the reporting of it and its presentation in the *EDP*.

Mark was attached to a young staff photographer called Dave and would go out with him in one of the pool vehicles when he was despatched out on a story. Dave was only a couple of years older than Mark and they were trusted with only the bread-and-butter stuff of local newspapers but for the young Mark Elwin, it was truly heady stuff: hot weather, crowds on a Norfolk beach, wet weather, flooded fields, car crashes, a couple's 60th, 70th, 75th wedding anniversary, the wedding of a local dignitary and agricultural shows.

After a couple of weeks, Dave let Mark take the photograph for the 100th birthday of Mrs Edith Thompson of Evergreen Care Home in Hethersett. It was printed along with three paragraphs written by Mark name-checking Mrs Thompson, the care home, the care home sister also in the shot and Mrs Thompson's key to a long life, a glass of brown ale every Friday during the whist night. Not much of a story but there it was in the next day's edition of the *EDP*. Mark considered himself a professional, published photographer.

His work placement in fact went so well that well that every now and then he did get the odd commission from the news desk. As Mark was in Dersingham and so over an hour's drive north of the *EDP* newsroom in Norwich, on the Norfolk coast, he'd get a phone call from the Picture Desk. He'd jump onto his recently acquired Yamaha moped, seat box and rucksack loaded with kit, and motor off to take a photograph of a house where there had been a murder, or a fire, or multiple pile-up on the A17 (quite often, actually, a real breadwinner) then the Royals at Sandringham Church at Christmas, Burnham Market Horse Trials, The East of England Game Fair, a shooting party at Holkham Hall, a celebrity wedding at Pentney Abbey even if he had no idea who the *Coronation Street* actress was. At 19, he may still be living at home but he was starting to earn a proper living. That, plus the occasional family photographs for his parents' friends.

He was, he liked to say if anyone asked, a freelance photojournalist. He had cards printed to prove it. He bought a car.

His pictures in the *EDP* gave him a portfolio to hawk around and hawk around he did. Mark was young, keen and not ashamed to sell himself. Soon he was picking up day shifts with the *Lincolnshire Echo*, a paper which sold in the Fens and around the Wash but these were areas that were far too far away from the Lincoln newsroom to send a staff snapper.

By the time he was 20, his pictures of the Royals—great and lesser—on the Sandringham Estate and his pictures of toffs at Houghton Hall, Holkham Hall and some of the lesser grand homes of the north Norfolk coast got him commissions from the *Times* and the *Daily Telegraph* magazine sections.

It wasn't the photo-journalism of the Vietnam War but by the age of 20, he was making a good living and starting to make a small name for himself among commissioning picture editors. He bought a better car.

If he wasn't working then Friday night was pub night, usually at the Feathers in Dersingham. He'd meet up with old school friends who hadn't gone to university and old friends who had when they were back on their endless holidays.

One night in the Feathers he got talking to one of the gamekeepers from the Ken Hill Estate at Snettisham about five miles along the coast, an estate which swept down the shoreline between the A149 and the North Sea.

"Terrible trouble with hare coursing," said the old gamekeeper, rolling a cigarette. "Come on in plain daylight they do. I can't stop them. I'm only one man and his dog, as they used to say. There'll be a dozen of them. Usually gypsies down from Newark. All got greyhounds for the hares and Rottweilers for me. Can't show them a gun or I'll have my licence taken off me by the Old Bill."

Mark Elwin had an idea.

The following weekend Mark and the keeper laid low until the rusted trucks loaded with big men, big dogs and lean greyhounds were out. A clear field. Nets were laid at one end, the dogs were released and the hares were chased, netted, chased again and then chased again until one exhausted bloody greyhound was declared the winner.

He sold the photoshoot to the Press Association and the images went on to make page lead after page lead in *The Guardian*, the *Mirror*, *The Times* and the *Telegraph* and in regional newspapers across Britain and then in magazines across Europe. Mr Bilson sent him an email of congratulation.

It wasn't the money, although that night's work earned him the equivalent of two months of commissions from the *EDP*, *The Lincolnshire Echo* and all the other family group photos put together.

It wasn't the fact that his pictures were used to successfully prosecute and convict the 12 quite unpleasant men behind the hare coursing.

No. It was the fact that he'd spotted the story. Found the story. Shot the story. Sold the story. He was, from that point on, a bona fide freelance photojournalist with a scoop to his name. And the work started to flow.

"Can you do a weekend covering at our Manchester office?"

Yes.

"Look I know it's short notice but you couldn't go with this chap, this hot shot, this ego and do the snaps for next weekend's celebrity magazine could you?"

Yes.

"You wouldn't follow Comic Relief to the Sudan, would you?"

Yes.

Yes, was always the answer.

He loved it.

Chapter 12
Norfolk, Present Day

Sergeant Dave Bartrum had pretty much seen it all in his time with Norfolk Constabulary and he could tell as soon as he pitched up at the scene of the crash that this was a 'nailed on cut and shut case' as he liked to call them. Cut the bodies out. Shut the file.

In 20 years as a traffic man and almost 10 as a lead road traffic accident man, he'd seen some pretty awful things. Kids were the worst. A baby once, a long time ago, a mum and a baby, a Nissan Micra against a sugar beet lorry on the A17. No contest. Beet lorries always win in a road fight. Yes, he'd seen some pretty awful things. This collision wasn't one of them.

PC Adams gave him the quick low down by the side of the road and the fact that the woman in the VW was 'a pot head'. Case closed, thought the sergeant. Emma McMillan had been whisked away. PC Adams was despatched to do the death knock duties.

Sgt Bartrum knew the outcome of this scene but there was a process to go through and Sgt Bartrum always played it strictly by the book—the lengthy book.

Forensics were there. Photographs were taken. Cars were examined at the scene but, he thought, no point delaying the good folk of Dersingham any longer than he had to. Besides, he had more interesting things to do.

From the look of it, and his eye was experienced, Mr Jones had suffered quite a spectacular broken neck. The fire crews were there cutting open a jammed driver's side door.

Odd that he wasn't wearing a seat belt. Silly bugger, he thought.

He interviewed the man in the brown jacket. He'd seen nothing, just been a 'first responder' said the man in the brown jacket.

You, Son, are not a hero, thought the sergeant.

He spoke to the woman with the kid who had "seen it all."

She'd seen nothing. But the nothing she'd seen took ten minutes to tell and while she looked around at the dwindling crowd, she felt important for the first time in a long time.

She'd seen nothing but he wrote it all down anyway. Bulk out the file.

The signs were put out. 'Fatal Accident Here' but in his experience this delivered the square root of nothing in the way of anything useful.

There were a couple of other things he'd like to check but they could wait until he got the post-mortem and the car boys had a good look at tyres, brakes, and anything that could have contributed to this fatal little shunt.

Two days later he had just about everything he needed.

Car reports. Both had valid MoTs and both were in decent nick.

Driver reports, both insured and both with zero points.

Initial post-mortem examination revealed a broken neck, just as he had thought. But it was worth a call anyway.

"Dave," said Sgt Dave Bartrum to the pathologist.

"Dave," said Dr Dave Cooke the county pathologist.

It was the Dave Game they both always liked to play.

"Dave," said the policeman again.

"Dave?" said the doctor.

"Dave…broken neck?" said the policeman.

"Yes, Dave. It is Dave, isn't it?"

"Yes, Dave." And both grown men childishly chuckled.

"Ah, yes," said the pathologist eventually. "Recoil almost certainly. Forward into the airbag, thrown back, snap, dead. If he'd been wearing his seat belt, he could be playing golf today. I know I wish I was."

"But not at 30 miles an hour surely?" asked the sergeant.

"Possible," said Dr Dave.

"But not likely?" said Sgt Dave.

"Possible," said Dr Dave.

"Get off the fence," said Sgt Dave.

"Ok, he probably needed to be going more than 30."

"More than 40?"

"That would definitely do it with no seat belt. But you'll have a witness statement letting you know just how fast someone thought he was going."

"Oh, very funny," said Sgt Dave.

Three days later Sergeant Dave Bartrum along with WPC Davina Clements in her role as family liaison officer drove down the impressive drive to Westfield Farm House to make a visit to Mrs Ellen Jones. Widow. Expecting them. Not expecting what he had to say.

Cheerful bell tones but she was already opening the door as he rang.

"Mrs Jones?" he said, showing his warrant card. "Mrs Ellen Jones?"

"Yes, of course. Come in."

"This is WPC."

"We've met," she said curtly. "Come in. What exactly do you want? Let's get this over with. I'm not offering tea and biscuits."

Okay, he thought. Okay.

"Sit down, Mrs Jones," he said, in his best, often used, authoritative voice.

"Oh fuck off, Sergeant, don't patronise me," she said with a vigour that took even the sergeant aback. "What do you want? My husband is dead in a car crash. Some woman ran him off the road from what I hear. So what do you want from me, exactly?"

Okay, he thought again. Not what he had predicted. Tears possibly. Sad, still grieving widow probably. Angry and aggressive woman, no.

"Mrs Jones," he said. "Are you sure you won't take a seat?" Straight from the manual. Bad news, sit them down.

"Get on with it, or get out?" she said, a matter of factly.

"Mrs Jones. Do you know where your husband was going to? He wasn't going to work, was he?"

"It turns out he wasn't," she said. "So what?"

"Does the name Susie mean anything to you?"

"What?"

"Susie? Did your husband or you know a woman called Susie?"

She knew. And Sgt Bartrum knew she knew, straight away.

"Why do you ask?"

He reached into his inside pocket and took out a plastic evidence bag inside which was a card.

"There was a bunch of flowers in your late husband's car and this card attached. It says," and he read it out deliberately slowly "To my beautiful sexy Susie, happy birthday darling, Simon. With three Xs. Do you know this Susie, Mrs Jones?"

She sat down.

WPC Clements sat down next to her on the arm of the sofa.

"Mrs Jones?"

"What does it matter?" she said.

"I don't know. Yet. It might. It might not."

"It doesn't need to come out, does it?" she said.

Not so cocky now, are we, he thought.

"As I say, Mrs Jones. I don't know yet. If it's relevant yes. If it's not, no."

"Susan Wilkinson," she said abruptly. "Nurse. Blonde piece. About 30. Dresses about 20 apparently."

"Lives?"

"How would I know? Somewhere local. Worked at the hospital with him."

And now she looked straight at him.

"He told me it was over, the lying piece of shit."

Time to go, thought Sergeant Bartrum.

They say that as you die your whole life passes before you. In this case, when she heard of her husband's infidelity, her whole life with Simon Jones passed before her.

She had been a young nurse once too. Pretty. She'd set her sights on the young Simon Jones and they'd become a "thing." She stuck with him while he worked his way through all the other pretty nurses, some of the not-so-pretty nurses and even a couple of King's Lynn slappers. When he'd run out of steam and out of new opportunities, she'd pressed the 'marry me now' button and she had her man.

She knew what he was like from day one but the money, the house, the cars and the nice holidays, not to mention the status of being the 'lovely' Simon Jones' wife, meant she endured each sordid little affair until he got bored and came to heel again, if only for a while.

Now that her philandering husband was dead, she didn't even have the status of Wife and she doubted she'd be able to keep the status of the house or the nice holidays either.

When the police officers had driven away and she'd closed the door and taken a seat on one of the high stools by the butcher's block in the kitchen she finally let it out.

"You complete shit," she said out loud. "You utter and complete shit."

Susan Wilkinson met both police officers the next day in the main reception area of the hospital. She was in her nurse's uniform.

"Sorry to bother you at work Ms Wilkinson," said Sgt Bartrum.

"It doesn't matter. Police are here all the time. It's the way into A and E. I know what you want," she said.

"Okay," he said. "How did you know the deceased?"

"Look Sergeant we both worked here, we'd been seeing each other for nearly two years. He was going to leave his wife. So he said. And I think he would have done it. So there."

"On the day in question, what were your plans?" asked the sergeant.

"Oh, use your imagination, Sergeant," she said.

WPC Clements nearly smiled.

"What time did he say he'd be with you at your house?"

"Quarter past eight. He always left the house at the same time. Waved the dragon and the kids off on the school run, leaving as if he was the ever-dutiful doctor off to work. Gets to me at quarter past eight."

"Then he was late," said the sergeant.

"Of course he was late, Sergeant," she said "he was bloody dead, wasn't he?" she said. And she might just have been about to cry.

"No. The crash. By every account just before 8.15. He was running late."

"Who the fuck cares, Sergeant? I mean, Who. The. Fuck. Cares?"

I do, he thought.

Chapter 13
Norfolk, Present Day

Emma McMillan was taken from the scene of the crash in Dersingham to King's Lynn police station where she was asked to wait in one of the police cells.

"Really?" she said.

They left the door open.

It was two hours before she was ushered into the formal interview room, where there was a police officer and tape recorder. She declined to call a solicitor.

She was talked through the drug blood test and was asked three times if she was alright following the accident—she said she was—and three times if she understood what was going to happen next—she said she did. It was recorded and it was written down.

The legal limit for cannabis is the system when driving is 2 milligrams per litre of blood in your body. Cocaine is 5. Heroin is 10. Alcohol is 80. Emma McMillan knew she was in trouble. She had smoked a single joint as she always did just before breakfast, just before Daisy got up.

After the blood sample was taken by a woman in what Emma assumed was a nurse's uniform, she gave her statement. It was read back to her.

Briefly, she agreed she had said she was on time for work, not in a rush, she dropped off Daisy at school, went a hundred yards up School Road to the little Deli, bought her lunch, as she always did, was edging out of her side road onto the main road and then out of nowhere came this car. Could she see both left and right down the road she was entering? Of course she could otherwise she wouldn't have pulled out. Why was she partly on the other side of the road? She didn't know she was. And so it went on, all neatly written down by the policeman. Then typed it out, and read back to her again. Signed by both as an accurate record of what she had said.

"What happens next?" she asked.

"Well, we add this to the evidence. We have, let's see, I think, it's Sergeant Bartrum out at the scene right now. He'll be taking photographs, and talking to any remaining witnesses. There'll be forensics there and then it all goes off with the blood test results when we have them to the Crown Prosecution Service who'll decide what to do. You should hear something within a couple of weeks," he said, patiently, for the possibly the 100th or maybe even the 300th time in his career. He stopped counting a long time ago.

"But what *might* happen?" she asked. "I've got Daisy. My daughter. Will I go to prison?"

"If I was you, Mrs McMillan, I'd see a solicitor."

"Oh," she said. "Okay."

And then "Do I get taken home?"

She really did not want the neighbours to see her delivered home in a police car.

"The bus station is next door," said the policeman.

Thank God she thought.

She had no sleep that night. Daisy wanted to know why Grandma had picked her up from school and where was the car. Emma said it had broken down. She hated lying but, right now, she hated the truth even more.

A couple of days later she arrived at Brannon and Brannon solicitors to speak to a Mr Eric O'Grady, one of the solicitors, one of the small team of solicitors and paralegals still left at Brannon and Brannon trying to make money out of low-grade criminal law.

He was routine and unsympathetic. He began to process her.

"For a start Mrs McMillan," he said after making a note of her name, date of birth and address, "having MS is not a defence, it's not an excuse and it's probably not even a mitigating factor certainly as far as the CPS is concerned. The magistrates—if it is the magistrates."

"What do you mean? Why wouldn't it be magistrates? Don't they do all traffic offences?" she interrupted.

"Well, to put it bluntly, Mrs McMillan," said Mr O'Grady, running a hand back and forth across his muzzle, "they, the magistrates, can only impose a prison sentence of up to six months. If they think the case is more serious, potentially requiring a sentence longer than that, then they can and would send it to Crown Court to be heard before a judge," he said.

She started crying.

"But let's hope it doesn't come to that shall we?" he said, with a voice without sympathy and which was, at best, matter-of-fact.

Her tears would not affect his professional routine, or, rather, his personal routine. Death by drug driving was not how he'd seen his future caseload when he was doing his law degree in Nottingham. This was beneath him and his contempt for the case, contempt for the client and mostly contempt for himself, all these things meant he was not kind to her in her current fragile state.

He pressed on regardless of her tears.

This woman and a yob charged with wilfully snapping off wing mirrors from posh cars in Burnham Market were his last two clients of the day and when they had been processed when they had been dealt with, he would take up his regular spot at the bar of his golf club.

"Given the fact you've admitted smoking cannabis then you'll almost certainly be over the limit," he said. "The limits for cannabis are the tightest of just about any of the drink or drugs limits. So, in the next couple of weeks, you will almost certainly receive what is called an NIP."

Before she had time to ask what an NIP was, he raised the palm of his hand dismissively.

"Please don't interrupt just now, Mrs McMillan. There'll be time for questions when I have given you my resume of where we are now. At this point in the process."

Emma was quiet. Dreadful man, she thought.

"An NIP is a Notice of Intended Prosecution. When you get that document, you will need to come back. We'll know then how serious is the likely charge against you," he said.

Eric O'Grady was 50, had been made a partner at Brannon and Brannon ten years earlier but had been told in no uncertain terms that he was very, very unlikely to be made a Senior Partner.

Several attempts at Law Society 'Interpersonal Skills' courses over the years had not advanced his career possibilities. Nor had they advanced his interpersonal skills.

Eric O'Grady was passing time until he felt financially secure enough to retire permanently to the bar at the golf club to bore his fellow members with tales of a career in criminal law.

"What are the options?" she asked.

"Well, causing death by dangerous driving while under the influence of drugs would be the most serious," he said.

"And that means what?"

"Well, technically up to 14 years in prison…"

The tears started flowing again.

"But that is very rare. In fact, possibly even unheard of, I think. If you were out of your mind on heroin and drove your truck into a minibus full of Brownies, I think that would get you 14 years. Anyway, we'll cross that bridge when we get to it. What we are looking for—what we are *hoping* for Mrs McMillan is a charge of Death by Careless Driving while under the influence etc."

"And that?" she said, tears running down all over her cheeks.

"Only up to five years in prison depending on all the circumstances. And we don't know those yet. Really don't. No point speculating at this juncture, eh?"

"Why not? In your experience Mr O'Grady," she said "What do you *think*?"

"Wild horses couldn't make me guess what charge police evidence and the prosecuting authorities might produce. Not in the lawyerly way. Or shouldn't be, in my opinion."

This man has to be the most pompous man I've ever met, she thought. I bet there's no Mrs O'Grady.

He pressed on. "I'll need to see all of the evidence that the police submit and the police won't be submitting that for some a while yet. As I say, when you get your Notice of Intended Prosecution, we'll know much better where the CPS is going with this. It might be that the magistrates decide to handle it themselves and then we could be looking at anything as low as a heavy fine and community service."

Why didn't he say that in the first place, she thought. Give me hope. Then she realised she was only operating on hope itself and started crying more. She reached into her bag looking for a tissue. Even Eric O'Grady wasn't that insensitive and pushed over a box of Co-op tissues that were sitting on his desk.

"Thank you," she said.

"On more mundane matters Mrs McMillan, have you informed your insurers?"

"Not yet, no. Been a bit of a time."

"You'll need to do that."

"Of course," she said.

"And your employers?"

"Why do they need to know?"

"Well, you might receive a custodial sentence. And," he said, with deliberate, solemn impact, "it will probably be all over the *Lynn News*."

And the tears came again and lasted pretty much all the way home on the bus.

Chapter 14
Norfolk, 1933

Monty and Alfie left Sandringham village and headed up the hill back towards Hanging Wood at a sharp walk.

When they reached the spot where Monty had been tending to the game feeders, he collected a small heap of six dead pigeons he had shot earlier that morning and shoved them into the game bag he'd left lying there.

"How long are we staying in the woods, Father?" asked Alfie.

"We're not Son," his father said.

"But you said we'd be hiding in the woods?"

"That's only what I told your mother, just in case," said Monty.

"But you told her not to say anything?"

"Aye, I did," he said, but just in case, Monty thought.

"Come on Alfie. No time to lose."

Monty knew where he was going and knew the route he was going to take. It should give them the best chance of getting there without seeing anyone else or, more importantly, being seen by anyone else.

The Norfolk countryside was easy to walk. Not flat like the Fens to the west or the Broads to the east but gently rolling from the North Sea up to a long line of low hills sitting just back from the coast. It was June and the fields were still green, the ears of barley and wheat yet to turn golden and ready for harvesting, the potatoes in full leaf, feathery carrot tops blowing in the gentle summer breeze.

From Hanging Wood they headed north and, avoiding paths and bridleways, they tracked their way towards the coast always ducking behind hedgerows and walking half tilted forwards to keep below the hedge line. Monty knew the fields and the farms along the way intimately and he knew the rural calendar as if it was his personal diary.

Taking a high loop they cut across field after field of barley and wheat and at the Hare family pile just outside Docking, they dodged away from the village, the church and the school and round the back of the cow sheds. Monty and Alfie could now see the coastline from their position at the top of the rise of the land, the North Sea shining silver in the June sunshine all the way across the Wash to Lincolnshire.

The one place to avoid, thought Monty, would be Choseley Farm with its fine herd of dairy cows. They'd be bringing them in for second milking about now.

"Listen here Alfie," he said, and Father and Son stopped for a moment. "Listen, we need to get down to the Staithe you see."

"Why?" asked Alfie.

"We're going to see Uncle Jethro."

"Why?"

"Never you mind about that now boy," said his father. Monty knew the time for talking would come, but it wasn't now. Now was the time to get away.

"Look Son, this is a terrible day. I just need you to stick close to me. The tricky bit of getting to Uncle Jethro will be getting across the coast road without being seen. You understand?"

"Not really, Father," said the boy.

"Look now, a lad with a school satchel with his father won't attract attention today, right now, but if they do come looking for us, and I'm sure they will, it might stir someone's memory if the police started issuing descriptions of us. You see now?"

Monty could see Alfie for just what he was, a slightly scared, shocked, bewildered little boy. He put his hand on his son's head.

"Try not to worry Son. I'm here. We stick together. I promise you everything will be just fine. Now stay close. Let's get on. No time to lose."

And with that, they were off again. In just under three hours the two of them had covered nearly ten miles and they could now see the fine church at Brancaster about 300 yards ahead of them, the road that ran along the coast in between. They stopped in a little copse and swigged water from their canteens.

"You alright lad?" said Monty.

Alfie just nodded and wiped the sweat off his forehead with the back of his sleeve.

"Here, have a bit of bread and cheese," the father said to the son.

Alfie made to tear off a chunk but his father put up a finger to stop him. "Not too much now," he said. "We need to save it for later."

They sat for a short time behind a hedge out of view. It was a beautiful day. It was a terrible day. If anyone did see them, they could easily have been out for a day's ramble on a warm June day. As it was, the events of the day hung heavily in the air between them.

"Father," said Alfie.

"Not now Alfie lad. Not now. There'll be a time to talk, but it's not now. Not now."

There was a little corner village shop in Brancaster, just back from the main road. That was to be avoided. There was a smart Victorian school which more than likely would be having lessons in the playground on such a day. So that was to be avoided too. The Ship Inn would be closed and most likely the landlord would be having a couple of hours rest after beer deliveries and bottling up in the morning and a smattering of lunchtime drinkers.

So the pair cut behind a couple of cottages, then nipped through the garden at the back of the pub, they looked left and right and with no one in sight they ran across the road and quickly over the low wall surrounding the church, then across ancient graves to the back of the church where nobody could see them.

From there it was easy to find the track that ran parallel to the main route down to Brancaster Golf Club, and between the church and the golf course was the wide-open marsh.

The marshes were treacherous especially when the tide was in and the North Sea filled up all the creeks. That day the tide was just on the turn, starting to come in, but with the network of banks and paths still exposed leaving just shallow water in the creeks.

These were the marshes of Monty's youth, where he'd come with his grandfather wildfowling, looking for a pink foot or a greylag goose to shoot for the oven. A place where a fast, incoming tide could leave you cut off for hours and in winter, at night, that was almost certain death.

Zigzagging left and right they made their way east, using the exposed banks to crisscross back and forth, the high reeds and rushes of the creeks offering cover.

With Brancaster village about half a mile to their right they pressed on, just stopping once so that Monty could peer inland to see if there was anyone out and about around a couple of cottages closest to the marsh. There wasn't. It appeared the coast was literally clear.

Off again they pressed along the tracks through the marsh until they could see the Staithe itself. They pressed back against a wild hawthorne hedge to see if there was anyone about. Again the coast was clear. No one on the path, no one on the decks of the eight or so fishing boats tied up waiting for the returning tide so they could go out again into the North Sea.

In the main creek to their left were some pleasure boats, dayboats, sailboats and more tied to buoys, some the playthings of the local gentry, others for getting out to distant sandbanks on a falling tide to dig the mussel and cockle beds in the bitter winter months or in a few weeks' time to harvest the wild samphire to be served up on the fine dining plates of London. From behind their hedge, they could see a couple of young men pulling a dayboat up onto the shore. Monty could see them. They couldn't see Monty and Alfie.

Here was the risk. Here was the faith that Monty was about to put in his oldest friend. Here was when he needed someone to count on in his time of need. And this, right now, was his time of need.

One of those fishing boats, the Belle Star, belonged to Jethro Springer. More accurately it belonged to his grandfather but Old Man Springer as everyone called him had long retired from the truly gruelling life that was being a fisherman in the North Sea.

Jethro and Monty had shared their lives from the age of five when they'd both started at the Brancaster End Boys' School. Jethro came from a long, long line of fishermen, hauling in crab and lobster in the summer, digging for mussels and cockles in the winter, the family had oyster beds at Thornham to harvest all year round and there were occasional mackerel and bass trips if the shoals got down as far as Norfolk on their summer feeding migration from Scotland.

Jethro learned his trade from the age of 11 going out with Old Man Springer and his own father until his father was taken away to the Great War and never came back. At least, he knew his father. Monty's father just left Brancaster one day and never came back leaving young Monty to be raised by his grandfather.

Monty could see the tide was coming in so the boats would have been back in the Staithe hours ago to be unloaded, cleaned down and the catch taken away for wives to dress and prepare and even make a few local deliveries. The lorries from King's Lynn would have taken most of the catch away.

There was a large wooden hut about 50 yards ahead of them which was used occasionally, very occasionally, by the local customs men when they carried out spot checks. These spot checks were usually very well telegraphed by loose talk in the pubs. Monty couldn't remember when anyone was caught with any kind of contraband, although some of the fishing lads were known to nip over to Holland and return laden with gin and tobacco, or to Belgium for wine and French brandy. It was easier money than fishing.

Behind the wooden hut was a row of four tiny fishermen's cottages.

They quickly covered their ground and Monty knocked on the blue-painted door of Gull Cottage and almost immediately a man in a matching blue sweater and a beard a squirrel could hide in opened it.

"Monty and young Alfie," he said, delight across his face, "What are you doing here? Come on in, I'll put a kettle on."

"Jethro," said Monty, "there's been a spot of bother."

Chapter 15
Norfolk, 1933

"I didn't do it," said Monty after he'd given an increasingly shocked Jethro the story of the morning.

"He didn't," said Alfie, sucking on a mug of hot sweet tea and tucking into a slice of cake made by Jethro's wife the day before.

Monty looked at his friend.

Jethro paced four steps across to the fireplace, and then four steps back. That's all it took to cover Gull Cottage's front room.

"What's your plan?" said Jethro.

"Get out of Norfolk," said Monty.

"When? How?" asked Jethro.

"Now and you," said Monty. "If she does as she's been told then the police won't even have been called yet. So long as she keeps to her part of this bloody mess me and Alfie have got a good head start."

"Aye. And when they do start looking, they'll start in the woods," said Jethro.

"And more than likely watch the roads and train stations," said Monty, and raised his eyebrows and looked at his old friend with a smile.

"Aye," said Jethro. "Roads and railways. But not so easy to check the North Sea, eh?"

"Not so easy, no," said Monty.

"I think Boston will do you?"

"I thought so," said Monty.

"Boston is perfect. Boats are in and out of there all the time. None stay for more than a couple of days. I know quite a few of the lads there too. Nobody will take any notice of us," said Jethro.

"I'll need to be able to get me and Alfie to the train station first thing," said Monty.

"If we take Lucky Jim and not Belle Star, we can get off now. Throw a few lines out, put a few mackerel in the tub and at worst it'll look like a pleasure jaunt for a man and his lad. I do it often enough. 'sides, as I say I know some of the lads over there. Boston is the best bet. Where are you heading for?"

"Probably best not to tell, eh?" said Monty.

"Aye, probably best."

"What about Zither?" asked Monty after Jethro's wife.

"Zither? She won't be back until later. She's dropping off a couple of lobsters at the big house. I'll leave her a note telling her the truth. I've decided to take the evening tide up to Boston for a go at some mackerel and a beer with the boys up there. She'll be right."

"But you'll miss tomorrow's tide? You'll lose a day's fishing?"

"Nah, you two hit the road just before first light and I'll get to sea. I'll be back by seven tomorrow morning. Easy getting out of Boston. Not like the bloody shifting sands here. Soon catch up."

"Here," said Monty as Jethro was leaving a note for his wife, "have half a dozen pigeons."

"Don't be daft," said Jethro, "Missus'll know you've been here. When did I last shoot a pigeon? We'll take them with us. And here, Alfie, grab a couple of blankets from over there. It'll get cold enough on the water once this sun goes down."

The three of them closed the door of Gull Cottage behind them and checking no one was around they hurried the hundred yards or so to a rowing boat tied to the Staithe wall.

"Under the blankets boys," said Jethro.

Monty and Alfie lay on the bottom of the rowing boat under the blankets and Jethro started to row out to the Lucky Jim moored against a buoy at the edge of the channel near a red channel buoy.

"Alright, Jethro!"

Monty and Alfie stayed dead still under the blankets breathing in the salty, fishy air.

Jethro carried on rowing and looked over his shoulder.

"Where you off to boy? Do you know something I don't? That'd make a first!" and the voice burst into laughter.

"Just thought I'd take Lucky Jim out and see if the mackerel have made it down yet. What you up then Vern?" Jethro knew Vern Coleman well. They weren't friends as such but the Coleman's had been fishing these waters for as long as Jethro and his family.

"Ah, just a bit of tinkering with the gear. The engine ran a bit rough yesterday. I'll be out later. Let me know what you find!"

Jethro was past Vern's boat by now.

"Of course I won't!" he shouted.

Jethro rowed the boat around the back of the Lucky Jim and said "Right lads, let's go. Climb on then on the deck under the blankets."

They climbed in and silently pulled blankets over Monty and Alfie.

"Who is Vern?" whispered Monty.

"Boat called Two Brothers after his grandad and his brother," said Jethro. "If anyone asks, which they won't, but if anyone asks him if he saw anything tonight then he'll say he saw me heading for Lucky Jim to go and throw a few mackerel lines out. Perfectly normal. Exactly what I told the missus. And he'll say there was only me on board. Perfect. Now stay low. We'll get off."

Lucky Jim was a fine little day boat. 18 feet long, small cabin with a tiny thin bed and a 20 horsepower engine that coughed into life first time. With the rowing boat tied to the buoy in the creek, they nudged out past the sand bar, past the huge sand dune known as Scolt Head and out into the open North Sea.

It was a journey Jethro had done a hundred times before and more. In fact, on a clear early summer evening in June like today you could pretty much see Boston with the mighty Boston Stump building all the way from Norfolk. All you had to do was point the boat and open the throttle.

When they were past the Wash and well into the journey Jethro gave them the all-clear to come out from the blankets.

Jethro dug out a bag from inside a hatch and tossed it to Alfie.

"Get the lines out, boy. We need to look the part. And we'll need some supper too," Jethro said to Alfie.

Alfie hadn't been in a boat before and had no idea what to do.

Jethro laughed.

"Look, see these hooks on the sides of the boat," he explained.

"Yes," said Alfie.

"Wrap that end of the line, yes that end there," he pointed, "and mind those feathers boy, they've hooks in them. Then wind that end round the hook there and chuck the line and the feathers and that little weight out over the side."

Alfie took out ten lines each with four hooks on them. The hooks all had something shiny or bright tied to them, some twisted metal, some a bit of red feather from a pheasant tail.

Around the back and both sides of Lucky Jim Alfie found the coat hooks which had been screwed to the boat and one by one he tied one end of the lines to the coat hook and let the fishing hooks out into the sea.

Ten lines then trailed out in the wake of the boat.

And then nothing. Nothing for over an hour. The three of them sat still and mostly quietly as the engine put-put-putted.

Finally, Monty said "You could starve to death on this boat," and the three of them laughed.

"The alarm will surely have been raised by now?" said Jethro.

"Oh yes," said Monty. Then "Bread and cheese!" he said, shifting the subject away from events back at Keeper's Cottage. "Let's eat. In the absence of fresh fish, let's eat."

"No thanks. I'm waiting for fresh mackerel," said Jethro.

"Why, are we going to buy some in Boston?" joked Monty. And the two old friends relaxed, just a little, for the first time that day.

"You wait. Last hour into Boston," he said. "You just wait. I'll not tell you how to shoot a pigeon, you don't tell me how to catch a fish."

And he was right. When they could see the Lincolnshire coast Lucky Jim hit the mackerel shoal and it was all Monty and Alfie could do to pull in the lines, pull off the fish, chuck them in the tub and put the lines out again.

By the time, Jethro steered Lucky Jim into Boston harbour they had over 150 fresh mackerel and had thrown back fifty or more tiddlers.

They tied up away from the harbour buildings and the fish sheds and Jethro told Monty and Alfie to lie low in the boat.

"In fact, Alfie, get in the cabin for now. Two men on a boat is one thing. Two men and a boy on a boat is another."

"I'll stay low too. If I'm seen I'm seen but no point shouting about being here," said Monty and he said on the deck with his back against the side.

"I'll just go and check-in," said Jethro. "Chuck us those pigeons," he said.

And off Jethro went to the harbour master's hut.

He was back in ten minutes.

"No worries, it's all fine," he said. "Pigeons went over well. I told him I'd shot too many on a farmer mate's land. He was chuffed to bits. Now. Supper. Alfie pass me out that little stove and that fry pan. Thanks lad."

By the light of the stove Jethro gutted the shiny mackerel, chucked the guts over the side to the delight of a couple of nocturnal gulls bobbing on the sea, and rustled up supper.

The three of them feasted on fried fish and bread, Monty and Jethro chatting about this and that and Alfie drowsing in the cabin. When he finally fell asleep Monty covered him with a blanket.

"Good night, good lad," said Father to Son, "sleep well. Long way to go yet."

At three o'clock in the morning, Monty shook Alfie awake.

"Come on, lad. Get yourself together," said his father.

"Where are we going?" he asked, groggy and rubbing his eyes. It was still dark but the moon was clear and he soon got his night sight.

"We've just got to get off," said his father. "Off the boat now. Come on. No time to lose. We can get off the here, there's no chance of being seen at this time of day. Jethro's got to get home and get off to work. We've troubled him enough."

Monty climbed onto the harbour side and with Jethro giving him a push up from behind he hoisted his son onto the harbour wall with him.

He turned to his old friend.

"Jethro," he said.

Jethro put his hand up to stop Monty from saying thank you.

"Well then," said Monty "I hope this doesn't get you into trouble."

"How can it? You came to me and asked me for a lift to Boston. If anyone has seen you, which I doubt. Anyway, if they did, then an innocent man can go to Boston any time he likes. Anyway, no one will know except us three. No one."

"I think that's right. I'll still not tell you where we're going," said Monty.

"No, best not," said Jethro.

"Well then, goodbye old friend. Good friend," said Monty. "See you again sometime. Soon I hope."

"I very much doubt that," said Jethro. "Now get off, and quickly."

With that, and without looking back, Monty and Alfie slipped off the harbour wall and dropped down onto the road which would take them into Boston town and the railway station.

Jethro fired up Lucky Jim and headed home.

Chapter 16
Norfolk, Present Day

Mark Elwin opened the shop door at 9.30 most mornings, alarms off, sign turned to say "Yes, we are open!" in a cheesy 1950s font with a gurning child with slicked back black hair and a reassuring thumbs up. It was not an original.

He had a variety of signs for the door. "Sorry, We're Closed. Open Tomorrow!" was the most used. Passing footfall along the main drag in Dersingham was slight and regular planned jobs often required both him and Trish to be out on the job. Certainly weddings. And weddings were looming large on the horizon. His heart sank.

The upside was that he'd already got eight Saturday weddings in the diary and a handful of mid-week jobs all at the upmarket venues that recommended his services, for a small commission. There was no bargain basement at Visionary.

All bar two of them also wanted drone video aerials and stills, especially of the happy couple leaving their chosen venue as brand-spanking newlyweds. The venue was sometimes a church but increasingly a civil wedding licenced venue, fancy hotels, small country houses, medieval barns, and the nearby Pentney Abbey. To be fair, even the wedding-cynical Mark Elwin thought Pentney Abbey was a stunning spot.

Over the years he had pretty much migrated all that side of the business over to Trish. She had so much more patience than he did.

Last year on one wedding job, there were so many late changes to where the photographs would be taken and who was to be in them that Mark had said to Trish "You know I wouldn't mind doing these weddings if they would only shoot the mother of the bride at the engagement party."

The look of horror on Trish's face told him exactly what was going on.

He turned.

"Mrs Timpson," he said to the mother of that particular day's bride, "not you of course," and he gave her what he hoped was a winning smile.

"Mr Elwin," she said, smiling at him with the confidence of a woman who would be paying his invoice, "I would probably agree with you, if only the mother of the bloody bridegroom was shot at the same time," and she gave herself a little smile as she turned and shooed a brace of page boys back towards an assembling line of relatives.

"No, no, no Dennis and Violet," she commanded. "You're not in this one. Get out of the line. Get out. Shoo. Wait over there. You're in the next one with friends of the parents." And she strode away.

Mark turned to Trish and pulled the face of a man who may, or may not, have 'got away with it'.

No, Trish was the designated 'Visionary' wedding coordinator and all Mark did was pretty much turn up on the day and act as a second camera and operate the drone.

Anyway, there were 13 weddings on the books in total and there were always some late call-ups when a fellow photographer just packed up work or had been offered a better job somewhere. That would be north of £40,000 of business.

Mark was close to saving a 50% deposit on a newly built two-bed terraced house in King's Lynn. That'd be three he'd have. He'd set himself a target of eight by the time he was 50. Ten more years and he'd be financially as free as a bird, income flowing and house prices rising. No more bloody weddings. Happy days.

In the meantime, Trish had hundreds of school photographs to print up and slide into their cardboard frames from the school shoot on the day of the crash. Contacts had been sent out, by Trish, and the orders had come flooding in. As usual the most popular were ones where two or more siblings were at the same school. Family shots sold well and were despatched to grannies, aunties and Godparents all over the world.

An email confirmed that another one of the local game shoots had booked the souvenir glossy coffee table book for their guns.

Yes, business was good.

But he was bored. Really, quite bored.

The solution, he thought, might lie in the old-fashioned blue cardboard A4 folder on his desk in the office at the back of the shop onto which he had written: "Find Alfie Sidebottom."

He made himself a coffee, a cappuccino, 'frothy coffee' his mother had called them back in the day, no chocolate sprinkles though, and opened up the folder.

There was not that much in it so far but he had written up the conversation with his grandmother and had spent a couple of hours one night with a beer, or two, in the flat, skimming the internet.

The *Eastern Daily Press* reports from 1933 had been printed off and added to the file. He'd signed up to a couple of these 'find your ancestors' sites that would give him access to tracing documents such as birth certificates, weddings, deaths and more. No scrabbling through old dusty parish records for a genealogist any more.

The most interesting thing he found so far though was the *EDP* newspaper archive. It was the report of the Coroner's Court Inquest into the death of Mr Clement Sidebottom, farm labourer.

He lifted a couple of pieces of blank white A4 from the paper tray on the printer, took a swig of coffee which was a bit too bitter despite the frothy milk, and raised a pen for action.

Unlawfully killed, eh?

Well, it wouldn't take a genius to work that out.

Sandringham Labourer
"Unlawfully Killed."

The labourer murdered in the so-called 'Royal Gamekeeper' case was unlawfully killed the King's Lynn coroner has ruled.

Mr Clement Sidebottom, 30, of Apple Cottage, Sandringham was found dead at Keeper's Cottage, Sandringham the home of his brother Mr Montgomery Sidebottom, 32, who is now being sought by Norfolk Constabulary as part of a murder enquiry.

The Coroner, Mr Jeremy Thwaites, sitting with a magistrate, heard evidence that Mr Clement Sidebottom had been found dead at Keeper's Cottage at around 5.30 pm on June 8th by Mrs Nika Sidebottom, 28, the wife of Mr Montgomery Sidebottom.

She told the court "I'd been spending the day with my mother and returned to the cottage at around tea time, about half past five. I couldn't open the front door which I thought must be stuck. It was never locked. I went round to the back and into the house and there I saw him slumped against the front door. There was blood everywhere."

Mrs Sidebottom, who cried throughout her evidence, said her first thought had been for her son Alfie who should have been home from school about an hour earlier. His tea of cheese and ham and bread had been left in the larder for him. He was nowhere to be found. Nor was the food.

The murder weapon was the victim's own 12-gauge shotgun, found at the scene and placed on the kitchen table by Mrs Sidebottom she said.

"I broke it. I was loaded. One barrel anyway. I broke it and left it on the table so it wouldn't go off," she said.

Evidence was also given by Sergeant Christopher Killingbeck, a detective with Norfolk Constabulary.

He told the court that he and three other policemen had arrived at Keeper's Cottage around 7 pm the same evening. It was still light.

An initial statement had been taken from Mrs Sidebottom and photographs taken of the scene. Two of the policemen were sent to take a walk around the village and knock on doors to see if they'd heard anything unusual.

Sergeant Killingbeck said that unfortunately, the sound of shotguns being discharged was not unusual on the Sandringham Estate.

He said the systematic search of the area had started the following morning and encompassed the whole of the Sandringham Estate with police watching the railway stations at Wolferton, Hunstanton and King's Lynn.

The court heard that in the weeks since the killing, there had been no reports of any sightings of either Mr Montgomery Sidebottom or his eight-year-old son Alfred.

Sergeant Killingbeck added that descriptions and photographs of the two had since been circulated to surrounding police forces in East Anglia and to Scotland Yard.

A ruling of unlawful killing was recorded.

Chapter 17
Norfolk, Present Day

Trish didn't start work until ten in the morning so Mark thought he'd give himself half an hour with his 'Find Alfie Sidebottom' file and the great Google search engine in the sky before steeling himself for wedding day planning.

"So," he said out loud while making himself another coffee, this time with half a spoon of brown sugar to take away the bitterness, "next time buy better coffee."

Back at his desk, he reread the *EDP* report again.

"Unlawful killing, eh?" he said to himself. "Well, I agree with them there," and pulled some white A4 sheets towards him and started making a list of things that didn't make any sense, things which he wanted to know and things just to consider. What was needed, he decided, was a list. He wrote carefully:

1. Why was only a policeman of the rank of Sergeant assigned to the case?

This perplexed him. A murder? On a royal estate? Of course, it may well be that the sergeant was simply the first on the scene and knew everything the Coroner's Court needed to know. But a Detective Inspector had been quoted as leading the inquiry in earlier *EDP* reports. This was something to follow up on in the *EDP* archives to see if anyone more senior was ever subsequently involved or quoted. Or, and far more sinister, were only junior officers involved to brush the incident under the carpet with as little fuss as possible? Better for the King if Monty and Archie weren't found. No subsequent murder trial. No lurid coverage. No hanging.

Mark paused, mentally lining up the questions in some sort of importance.

2. Why didn't the police turn up until 7 pm?

This seemed a strangely long time from the body being discovered at half past five that evening. There was no mention in court of how Nika Sidebottom had raised the alarm. A quick flick through the internet revealed that when the murder took place the classic Sir Giles Gilbert Scott design number 3 telephone kiosk was being deployed in all rural areas, so it was safe to assume there would have been a public telephone kiosk nearby, especially on the Royal Sandringham Estate. Might be worth a check, he wrote.

So the alarm could have been raised quite quickly.

So why the delay? Maybe things just took longer in those days. The internet again revealed a handsome-looking Morris 6 as the police car of choice in 1933. He added that to the conspiracy theory. Don't rush over there boys, we need to kick this one upstairs first to see what we do about it. Was that it? Royal protocols? Checking if there were any Royals there with a murderer on the loose? Did the senior police officers go to Sandringham House and send the B team to Keeper's Cottage?

Ooh, he thought, this is much more interesting than snapping the happy smiling couple under some honeysuckle-covered arbour.

Of course, Mark had the advantage of reading the report knowing that Nika Sidebottom was pregnant at the time of the shooting. So, had Monty found that out? And if he had...

3. If you've just found out your wife is unfaithful, how come she is going about normal business by visiting her mum?

Maybe he just wanted her out of the house. Maybe there'd been a massive row and she'd just walked. But she said nothing of this at the court hearing. Of course, she wouldn't, he thought.

4. Why shoot his brother in his own home?

Yes, why? If he'd found out that his wife was pregnant with his own brother's child, why did he not confront his brother in his brother's home? Surely by shooting his brother at Keeper's Cottage, he had no chance of getting away with it. Brother shot dead at Brother's house could have been, well, anyone. No tracing a shotgun cartridge like you can a pistol or a rifle bullet. The brand of the cartridge may be but virtually impossible to tie it to an actual weapon.

"If I was mad with rage at my brother, I'd have gone round to his house to have it out," he mused.

5. How come his brother's gun was the murder weapon?

This is very odd, thought Mark. How come Clement was at Keeper's Cottage with a gun? Clem was a farm labourer not a gamekeeper so presumably would not routinely carry a gun? Or maybe he would? Nothing to stop him from shooting a rabbit, or a hare or even a squirrel or two, for the pot. Certainly pigeons. Perfectly acceptable. But why take a gun to your brother's house, if it was a social occasion? Or maybe Clement had gone round to have it out with Monty?

And if I've got murder in mind why rely on the victim to bring his gun round? Weird. So Monty probably didn't have murder in mind? Was there a stand-off, anger, a struggle then boom?

Mark realised he probably could never find out. All the players would be dead by now. Except Alfie. He might still be alive.

"Find Alfie Sidebottom," he said to himself. So then…

6. Alfie

This was the big one. Where was Alfie? If Monty had taken Alfie with him, why? If he hoped to evade capture by going on the run why take the boy with him? This would make life incredibly tricky for him to get away.

And if Alfie had come home at half past four and seen his murdered uncle, why would he go with his father? Taking a child was risky enough but taking a frightened and reluctant child…it didn't make sense.

No wonder the police manned the local train stations. A man with a boy not at school would be noticed even by strangers. Catching the train at Wolferton or Hunstanton would have been very risky for the runaways. Surely a Sandringham gamekeeper was well-known enough locally to be spotted a mile off?

And Monty must have known he couldn't hide out in the woods and fields of Norfolk forever so.

7. Where do you run to?

The court reports showed that a superficial search of the village of Sandringham had taken place the first evening but the substantive search of Sandringham, the wider estate, and the watching of train stations hadn't begun until first light the next day. Why the delay?

Had Monty and Alfie already made good their escape? On foot? And was Alfie actually with his father or had something much more sinister happened?

Oh, that was a new thought which just popped into his head. Surely not a double murder? These things were not unknown these days. A father kills his children to deprive an unfaithful mother of them. But they usually kill the mother as well.

"No, that's not it," he said out loud. "Or is it? Who knows?"

Yet.

Yes, where to run to? Further than Norfolk, for sure. You can't hide in the countryside. People know all about you and strangers stand out like a sore thumb. Even these days, he thought, rifling through memories of dozens of matey chats in the bar at the Feathers. People in villages know everything about you.

"Did you see that white van parked up on Lynn Road the other day?"

"I see Mark Smith was in the Bircham shop this morning. What's he doing back over here?"

"Tracey and Jim are back together…are they? …yep, saw them out with the dog on Snettisham beach yesterday."

No, you couldn't breathe in Norfolk villages without someone seeing you and passing it on. It would have been even worse in 1933 he thought.

So a city then. Yes, much easier to lose yourself in crowds. Norwich? Unlikely. Norfolk Constabulary and the *EDP* and plenty of other newspapers were everywhere and especially in the days and weeks after the murder. No, if it was the two of them on the run, Father and Son, then they would surely need to be out of the countryside and out of the county.

So, where did you run to, Alfie Sidebottom?

Chapter 18
Norfolk, Present Day

Manilla envelopes from government bodies are rarely good news and Emma McMillan looked down at the two in her hands with a deep, deep sense of the enormity of what was swarming around her.

For a week and more all she could think of was what would happen to Daisy if she was sent to prison? I mean seriously? Absentee father. Her parents elderly and, to be honest, simply not capable. Or willing, she knew.

Weren't Godparents traditionally lined up to step into the breach? Not a hope. They'd both been chosen by Daisy's father and proved as unreliable as he had.

That and the house, the payments on the car…oh no. Just, oh no.

A heart sinking is a real thing.

The Notice of Intention to Prosecute was exactly that. An intention to prosecute. The first one stated the offence to be prosecuted was driving under the influence of drugs.

Fair enough, she thought.

The second one would be crucial.

"Careless," she said out loud. "Let it be careless."

She opened it.

"Dangerous," it said, and her hands dropped to her waist and she looked up to the ceiling in her hallway.

"Oh God," she said.

She telephoned Brannon and Brannon and made an appointment to see Eric O'Grady in a couple of days, after work.

"Come in, come in, sit down, Mrs McMillan," he said.

Was he cheerier than last time? Had he taken a humanity pill?

She handed over the letters, but she'd already passed on the vital details via the receptionist.

"Sit down, sit down," he said, then scanned the letters and said eventually, "Hmm, okay."

"Give me hope, Mr O'Grady. Please," she said.

And he looked at her as if she'd just spoken in tongues.

"Well, okay. I have here the two NIPs. It's a question of tactics. Now I haven't seen the police files, the Crown Prosecution Service evidence or, really, anything yet. But, first of all, we'll go to Magistrates Court. Now, the driving while under the influence of drugs is a straight guilty plea," he paused, she didn't reply, "so really what we're looking at is the death by dangerous driving intention to prosecute."

"Could they change their mind?" she asked. Give me hope.

"In theory, yes. In practice, unlikely." he said "So we don't have to make up our minds about the plea until I've seen the files. We don't have to enter pleas until the first magistrates hearing. Then, if we go with not guilty."

"Yes," she said.

"Let's see the files first, eh? But if we go with not guilty two things could happen. The magistrates could decide to try the case themselves, in which case we're already down to a maximum sentence of six months in prison. Out in three."

"I can manage that. I can find somewhere for Daisy for that."

"Or they can decide that on the evidence they've seen, they reckon it's too serious for them to handle and it's a trial by jury at the Crown Court."

Trial by jury. Oh my god Emma, what have you done?

"There's a third option which is they take the case themselves, hear all the evidence, find you guilty and then send you up to Crown Court for sentencing as they think it's too serious for just six months."

With every word that passed his lips the little hope left in her soul drained away.

"Is there anything going for me?" she asked. Give me hope you cruel, cruel man.

"Well," he said, as if flicking through an old internal notebook of classic defences he had presented, "you were not speeding."

"And?"

"We don't really know what he was up to. Was he in any way responsible? Partly responsible? All these things are taken into account."

"And?"

"Well, if you plead or are found guilty then before sentencing, I get to plead mitigation on your behalf."

"Like what?"

"Well, we are on stronger ground there, I think, at the moment. Firstly, you admitted smoking cannabis at the scene of the accident. Early admissions count in your favour. Secondly, you're not wildly over the limit. The cannabis limit is set very, very low certainly when you compare it to drink drive."

"And?"

"Daisy. If it stays with the magistrates, they'd be thinking about her welfare too. The courts aren't keen to separate a single mother from their child. It happens, though."

"Anything else?"

"Well, finally, your MS. I'll need a letter from your GP as to the seriousness of the condition. If he could give a view on whether cannabis might help your symptoms that would be ideal. The view of medical cannabis is changing right now."

"My doctor a bit old school."

"You never know. Anyway, that's what we have so far. As I say, we'll need to see all the evidence in the files."

"And," she said, "timescale?" It wasn't the prospect of what lay ahead that was torturing her but the waiting.

"Well, could be as soon as a month, could be as long as six or more."

Oh god, she thought. Six months of coming home every day looking behind the door waiting for the dreaded letter.

At Westfield Farm House, it wasn't dreaded letters but a ringing phone that had become something of a messenger of further gloom for the newly widowed Ellen Jones.

In the two weeks since that horrible day, her life had gone from chaos, despair and long silences to at least a routine, if not to normality. The children were got up, washed, dressed, breakfasted and driven to school with perhaps a little too much firmness and definitely too little empathy.

It was all Ellen could do to keep herself and Sam and Gemma together. What she did not need was having to hear friends, once upon a time friends, long lost friends and especially long lost friends of Simon's, crying and blubbing down the telephone or, worst of all, trying to make out what a good chap Simon was.

He was a lying, selfish piece of shit, she thought during these calls, but I'm never going to tell you why that is.

There was one person, however, who was definitely going to know the truth. His mother. Ellen's end of that conversation went like this:

"No Eileen, Simon wasn't such a lovely family man… Yes. I'll grant you that. He was a fine doctor. Yes, probably very caring. Saying 'well then' doesn't make him a lovely family man. He was an adulterer. Nearly two years fucking some nurse. No, you listen, I'll use whatever language I like in my own home. And then he was a world class liar telling me it was over. He was a bloody liar, Eileen. Your son, listen to me, was a lying, adulterous, selfish, little shit. Make that big shit."

Listening to her daughter in law Eileen Jones didn't hear anything after 'listen to me'. She put the phone down in the hall of her new McCarthy and Stone retirement apartment and wondered if she'd ever see her gorgeous grandchildren again.

The phone rang again and as she went to answer it, she steeled herself for more dead husband worship from his friends and colleagues.

But this phone call to Ellen Jones was better news. It was the Family Liaison Office of the police telling her that there was a definite intention to prosecute Emma McMillan over the death of her husband.

"You have the right to enter a Victim's Statement which will be taken into consideration by the Crown Prosecution Service. If you do, you may be asked to present this in person, in court. Would you like to make a Victim's Statement Mrs Jones?"

"Oh yes," she said. "I really would."

Chapter 19
Lincolnshire, 1933

Monty knew it would be getting light by five o' clock in the morning, but a man with a child wandering the streets of Boston at first light would have been noted and talked about, especially as the town's port was full of boats and men would be coming down ready for a day's labour on the North Sea.

Father and Son took a short but brisk walk on the harbour wall at a good pace, stopping well short of the urgency of running, which might attract attention if anyone was around.

Eventually Monty dropped down off the wall and onto a bank, with Alfie just behind, following his father. The bank took them along a half-sand, half-marsh mud fringe towards a short jetty. Monty tucked himself under the jetty and pushed Alfie behind him so he could sit with his back to the support timbers.

Jetties were for walking on, not under, thought Monty, and even if there was an early dog walker or trade delivery van along the bank then, with Archie tucked away out of sight behind him, to all intents and purposes, Monty was just one man sleeping rough for the night.

"Father," said Archie, once they were settled, "where are we going?"

"Shush now, Son," Monty said.

Monty knew exactly where they were heading, but he didn't want to alarm his son. He was the fox now, the quarry, not the hunter. He knew where he was going to ground but he needed to be cunning to get the two of them there safely.

Alfie looked down at his lap. His father put his hand under the boy's chin and lifted up his face.

"We're going to get a train."

"Where to Father?"

"Shush now, Alfie lad. We'll be getting a train soon and some breakfast. You'd be ready for a spot of breakfast, eh, lad?"

And they sat in silence and watched the sun fully rise over the North Sea. Looking back across the Wash in the distance, they could begin to see the Norfolk coastline being lit up by the sun.

Would either of them ever return, wondered Monty?

By half past seven, there was clearly some action on the jetty above them and Monty could hear cars and vans moving along the narrow delivery road to one side. He gave it another half an hour and then they clambered up onto the road, then along the main road, and, following the signs, they headed for 15 minutes or so to the station.

Inside the station, they went straight to the ticket office, where Monty bought two tickets on the 0914 to Nottingham via Grantham.

With 20 minutes or so until the train was due to leave, there was plenty of time to go to the station café for bacon sandwiches and mugs of tea.

"Father, why are we going to Nottingham?" asked Alfie.

He'd never been on a train before, and Nottingham was just a name he'd heard of, and that name was Robin Hood. "What's there?"

"Now look, Alfie," said his father as they put their bags down and tucked into breakfast. "Just stick close to me. Do you understand? We've got quite a long trip ahead of us. We should just get on with it. Do you want a *Wizard*?" he said, pointing to the comic book on the newsstand. "It'll give you something to read."

"Yes, please!" said Alfie. A comic was a treat usually sourced on rare outings to Hunstanton.

The train was in the station, and there were only a handful of fellow passengers on the mostly deserted platform when they boarded.

Monty and the boy walked down the corridor of the carriage and, looking into each compartment as they went, finally settled into a compartment they had to themselves.

It was just the two of them all the way to Grantham but at Grantham station the platforms were full and there seemed to be platforms everywhere.

Station masters in sharp blue uniforms, carrying flags, moved around with purpose. Dozens of people stared up at clocks, peered down tracks to spot oncoming trains, or, for the more fancily dressed passengers, discussed with porters with carts loaded with luggage or packing cases, exactly who they were and where they wanted their luggage loading.

Monty and Alfie waited in their compartment. Monty hoped they'd be able to keep it to themselves, but it wasn't to be.

An elderly man in napless trousers and a heavy jacket, too heavy for June, slid the door to their compartment back and nodded as he stepped in.

"Morning," he said.

"Morning," said Monty.

Alfie was transfixed by the man's whiskers, which were white, bushy and unkempt.

As the elderly man was about to slide the door closed behind him, two young women appeared at the door's window and put up a hand to halt the operation, and they also came into the carriage.

"Gentlemen," said one of them, the taller of the two, wearing a green suit, the jacket nipped in at the waist, as was the fashion.

"Ma'am," said Monty. The elderly man nodded and removed a serge cap to reveal an explosion of white hair.

Alfie has never seen anything quite as unusual as their male travelling companion. His was a world of uniforms, formal dress and tweeds. Well, it had been.

The two women came in and sat opposite each other. One sat next to Alfie, one next to the elderly gentlemen, both nearest the door to the corridor, and they immediately started chatting about the lace doilies they were going to source in Nottingham for the family haberdashery shop in Grantham.

Monty wondered if anyone would be looking for him and Alfie on the train. Unlikely, he thought, and he needn't have worried. He had no way of knowing, but back in Norfolk, two policemen were wandering the platforms at King's Lynn station; one was at Wolferton station; and two more policemen were at King's Lynn port. There were twenty or more sweeping the woods and byways of the Sandringham Estate. But there were no policemen looking anywhere other than in Norfolk, and even then, no more than 15 miles from Keeper's Cottage.

From Grantham, it was a journey of about an hour or so to Nottingham, where Father and Son got off. If anyone ever gets as far as tracing them to Boston, reasoned Monty, and even if anyone recognised them at Boston station, his logic continued, then the hunt would only shift to Nottingham.

He now had a very clear plan of action in mind and there were things to do.

He took Alfie by the hand and, leaving the station, turned right where he could see shops lining both sides of the road which rose up over the canal and led into the city.

Monty stopped at one of the first shops available, a general hardware store, where he bought a suitcase.

Next in a men's outfitters, he bought three sets of socks, underpants, vests, shirts, a new pair of trousers, a light coat for Archie, roughly the same for himself and a cloth cap each for each of them.

Stuffing them into the newly acquired suitcase, they crossed the road and into a smart new Boots the Chemists shop, where they ordered at the counter some basic things they'd need on the journey, such as toothbrushes, soap and a couple of face flannels.

The nice young woman behind the counter put it all into a little cloth bag for him, "Free of charge," she said. "For the little 'un. Alright me-duck?"

And then, to Alfie's surprise, they left the shop and headed back towards Nottingham station and straight to the ticket office.

"One for me and one for the lad, two singles to Manchester, please," said Monty and, with their train already waiting at the platform, within ten minutes they were off again.

Once they were settled in, Monty said "Right, Alfie, pick out your favourite shirt and put these new trousers on too."

Alfie thought this was rather odd but odd seemed to be happening all the time, so he picked out a blue shirt from the three they had bought less than an hour ago.

When Alfie was dressed in a brand-new shirt and trousers, Monty pulled the compartment's door blind down and telling Alfie to mind the door, Monty got changed as well.

He then put their old clothes into his haversack and shoved them down next to his gun parts.

"Father," said Alfie.

"Don't worry, Son," said Monty, anticipating his son's line of questioning. "We're not going to Manchester. We're going to Liverpool. And when we get there, we're going to find us a nice lodging house for the night, then go out for a proper, nice fish supper. How does that sound?"

"Alright," said Alfie. Grantham, Nottingham, Manchester and Liverpool were all unknowns to him. A fish supper, he understood. Anyway, within five minutes, the rickety rack and clickety-clack of the train journey had lulled him fast asleep, and he slept all the way to Manchester.

While he was asleep, Monty pulled down the compartment window, and, as they were chugging across wide-open countryside, he threw out their old trousers and shirts. If there was a description of them out there, then at least they couldn't be spotted by their clothes. Monty was keen to do anything to blur the description of them at any point in their escape so far.

As the train pulled into Manchester's London Road station, Monty roused Alfie and they went out of the station and walked quickly through the streets of the huge grey city to Manchester Victoria Station.

Alfie had never, ever seen anything like it. Towering soot-blackened buildings, pubs, shops, double-fronted stores, and so many cars, vans and lorries that Monty had to drag him along following directions he'd gotten from the newsstand vendor on London Road.

Then, straight after the visit to the ticket office the Liverpool train was boarded, and they were off again.

"When will we be there, Father?" asked Alfie. "I'm a bit bored. And I'm hungry."

"Think of those fish and chips, Alfie boy, think of those fish and chips," said Monty. "I know I am."

Alfie reached for his *Wizard* comic again.

Monty looked out of the window and thought that in a day, in less than 24 hours, they would have gone from one side of England to the other.

Monty knew it was nowhere near far enough.

Back at Wolferton station, less than two miles from Keeper's Cottage, Sergeant Christopher Killingbeck paced up and down, ready to act should any fugitive cross his path.

Chapter 20
Norfolk, Present Day

Mark was giving himself a reasonably firm talking to as he snapped open a bottle of Corona beer and squeezed a wedge of lime into its neck. He was prone to letting his mind roam aimlessly in several directions at the same time. He needed a To Do list every day. He was at least that self-aware. Patience was not his strong suit. Ask Trish what it was like during wedding planning meetings.

"Focus Elwin. Focus," he said to himself, as he settled down at his kitchen table. "What do we know to be absolutely true so far?"

He pulled the Find Alfie Sidebottom file across the table, opened his laptop and tapped in his password.

He reckoned with almost absolute certainty that Monty did not kill his brother, his son and himself on the same day. If he had then Monty's body would have to be a. above ground.

b. a maximum of one day's walk—a 15-mile radius of Keeper's Cottage at the most—and that radius included an awful lot of the North Sea.

c. certainly discovered eventually, if not at once.

As there was no discovery of a body then, Mark deduced, the worst-case scenario, the bloodiest possibility, had definitely not happened.

Next, he knew for certain that Monty and Alfie had not been found.

There was not a single newspaper report of them being found. There wasn't a single newspaper report of anyone, ever, being brought to trial over the death of Clem Sidebottom.

So let's, he reasoned, for the sake of this entertaining ancient game of hide and seek, let's assume that the worst-case scenario that Monty killed his brother, his son and himself on the same day, never happened.

Let's assume they successfully scarpered.

So, where did they go?

A slug on the cold Corona and occasional scribbled notes meant he could always read himself back up to speed when the file came out.

'Focus' he kept muttering as he jotted. Monty and Alfie had at least 14 hours start on the police search proper. From 5.30, the first afternoon when the alarm was raised by Nika Sidebottom, right through until the next morning at around 7 o'clock when the police search of the Sandringham Estate started in any kind of determined fashion and the train stations and King's Lynn port were being watched.

How far, on foot, can you get in 14 hours with an eight-year-old boy who may, or may not, have been a willing companion?

The great Google would tell him but instead, he went to a drawer in the kitchen, took out his old Ordnance Survey Landranger map number 132, opened it out, spread it on his kitchen table and took another slug of cold beer reflecting with pleasure the sharp hint of lime.

So, 14 hours minimum to walk, with rest periods for the boy, across open land and through woods, who knows, maybe 25 miles? Could he himself cover 25 miles in a night? He supposed he could if he thought the cops were on his trail.

In that case, which way did they go?

He put a finger on Sandringham village.

To the south and west that took them way beyond King's Lynn and with his finger tracking along the River Great Ouse then 25 miles would have got them as far as the small town of Watlington and possibly even further. But in the dark? There was a railway station at Watlington. Would they head for there? Possibly. He put a red ring around Watlington.

To the west of King's Lynn, across the bridge over the River Great Ouse and pushing on due north to Sutton Bridge, that would get them as far as Lincolnshire. Perhaps not in one night, but soon enough. At least, they'd be out of the searchlight of the Norfolk Constabulary. Sutton Bridge was off his map so he wrote "Sutton Bridge/County boundary west and north?" onto his white A4 notes.

East would have got them as far as Fakenham or possibly even further to Thursford and beyond, but why would they go in that direction? That would only mean that after a very long slog overnight and most of the next day they could make it to the far east coast, Bacton and Great Yarmouth. Surely, they'd need to sleep at some point. Mark didn't think much of this option.

North? Well, the coast. Easy to reach. Anyone of a dozen little fishing harbours back in those days, Thornham, Brancaster Staithe, Burnham Deepdale, Burnham Overy Staithe all the way along the coast to the bigger port at Wells-next-the-Sea, still a vibrant fishing port and a port servicing the wind farms out in the North Sea.

He went to Google and, yes, lots and lots of boats pottering in and out of the North Sea coast from a whole string of harbours.

"There be smugglers," he said in a piratey voice.

He mentally discounted an escape route to the east. It looked to Mark like a dead-end route for a man and a boy on the run.

So, west? Avoid the prying eyes of the police in King's Lynn. Pick up a train further down the line?

"Nah," he said out loud, wandering to the fridge for a second beer. The first beers were the equivalent of a marksman's sighter. Get a first round away, take your time and concentrate on the second. "Doesn't make sense. All the drivers and guards and station masters along the line to Cambridge would have been told to be on the lookout at King's Lynn."

But north?

Of course, Monty and Alfie could have had much longer ahead of the cops, he thought. He had no idea from the *EDP* report of the inquest what time any coroner, autopsy or post-mortem examination had put the time of death. All he'd managed to unearth was when the death was reported, not when it occurred.

The police files. Can you get to see the police files? He thought he probably could after all this time. He made a note "Check on access to police files."

He went back to the *EDP* report. Nika Sidebottom said she had 'spent the day' with her mother. If Alfie got home from school at what? Four o'clock-ish and arrived home to surprise his father standing over the dead body of his uncle at say half past four, then that would mean they had not 14 hours but at least 15 hours, maybe more.

"Wow, that's a pretty big head start."

But would that mean they just used the time simply to run as far away as possible? Just head off in one direction and keep going and going?

Mark thought not.

Okay, he thought… Monty Sidebottom was an experienced gamekeeper. He must have been a good one to work for His Majesty King George V. His craft was to plan and execute—literally on some occasions—the driving and stalking of game. He knew how to track quarry. He knew how to find quarry. He knew where to look. He knew where they hid. His job was to outfox a fox. So when the tables were turned, when he was the quarry, when he was the hunted, he wouldn't just run. Just like the roe deer doesn't just run. Like a fox, wouldn't he just get so far, then simply go to ground?

"Where would you go to ground, Monty Sidebottom? Where could you go and evade capture for the rest of your life? What could you do? An anonymous factory job in London or Manchester?"

Yes, he could but on the briefest reflection, no, thought Mark. Monty was a countryman. City life was both unknown to him and almost certainly unappealing. He was a gamekeeper with a singular set of skills which were almost worthless in any other profession.

Mark woke up his laptop which while he'd been musing over his map had gone into sleep mode. He opened up the desktop file marked "Find Alfie Sidebottom," left it open, turned to the Great God Google in the sky and typed in "List of English Gamekeepers 1934."

"Let's see if you found yourself another job somewhere, shall we Monty?" he said.

Three more beers and endless Google searches later both he and the GGG in the sky decided that no, there wasn't a list of gamekeepers anywhere. No *British Union of Gamekeepers* handily recording who was working where, when and for how long. No *Track My Gamekeeper* website faithfully listing every transfer of gamekeeper from one estate to another.

Occasionally there was a newspaper article thrown up from Devon or Northumberland announcing the appointment of a new gamekeeper to Lord Somebody of Somewhere or naming a gamekeeper in local assize courts during prosecutions of local poachers. There was, noted Mark, an awful lot of poaching going on. Let's face it, 1933 was the depth of The Great Depression. Poaching would have been beyond rife in the shires of England.

Occasionally a gamekeeper was named in a newspaper photograph standing close to, but not with, a group of gentry standing over a bag of 650 pheasant, partridge, woodcock, magpies, duck, teal and more.

Captions along the lines of the Duke of Devonshire with his guests at the Chatsworth House Boxing Day shoot including the industrialist Sir Richard Jennings of Cromford (second right) and others. Gamekeeper William Hodges (l).

This photograph was dated *Derbyshire Times* Dec 28 1933. Six months after Monty and Alfie went in the run. There was not much sign of The Great Depression in the world of the Duke of Devonshire.

If he had to look at every gamekeeper photograph from every local newspaper archive and every report of every assize court listing of poaching fines, then Mark would need to live to be as old as Gandalf.

And still not certain of success.

No, thought Mark, closing down the laptop and packing away his notes. Let's not start at the beginning of your flight from Sandringham. Let's have a little think about where you might be aiming for. Where do you know or, possibly more importantly, who do you know outside your life in Sandringham?

Who could you turn to for help?

Chapter 21
Liverpool, 1933

It was still daylight when the London Midland and Scottish steam train pulled into Liverpool Lime Street station.

Monty and Alfie got off and headed out of the station and down towards the Royal Albert dock. Within ten minutes, Monty had found exactly what he was looking for. A lodging house and a fish and chip shop.

"Perfect," said Monty to Alfie. "Now listen Son, say nothing. Doesn't matter what you hear, just say nothing for now. As soon as we get in and drop off our bags then we're going to go to that fish and chip shop over there. Then we can have a talk, Okay?"

Alfie looked to where his father was pointing, saw the fish and chip shop, and a couple of likely lads in rough-knit jumpers and flat caps outside and nodded his agreement.

Mrs Kendrick kept a clean house she said. She didn't mind the Irish, she said, so long as they were clean and sober. But she wouldn't have foreigners or dogs. The sign in the window said exactly that. She wouldn't normally let a room for one night as it meant washing the sheets but the lad looked tired, she said.

There was a washbowl in the room and a water closet out in the yard. It was money up front she said, and Monty paid.

"You catching a boat tomorrow?" she said as she led them upstairs.

"Yes," said Monty.

"Where to? Anywhere nice? Here's your room."

"Not really," said Monty. "Relatives. Family business."

"Oh, I see. Now then, not that you will, having the lad and all that, but I lock the front door at 10 o'clock sharp. I'm up at half past seven in the morning but if you are gone before then just leave your key on the hall stand and pull the door closed behind you."

"Okay," said Monty. "Thank you, Mrs Kendrick. Very kind."

"I'll bid you good evening then," she said and, turning, went back downstairs.

Monty put their bags at the bottom of the bed.

"We'll have a wash when we get back, Alfie lad. Same clothes tomorrow, alright? Now, fish and chips!"

Father and Son made their way across the cobbled street that separated two lines of identical tiny houses, two rooms down, two rooms up, built almost back to back with just a tiny alley running between them. Four scruffy lads with grey flannel shorts, and knee socks flapping around their ankles, played a game of marbles in the street gutter. A mother in a head scarf and house coat emerged from one open front door and bellowed down the street in a broad Liverpool accent "Jamie. Jamie! Come home your tea's ready!"

The call was picked up by another mother 200 yards or more along the street.

"He's down by the foundry with our Billy," shouted the distant mother back up the street and turning away she bellowed "Jamie O'Donnell! Get you home. Your mam's calling you. Jamie O'Donnell Can. You. Hear. Me?"

"Coming." A light treble voice came floating back through the early evening air. So the urban maternal telegraph rang out again and again until all the children were back in their little brick hutches.

Monty breathed in the wonderful fumes of frying fish and chips as he waited in line for supper. He ordered two lots of haddock and chips, with mushy peas, and four pickled eggs which were wrapped separately in a double page from a week-old edition of the *Liverpool Daily Post.* The eggs Monty put in his pocket. The haddock and chips he sprayed with malt vinegar and sprinkled with salt. As soon as the vinegar hit the chips it burst into familiar and comforting smells. For a second, he was back home, home in his own childhood at a chip shop with his mother just off the promenade at Hunstanton.

Monty went out of the shop, and gathered up Alfie who'd been waiting patiently, if a little nervously, in front of some much bigger boys. and the two of them wandered down towards the docks looking at the various posters and billboards as they went.

They sat on the edge of the road on the kerb.

"Father," said Alfie when his fish and chips had just about filled him up "are we going to see relatives like you said to the lady?"

"We might be Son," his father said, "we might be."

"And are we getting on a boat?"

"We are Son, we are."

"Which one?"

Monty looked up.

"That one," he said, pointing a finger at a poster featuring an impressively romantic oil painting of the MV Ulster Queen. "Daily sailings from Liverpool to Belfast at 0930," it said.

"Belfast?" asked Alfie, who'd never heard of Belfast in his life.

"That's right Son. Belfast. It's in Ireland."

"Ireland?" said Alfie. He'd heard of it, vaguely, when geography had featured at school. "Do we have family in Belfast in Ireland?"

"Not quite," said Monty. "But not far. It's where Granny Kathleen came from. I know you don't remember her. You were only little when she passed away. But Granny Kathleen, she came from Ireland."

Alfie had no idea about Ireland and only knew one or two well-told stories about Granny Kathleen that his father often repeated, mostly featuring her ability to turn out a feast from a potato and some lard and one about how savage her tongue was if she was crossed or if she thought that anyone in her presence had "taken drink."

He scrunched up his fish and chip newspaper and the two of them retraced their steps back to Mrs Kendrick's lodging house and went up to their room. They stripped off and washed, laid their same clothes out for the morning and slept top and tail until it was light again.

No one paid them any attention at all at the Belfast Steamship Company ticket office as Monty bought two one-way tickets as foot passengers for himself and Alfie and they were paid even less attention as they climbed the gangplank.

At precisely half past nine in the morning there was a long blast on the ship's horns, the engines roared into action and Father and Son left England.

Probably forever, thought Monty.

Alfie loved it on the ship. It was huge and Father and Son walked around the deck time after time. They counted their strides and Monty reckoned the sparkling Ulster Queen must have been 100 yards long. While their tickets said the Belfast Steamship Company this was no steamship, but a brand-new glittering diesel ship and it chewed its way over the Irish Sea and into Belfast in a little under 10 hours.

When they disembarked, they repeated their manoeuvres from the night before in Liverpool looking for a lodging house near a fish and chip shop. Two pickled eggs each had been their only food all day and it meant Father and Son were famished.

Mrs O'Grady could have been Mrs Kendrick's sister.

Blousy with a tweed skirt and a gingham apron she informed them that there was no drink allowed on the premises, not that you would with the little one and all, that the door was closed at 10 o'clock sharp and that there too was a water closet in the back yard.

"You here on business?" she asked, wondering who came on business with a young boy.

"Family business," said Monty and asked where the station was. She gave Monty directions.

"Where you off to then?" she asked.

"Newry," said Monty.

"Oh, aye. It's a pretty town Newry is," said Mrs O'Grady but she'd lost interest by then and went back downstairs. She had a pudding steaming on the range and she was keen to get back to it before it spoiled.

Monty and Alfie looked at their room.

"I like this one," said Alfie.

"Me too Son. Right, clean shirts tomorrow I think," he said opening the suitcase. "New shirts, eh?"

"Yes!"

They soon found themselves in their fish and chip shop and judged that these fish suppers were better than the ones in Liverpool.

Sitting on the pavement kerb halfway between the chip chop and the lodging house they ate in silence until Alfie finally spoke.

"Father, who do we know in Newry?"

"Absolutely no one, Son," Monty said and started laughing, "absolutely no one at all." And Alfie joined in the laughing, not really knowing why, but it just felt good to be laughing. The first time he'd laughed since he saw his mother and Uncle Clem. He shook the memory from his head.

"Father," he said as they walked back to Mrs O'Grady's lodging house.

"Yes, Son?"

"Will Mother be alright?"

It was the first time in three days that either of them had mentioned her.

"Yes Alfie," said Monty. "She'll be fine. This is why we've gone away. You and me. Going away will make sure that she is fine. So long as we go away and remember never to tell anyone, anything, ever. You understand?"

"Yes Father," said Alfie.

And they never mentioned her ever again, although Alfie thought about her for the rest of his life. Mostly at night, in his bed. Sometimes it made him cry.

Chapter 22
Norfolk, Present Day

Friday morning and all that the day held for Mark Elwin was yet more changes of plan to the Vickery wedding which was taking place the following day at Sussex Barns.

Wellies, they wanted. They had asked all the guests to bring wellies, as wacky as possible. Not any of your classic British green jobs, and certainly not one of those rather superior French brands. No, the newlywed Mrs and Mrs Vickery wanted everyone to go to their favourite market stall in Anytown and buy wildly coloured, patterned or even home-decorated wellies. To go with the Vickery country house wedding.

The Vickerys were from Leicester.

Anyway, thought Mark, Trish could handle that. All of that.

He plugged in a spare set of batteries for the drone camera so they were fully charged for the wedding ahead and then he settled down with a slice of toast and a super strong Nespresso. Those black Nespresso pods were definitely the right colour. He added half a teaspoon of sugar just to edge the bite off the caffeine.

He opened up his laptop and gave himself just an hour with the 'Find Alfie Sidebottom' file on his desktop.

Success, so far, had been pitifully thin.

He had signed up to a whole raft of historic search engines starting with Free Genealogy, Free Newspaper Archives, Free Parish Records in fact anything with the word free in it but they were either American-based or were so clogged up with adverts that they drove him mad.

In the end, he'd got his credit card out and invested in sites which promised the earth, charged accordingly but reassuringly had.co.uk on the end so at least he wouldn't be scouring the town records of Nowheresville, Wisconsin looking for a Norfolk gamekeeper and his son.

He thought his first brainwave would be a winner.

The advantage he had, so reasoned Mark, was that Montgomery Sidebottom was not your run-of-the-mill name. So instead of finding out where the fugitives had gone on that day in 1933, he decided, let's find out where Montgomery Sidebottom had ended up.

searchbritishgraves.co.uk was a much more cheerful website than the name suggested. Not only did it contain what it claimed was the UK's largest database of burial sites but also was an online forum for people who "just like graveyards." Surprisingly there were lots of people who "just like graveyards." And they also like a popularity poll. Mark revelled in the competition for the prettiest local authority graveyard (Ashford in Kent), the spookiest graveyard (Whitby, Dracula helping to secure a big vote) the best Jewish cemetery (Golders Green, London, obviously) and so on.

Mark entered Montgomery Sidebottom and waited to strike oil the first time. No chance.

There were a few Montgomery Sidebottoms to be fair. There were three in Lancashire, all the wrong dates, but nevertheless, Mark was sidetracked by one Montgomery Sidebottom in particular, a 17th-century undertaker in Clitheroe Parish Church. There was something inherently interesting about the grave of an undertaker.

Anyway, no Montgomery Sidebottom fitting anywhere close to the dates of his quarry.

Alfred Sidebottom threw up dozens. None was a match.

This was not a wasted effort though. Perhaps it was a waste of the £27.50 he'd paid to sign up to the site for three months but while he was trawling through searchbritishgraves.co.uk he put in Nika Sidebottom and found she was buried in Dersingham parish churchyard. She had died in 1966. She was just over 60. There was no one else recorded in the grave with her. Mark made a note that her surname remained Sidebottom and so she had clearly not remarried. Perhaps she never had Monty and Alfie listed as dead. A line of enquiry to pursue? Perhaps not.

The lack of an easily located grave for Monty meant one of three things thought Mark. Option one: Monty was dead but with no grave. Well, thought Mark, if that was the case he may as well give up now.

Option two: he changed his name. This seemed more plausible. He wondered what the system of National Insurance numbers was in 1933. Not National Insurance numbers that's for sure. Post-war surely? Check.

Could a jobbing man in 1933 simply fetch up in a new town, declare his name was Basil Brush and start a new job? Mark thought he probably could. In which case his search was also, again, probably in vain.

Option three: Monty wasn't buried in England at all.

Blimey thought Mark. For a start that's a waste of £27.50. And a waste of a good life. He could spend the rest of his life searching every grave in the world and still end in epic failure.

yourfamilytree.co.uk proved much more productive in that he turned up a lot about Monty's past. It helped not one jot about what happened after the fateful day, but it was fun finding out more about his running man.

To start off with he got Alfred Sidebottom's birth certificate and printed it off, then Montgomery Sidebottom's birth certificate, Monty and Nika's wedding certificate and Monty's parent's wedding certificate. Now that was interesting.

Marriage certificates in 1900 carried just about as much information as Mark remembered was recorded on his own marriage certificate. I wonder where that is, he thought.

Monty's father was recorded as Arthur Sidebottom, an estate worker. Fair enough and it makes sense. Social mobility was glacial back in the day thought Mark. Estate workers shall beget estate workers and so on.

Monty's mother was Kathleen Sidebottom, a scullery maid. Fair enough again, and, Mark reasoned, it probably explained how they met. Both worked for the big house, probably Sandringham, as Arthur's address was listed as estate worker of Number 4 Cottage, Anmer and Anmer was a Sandringham estate village. A pretty one too.

The real interest lay written under Kathleen's maiden name. In the looping copperplate handwriting of the registrar, it stated "formerly the wife of Patrick O'Malley of Donegal from whom she obtained a divorce. Nee Casey."

Her father was named "Declan Casey, a whiskey distillery labourer."

Divorced?

Wow, that took some doing in 1900 thought Mark. And surely impossible in Ireland? Something else to look up. He made a written note and then remembered to add it to the Notes file on his laptop.

And her father a labourer in a whiskey distillery. Whiskey with an 'e' so Irish. Scotch whisky has no 'e'. And she had married a man from Donegal.

One thing more caught his attention. The marriage was in January 1900. A quick cross-reference to Monty's birth certificate showed he was born on April Fool's Day 1901.

"That was cutting it fine," said Mark out loud. "You naughty downstairs girl!"

One more quick search for Kathleen and Arthur's birth certificates revealed that Arthur was 51 years old when he married and that Kathleen Casey did not have a birth certificate in the UK. Mark thought about getting out the credit card and looking for a website called something like findmyirishfamily.com but he realised it didn't matter.

He had enough to be going on with for now. Going back to his original list of things to find out he realised that 7. Where did you run to? should have been followed by 8. What were you called?

That evening, at Lower Farm Care Home, after he'd extracted from her handbag a portion of fish, three ketchup sachets, around twenty packets of sugar cubes and, oddly, if it really was that odd any more, three teaspoons, he looked at his grandmother.

"I don't know who put those in there," said Lauretta Carey and Mark knew that she was telling the truth, she really didn't.

"Grandma," he said, and she stared blankly out of the window into the car park.

"Lauretta," he said, and she turned and looked at him.

"I've started looking for Alfie Sidebottom," he said.

"Who?" she said.

"Alfie Sidebottom. You told me about him. Alfie Sidebottom who got you into trouble at school."

"Never heard of him," she said and turned back to her car park.

Chapter 23
Belfast, 1933

Monty woke at first light in Mrs O'Grady's lodging house and, planning the day before them in his head, he waited an hour or so before rousing Alfie.

They dressed in silence and slipped out into the crisp early Belfast air. The seagulls yawling overhead reminded them both of home.

The station they wanted was Lanyon Place but when Monty asked for two tickets to Strabane, he was disappointed.

"Station closed not six months ago. And Castlederg. The boys are on strike trying to get it open again, but they're eejits wasting their time," said the ticket master behind his glass partition.

This was the first stumbling block in Monty's planning.

"Where's the nearest station to there then?" he asked.

"I can get you Belleek via Enniskillen if you like. Or you can always get the bus to Strabane."

"Give me a minute," said Monty and he went over to a huge map on the station wall with various lines marked on it. The line to Strabane was still marked. Then he found Belleek. Just as good, he thought, and his plan was back on track. He went back to the ticket desk.

"Singles for me and the boy to Belleek then," he said.

"You'll be getting a bus up to Strabane after then. There's one that goes from right outside the station at Belleek. Right outside," said the ticket master.

So what, thought Monty as he pocketed the tickets.

Bacon sandwiches were found in the station café and mugs of hot sweet tea.

"These are the best bacon sandwiches," said Alfie who had by now fallen into the rhythm of life on the road. Well, life on boat and rail.

On the train, he took out his *Wizard* comic and started reading it for the fourth or fifth time and pretty soon they pulled into Enniskillen and pretty soon after pulled out for Belleek.

"When we get to Belleek Son, we're going to have a lazy day ok? We'll find somewhere to stay for the night, find something to eat and get a good night's sleep."

"Alright Father," said Alfie and didn't ask anything more.

"We've got a big day tomorrow."

"Yes, Father."

"Don't you want to know why?"

Alfie was engrossed in some hero's adventure in *Wizard* which he reluctantly put down. He looked at his father.

"What do you think of the name Alfie Casey?" asked Monty.

"Who's he?" asked Alfie.

"You," said his father. "And I'm Monty Casey. From tomorrow anyway. It's your Grannie's Irish name. It's our Irish family name. And we're going to be in Ireland for probably a long time, so I think it's a good idea to have our Irish name."

Alfie stared at his father.

"Go on, say it," said his father.

"Alfie Casey," said Alfie, without enthusiasm.

"Brilliant! Pleased to meet you, Alfie Casey. I'm Montgomery Casey. Monty Casey," said Monty with a grin. "You can call me Father!"

"Okay… Father," he emphasised starting to play along with the sport. "You can call me Son!"

"That I will Alfie Casey! My son, Alfie Casey."

"Are you sure Father?" said Alfie.

"I am," said Monty.

And with that Alfie Casey went back to his *Wizard*.

Belleek was a close-knit, charming little border town tucked up on the east bank of the River Erne. Father and Son got off the train and walked out of the station, past the bus stop for Strabane and into town past neat houses and shops until they reached what was clearly the marketplace where the road bowed out on both sides to leave an expanse of grass in the middle and two benches, back to back.

The Fiddlestone Bed and Breakfast looked onto the common. It was probably, to Monty's eyes, ideal but after a couple of knocks on the door and a bit of standing around it was clear there was no one at home so they found a tea room where they had sandwiches and cake and more mugs of tea.

When they'd had their fill under the curious watchful eyes of the pretty serving girl, they stepped outside into the Irish sunshine and Alfie sat on one of several three-legged stools outside the tea rooms.

"Stay here Alfie Casey," said his father, "Mind the bags while I go and get something."

"Okay," said Alfie. The whole Casey name thing had already been going on long enough for Alfie not to pass comment.

Monty went to the other side of the common to the Post Office where he bought a map of the whole of the northwest of Ireland which he tucked into his pocket then he returned to the tea rooms and Father and Son sat on the stools watching the Fiddlestone Bed and Breakfast house.

Eventually, a man in a baggy green suit and a flat cap turned up on a bicycle, dismounted, parked the bike outside the B & B and let himself in.

They wandered over.

"Good afternoon to you," said the man taking off his cap.

"I was wondering if you had a room for me and the boy for tonight," said Monty.

"The one room?" asked the man.

"Yes," said Monty.

"Aye, we have. Just the one night? You'll not be staying with us for longer?"

"Not this time," said Monty.

"Holiday?" asked the man.

"Not this time either," said Monty closing down any further line of enquiries the man might have.

He paid for a room, bed and breakfast.

"Instead of breakfast we couldn't just have a couple of sandwiches and these canteens filled with water, could we? Tonight? To take with us. Going to make an early start tomorrow," said Monty "Don't want to trouble you for breakfast,"

"Oh aye, I'll ask the missus when she gets in. Cheese and pickle suit you?"

"That'll be fine."

"Off anywhere nice?" asked the man, keen to extract at least a morsel of information about his English guests.

"Family business," said Monty.

And that was that.

Later that evening there was a knock on their bedroom door but when he answered it there was just a tray with sandwiches on greaseproof paper, two apples and freshly filled canteens.

It was the dark, dark time before dawn, when Monty said "Come on Alfie Casey, let's be having you up. We've a long, long day ahead of us."

The two dressed, slipped out of the house unnoticed and headed north in the moonlight, out of the little town of Belleek then a sharp left along Commons Road.

Within a mile and a half, they'd crossed into the Irish Free State.

The road took them over a little river and towards a farmhouse surrounded by sturdy looking barns. There were cows in the fields.

Monty took Alfie by the hand and they scrambled down a bank onto a footpath that headed north-west.

"Keep going, Alfie Casey. We've a full day walking ahead of us."

And it was a full day. Nearly 25 miles across open country, long forgotten footpaths, bridleways, tracking along hedgerows but always heading north-west with Monty aiming true by the contours marked on the map from Belleek Post Office and the position of the sun in the sky.

They stopped for lunch in a little copse just after one o'clock when the June sun was high in the sky. Monty was pleased this wasn't a foot slog in driving rain.

Their rest was short and both man and boy were a little stiff when they set off again. Never once did Alfie ask where they were going. He was used to long days on his feet. After all, he'd been a beater on his father's shooting days since he was five years old.

By four o'clock, they crossed the main road running north to a place signposted Ballintra and shortly after that, they saw the most beautiful beach and the sea beyond. Again, they both thought of home.

"That's the Atlantic Ocean Alfie Casey," said Monty using Casey every time he addressed the boy. "and if you keep going west, where would you get to next?"

"I don't know Father. Where would you get to?"

"America," said Monty.

"Is that where we're going?" asked Alfie.

Monty laughed. "No Son. Not today anyway. We're not going much further today at all."

Heading north now and risking tacking along the main road it was another two hours before they saw the town sign.

Donegal.

"Are we here Father?"

"Aye, we are here Alfie Casey."

"Where is it?" asked Alfie.

"Home," said Monty.

I hope, he thought.

Chapter 24
Irish Free State, 1933

Monty knew exactly where he was going. He was going to the Olde Glen Bar. He knew the Olde Glen Bar because his mother had told tales of her father and her brothers, her uncles and half the men in Donegal spending all night and all their money in the bar, singing to the fiddle and the accordion and coming home late at night stinking of whiskey. Kathleen Sidebottom did not drink.

Monty and Alfie sat outside the bar until six o'clock when the bolt behind the front door slid open and a man with the large broken veined nose of a hard-drinking publican stepped out and admired the early evening sunshine.

Monty stood up and the man with the nose said "Can I help you?"

"You can," said Monty.

"An Englishman in these parts, is it?" There was hostility in the man's tone, not inquisition.

"An English Irishman you might say," said Monty.

"And how might that be?" said the man with the nose.

"Would you be expecting either Michael or Patrick Casey this evening?" asked Monty.

"And who wants to know?" The hostility remained but hadn't grown.

"My name is Monty Casey. This is my son Alfie Casey. I'm their nephew."

"And how might that be possible?" said the landlord with the red-veined nose.

"I'm Kathleen Casey's son."

"Ah, well, that might be the case. It might not. What was your mother's name after Casey then?" he said. Mistrust now replaced hostility. Monty realised he was going to have to get used to that.

"I believe she was briefly called an O'Malley. Before a divorce." Monty was not ever going to mention the name Sidebottom again in his life.

"Oh divorce, was it?" said the man with the nose, "Divorce was it. Ah, you'll know Paddy O'Malley then, will you? No? Ah well, not the nicest of men, Paddy. Big man but only in size. So, you'll be Monty O'Malley then?" We've gone from hostility to mistrust to inquisition. Did this, Monty thought, count for progress for an English Irishman in Donegal?

"No. Never knew my father, left when I was little," Monty said "Always been Monty Casey."

It's true his father had 'left' when he was little. His father had died of consumption just before his first birthday but what he said must be substantively true. Monty couldn't bring himself to be an out-and-out liar. Not for any reason.

'So' he followed up quickly, "Michael or Patrick Casey. Do you know them? Will they be in tonight?"

"Ah, the Casey boys. Well, not Paddy Casey, he won't be in that's for sure. He went to ground in 1923 so he did. And I don't blame him. No, I don't blame him. Some say he's in Dublin. Some say he's dead. But we won't be seeing him round these parts again I can promise you that."

"And Michael?" asked Monty realising this might be his only lifeline.

"Now Mick Casey has been known to be in here from time to time," he said, the first smile to cross his face. "The tough old bastard—sorry Son," he said to Alfie "the tough old goat will be out on the farm in this weather. He won't miss a night mind. We'll be seeing him about nine o'clock I'd guess."

"Then I will come back then, Mr …"

"McLaughlin. Jimmy McLaughlin," he said and did not offer his hand.

"Thank you, Mr McLaughlin." Monty was waiting to be invited to call him Jimmy. He wasn't. "Perhaps then Mr McLaughlin you could advise me on a lodging house. Me and the boy are weary and need some food and a place to stay for a couple of nights."

At that moment a man who could have been fifty, could have been seventy, wearing an unseasonably sturdy, stained, stone-coloured mackintosh, tied at the waist walked straight past them into the bar.

"Declan," said the landlord in greeting, nodding.

"James," came the reply from the red-faced mackintosh man, nodding as he passed.

"Wait here," said the landlord to Monty, "five minutes. Need to get the Guinness going." And with that, he went inside.

Another man walked into the bar with just a nod in Monty and Alfie's direction.

"Father," said Alfie.

"Not now Alfie Casey," said Monty.

It was nearly 15 minutes before the landlord came back.

Now, Jimmy McLaughlin might have been suspicious of this English pair but money was money and he wasn't going to see the old bastard O'Donnell get his hands on the English money at his hotel down the road.

"I've got a room you can have," he said "Two nights. Eight shillings a night. One bed. Money up front. Bite of supper thrown in and a decent eggs and bacon breakfast in the morning. Do all the cooking myself since the missus died. So it won't be an early breakfast. And I'll be having one myself. I've got a delivery at 10. Shall we say nine o'clock for breakfast?"

"That will be fine. I've only got English money," said Monty.

"Ah, get away," said the landlord, "money's money and with the amount of smuggling going on around these parts in these troubled times half the county's carrying enemy coin," and there was a genuine laugh, but a laugh which didn't hide the menace of the words 'smuggling' 'these troubled times' and 'enemy'.

"What about the boy?" asked Monty.

"If he's quiet, he can sit himself in the corner. No one will pay any mind to him. And it'll be light enough until ten. Or he can play in the street. He'll come to no harm."

With that money changed hands, the cheapest room so far and with a spot of supper thrown in, thought Monty.

The landlord went inside and the two of them followed him through the surprisingly small bar and then up the creaking, bare oak stairs to by far their biggest room to date, clean, with a soft comfortable bed, a large window onto the street below, an impressive oak tree beyond, a washstand and a single set of drawers.

"You can fill your jug at the bar, there's an earth closet out back. I'll get your supper now before we get busy. I'll see you downstairs in 10 minutes. I've just heard the bell ring. That'll be Declan after another." And with that Landlord McLaughlin was gone.

Monty and Alfie put down their bags. Monty checked his gun parts wrapped in their cloth as he always did of an evening and then shoved them deep into the haversack.

"Same clothes tomorrow, Alfie Casey, wash when we come to bed. Depending on when Michael Casey comes in tonight you might be up here by yourself, is that ok?"

"Yes Father," he replied. He'd covered 25 miles and more that day. He was hungry and tired. Very tired.

"I'll only be downstairs," said his father "You can come and get me any time if you need anything."

"I know," he said.

"And remember Son, if anyone, ever, ever asks…" and here he whispered "You are Alfie Casey. Casey after your Granny Kathleen Casey, ok?"

"Yes, Father."

And with that, they went downstairs for big bowls of unnecessarily hot mutton stew—"it's what was on the range."—and lumps of heavy bread. It was superb.

Full and tired Alfie was sent up to bed and he went without hesitation or complaint.

Monty ordered himself a half pint of Guinness, returned to the table in the corner and sat and waited.

The two men at the bar, Declan in the coat and the one who followed shortly afterwards, looked over and then fell back into chatting with the landlord. Their conversation was animated but just too low for Monty to hear what they were saying.

As each new customer came in, words were exchanged, and the new customer would look over.

Monty knew what was going on.

They were all being informed by Mr James McLaughlin that the stranger in the corner was an Englishman claiming to be Mick Casey's nephew.

Chapter 25
Norfolk, Present Day

For Mark Elwin, it was the start of 'Operation Tail Chase' as he called it. From the middle of June until the end of August, it was shoulders to the wheel and all hands to the pump, if that was actually, physically possible.

For a start, it was the end of the school year and he had seven school photo shoots on the books. Over the years he had tried to move schools to an end of Easter term shoot with the promise of a discount on prints for the parents, just to make life easier for him. It hadn't worked. A couple of schools had taken him up on it but most still wanted the outdoor full-school photographs to be bathed in late summer term sunshine so that school memories would always be happy, sunny and tanned.

He split the school shoot preparations with Trish, Trish taking the small local primary schools, Mark taking the big ones, the vast Smithdon High School in Hunstanton, Fakenham High School and the big bucks money spinners, Wymondham, the boarding school near Norwich, Wisbech Grammar School and Gresham's, the self-styled Harrow of Norfolk.

These vast school shoots required planning, or at least update planning on last year, as Mark had fought and won these big jobs several years ago. For each, the full-school photograph required particular attention which now included temporary grandstand seating installed by outside contractors on school playing fields. Schools were not keen on their timetables being messed around because of trivial matters such as heavy rain.

The entire school cohort with gowned teachers at the front, principal non-academic staff to the sides and the whole school banked up from the little ones at the front to the potential V-flicking arseholes at the back always needed a clear, bright, dry day and that often meant a whole day's shoot scrapped at the last minute until better weather arrived. Mark was proud of the fact that he'd never failed to get the full-school shot, although once for Smithdon High School it was only finally achieved on the very last day of term.

The big secondary schools and the boarding schools were three- or four-day shoots, sometimes with Trish and Mark shooting separate classes in different school locations. Then there was processing, contact images emailed back to the school, relying on the school emailing out the images to the parents and then the orders for prints coming in.

From mid-June to the end of August Trish and Mark worked pretty much every day, Monday to Friday, from seven in the morning getting the necessary kit together and then travelling to schools, to 7, 8 and 9 o'clock at night processing images and responding to email orders, checking the bank account to make sure payments had been made, stuffing padded envelopes.

Sometimes the workload was so great that he subcontracted the printing out of the school images, putting them into cardboard frames and posting out to his chums at the camera shop in Hunstanton. It was dull work but altogether hugely profitable.

That was just the schools. 'Operation Tail Chase' also meant weddings. June to September was prime Saturday wedding territory. Mark tried to avoid mid-week weddings in June and early July as the school shoots were so time-consuming but weddings were also so lucrative.

Every Friday at 7 pm Trish would brief Mark on any wedding shoot coming up the next day. Mark knew they were in the diary. He often knew the venue. He'd know if he was required with the drone.

What he wouldn't know would be the wrinkles. The groom is in a wheelchair, how do we shoot the group shots? It's a Star Wars-themed wedding. Really? What was it with these people? Solemn vows? You're kidding. For this next wedding, they want to bring their dogs, dressed up. Then another, the groom is bringing his favourite tractors, a 1950 Ferguson and the latest Massey Ferguson combine harvester. One the size of a Ford Fiesta, one the size of a small office block.

Anyway, Trish's planning was meticulous and after an hour or so the two were always up to speed and knew what the next day held. A quick check of the weather forecast promised it would be dry. Thank God. And Trish went home to relieve her babysitting mother.

For two and a half months every summer Trish, and, by default, her mother, worked 12 or more hours a day six or seven days a week. The payback was that she always had the last two weeks of the summer school holidays off, two weeks at Christmas and two weeks at Easter, every bank holiday and as much flexitime as she needed the rest of the year when childhood illness struck in the night.

Mark's own children, Beth and Tim, were by now pretty much grown up and summers had been, for a long time, spent in Spain with their mother and her new husband at his villa on the coast somewhere. Beth sometimes called. She was a sweet girl, he thought, planning a gap year after A levels. Tim texted infrequently. Inquiries from Mark about their exam performances were usually out of date and concerned the wrong subjects. He'd been a mostly absent father making brief appearances on high days, holidays, occasional weekends, rare emergencies and on Boxing Day. He'd always paid his maintenance on time, every time. He was not proud of his record as a father. Neither did it trouble him unduly. Eight or so years after the divorce it rarely crossed his mind anymore.

Mark hated almost every minute of summer. Occasionally he'd make a Friday night at the Feathers after a visit to his grandmother but where he'd been young into fatherhood and then dropped off the social scene all his village and school contemporaries were now knee-deep in nappies and kids' party pick-ups. He was not a man awash with friends.

So Mark contented himself, when the workload allowed, with an excellent Sunday lunch at Rose and Crown in Snettisham where the front bar was full of old timers who'd been propping up the bar for 50 years. More in some cases. The former 'Visionary' proprietor Mike Clowser was always in place on bar stool number 2, asking about business and good for half an hour of chat about the good old days of school photography.

Mark also contented himself with the business bank account filling up. The money came tumbling in across the summer with every school shoot and every wedding and by late August Mark was spending his spare hours looking through estate agent websites for newly built properties.

He knew exactly what he was after in the buy-to-rent market. He already had two houses rented out. By early September the Visionary Ltd business account was once again groaning with cash that needed to find a home. Specifically, a two-bedroomed home, a new build on a medium-sized development which also contained three and four-bedroomed properties within easy reach of King's Lynn. Homes for aspirational young couples. Couples who saw themselves joining the three and four-bedroom set sooner rather than later. Couples who paid a decent rent, every month.

He easily found what he was looking for and emailed the builder's marketing suite to arrange a visit the following week. By the middle of September the deposit was paid, the local agents that handled his existing lettings were informed and he was pretty much home and dry on his third buy-to-let property.

His target of eight houses by the time he was fifty took another step forward. He imagined himself as a player at a customised Monopoly board, passing the 'Go' of summer 'Operation Tail Chase', collecting £200, reaching for the box the game came in, selecting another tiny wooden house and firmly placing it on the board.

The one thing he hadn't any time for was his laptop desktop file marked 'Find Alfie Sidebottom'.

Chapter 26
Norfolk, Present Day

The summer weeks passed much more slowly and much more painfully for Emma McMillan.

On too many nights she woke from a recurring nightmare in which she was sent down from a Gothically grim dock, her child Daisy wailing from a public gallery being half ushered, half dragged away, by her maternal grandmother.

When these nocturnal fantasies finally gave way to the reality of morning nothing at all could stop her mind from chewing away at the endless hours of not knowing what was to become of her or, more particularly, what was to become of her daughter, should she be sent to prison for the death of Simon Jones?

The post arrived mid-morning at her little house, while she was at work, and every day from 1030 onwards she wondered whether there was an ominous brown envelope lying in wait on the hallway floor.

It was all she could do but make an excuse and drive home to find out if the envelope was there. Each day, when she was finally home after a day at work and after collecting Daisy from Grandma's free child-minding service, it was all she could do to put the key in the door for fear of what lay beyond. She was torn, every day, between being desperate to know and never wanting to find out.

Then one day the letter was actually waiting for her. She picked it up and walked down the hall, shooing Daisy ahead of her and telling her to get herself some juice from the fridge and to set up her laptop on the kitchen table ready for homework.

Emma put the envelope into her pocket. It was as if she'd put a hand grenade in there. She filled up the kettle as she always did so Daisy wouldn't spot any change in routine, even though Daisy hadn't spotted the envelope on the hall floor at all.

Emma took off her jacket and placed it on the back of a kitchen table chair.

"Oh, I don't think so," said Daisy, wagging her finger. "I think we know where jackets live don't we?" she said, mimicking her mother's regular chiding.

"Yes, yes, we do," said Emma, "Now get on with your homework!"

Emma picked up her jacket and made her way upstairs, tearing open the envelope as she went.

She'd read it before she got to her bedroom door. It was not what she was hoping for. Death by Dangerous Driving and Driving Under the Influence of Drugs. A court date. Instructions to present by 0930 or else more dire consequences.

She sat on the end of her bed and let out a long, empty, tragic sigh.

A couple of days later she took half a day off work and presented herself at Brannon and Brannon for an audience with Eric O'Grady, solicitor for her defence.

"Come in. come in," he said, "have a seat. Have you been offered a coffee?"

"No thanks," she said, holding out the letter.

"Yes, yes," he said tapping a file in front of him "All present. Now at least we know where we stand."

You must be kidding, she thought, I have no idea where I stand except somewhere between freedom and prison.

"Now there's some interesting stuff in the case notes here," he said. "So before we think about what we might do let me just run through a few things, check again with your side of things and then consider our plan going forward. Okay?"

What does he expect her to say? No, let's just all go home and forget this ever happened.

"Fire away," she said using a phrase she was pretty certain she had never used in her life before. "Okay," she added. Much better.

"Okay then, well the charge is not what we'd hoped for but there are things in our favour," he said.

Hope, she thought. Really? From Mr O'Grady?

"First of all it seems the victim, for some reason, was not wearing a seat belt."

"What difference does that make?" Emma said.

"Well, courts will take into account if there are factors contributing to the death which were not down to you and not wearing a seat belt has long been established, not as a defence, but certainly a strong mitigating factor."

"Meaning?"

"Meaning it won't get you off but it might get you off more lightly."

What does that mean, she thought.

"Anything else?" she said.

"Yes, it seems he was possibly, probably even, exceeding the 30mph speed limit. Nothing from the police suggesting how much but certainly by the amount of damage to both cars, the likelihood that you couldn't have been travelling even 20mph, plus the small amount of skid marks from the deceased's Range Rover, the distance he'd travelled from his stop at the flower shop, then it looks like he'd put his foot down."

"But mitigation not defence?"

"Yes, I'm afraid so Mrs McMillan," he said.

"*Ms* McMillan," she said.

"Apologies," he said.

"Is that it in my favour?"

"Well, it's more than we had. You were not speeding, he was. Probably was. Not entirely certain. He was not wearing a seat belt. Definitely certain."

"And against me?"

"Ah," he said and slowly opened the file and took out his latest notes.

"It was a clear and dry day so road conditions were perfect for vision and driving. You should have seen him coming."

"But I didn't," she said. "He came out of nowhere."

"Ah, but you had a clear view both left and right when you pulled out into the road. Here," he fiddled in the file, "here…your statement to the police. Then there's the fact that you were partially on the wrong side of the road at the moment of impact."

"I see," she said. "Anything else?"

"Well, you had been using drugs immediately before driving… Ms McMillan," said the solicitor.

"But you said my multiple sclerosis…that could be used in my favour?"

"For sentencing Ms McMillan," he said now pointedly emphasising the Ms "for sentencing purposes, not in fighting a defence."

"Anything else?" she said.

"Well, for sentencing there's a powerful statement from his wife. His widow, that is. Her husband was a gifted and respected doctor, pillar of the community etc., churchgoer, dedicated father, there are two orphans and, of course, a widow now, loss of income and status etc.," he said. "I've never known a person who has died in an accident to be described in court as a bit of a bastard, Ms McMillan, but this widow statement is, by any standard, powerful stuff."

"Anything else?" she said, wearily.

"Well, at the end of the day," said Eric O'Grady, "At the end of the day…a man did die."

And his last words hung in the air until they settled like a dusting of gloom. She shook herself into practical mode.

"So, what next?"

"Well," he said "we appear before magistrates to enter a plea. Guilty or not guilty. Then, crucially, they'll decide if they'll take the case or not and even, given a guilty plea, if they'll deal with it there and then. This is the best we can hope for. It means the very worst is six month's prison but that would be unlikely on the day as they'd need to get reports on your personal circumstances and more. What would happen to your daughter, etc.? You understand?"

"What do you mean 'given a guilty plea'?" she said sternly.

Eric O'Grady looked quizzically at her.

"Mr O'Grady," she continued, her voice gaining strength and purpose "You have not asked me what I intend to plead yet."

"Well, Ms McMillan," the 'Ms' emphasis now becoming sarcastic, "what, given everything we've been discussing, have you in mind?"

"I'm not a dangerous driver Mr O'Grady. Never have been." She said, launching into what had long been rehearsed in her mind, "I'm not reckless. I'm not a reckless woman. Not in anything I do really. Quite a boring person in many ways. Certainly a boring driver. You can ask my daughter how boring a driver I can be. And I admit driving after having smoked a little grass that morning. But I wasn't off my head in drugs. I'm not sure exactly what happened that morning, to be honest, not sure at all, but dangerous I'm not. So I've been thinking of nothing else these past two or three months and I've decided that if they accused me of dangerous driving, I would plead not guilty. Can you argue that *Mr O'Grady?*" and her emphasis on 'Mr' went beyond sarcasm and veered towards contempt.

Eric O'Grady looked at his client through fresh eyes. There was a second's pause.

"Well, Ms McMillan," he said, the 'Ms' returned to a neutral state, "we can certainly give it our best shot."

Chapter 27
Irish Free State, 1933

Monty knew Michael Casey the moment he walked into the Olde Glen Bar, partly because he had a look of his own mother, especially around the eyes, and partly because Michael Casey scanned the bar looking for him. Word had clearly reached him out in the wider world that there was a stranger in town asking questions.

Michael Casey went to the bar, ordered himself a pint of Guinness and a small whiskey, chatted briefly to the men at the bar and then turned and purposefully came over to Monty's table and sat down on a three-legged stool opposite him.

"I understand you'll be looking for me?" he said.

"If you are Michael Casey or Patrick Casey then, sir, I am."

"There'll be no 'Sir' in the Free State," he said. "And friends and family call me Mick, not Michael."

"Then Mick it is," said Monty. "I'm Monty Casey," and he held out his hand for a shake. It was refused.

"I'm told you are Kathleen's son?"

"I am."

"We've never heard of you."

"Well, I still am her son." The bar was silent. Every eye was on the two of them. Monty looked towards them.

"Family business?" he said, expecting them to turn in embarrassment at being called out eavesdropping. They didn't.

"As I said Son, I've never heard of you. To be fair, never heard a word of Kathleen from the day she upped and went. So as far as I'm concerned, you're just another unwelcome Englishman in the Free State of Ireland."

The bar hummed in approval. One man said "You tell him Mickey boy," and another hushed him quiet.

Monty put his elbows on the bar table and looked at the man opposite him. It was no time to back off even if he could, what with Alfie asleep upstairs.

"Well then if you are Mick Casey, then I am your nephew, Monty Casey. Asleep upstairs is more of your family, my son Alfie. What do you say to that?"

"I say, Englishman, show me. I say show me something that proves you are the first Englishman not to tell a lie in Donegal. Would you be carrying a photograph of my little sister with you then? Or papers? Or a letter from the good woman herself?"

"No. I never knew there to be a photograph of her. And there'll be no letter. She's been dead these past dozen and more years."

That news at least blunted the pointed nature of the questions from the Irishman in front of him.

"So your mammy...she'd be how tall?"

Monty held out an arm and indicated around five feet from the floor.

"Aye, that'd be about right," said Mick Casey. "And her hair?"

"Mostly greyish as I remember it but she claimed to have been a redhead in her youth," said Monty.

"Aye, with piercing green eyes," said Mick Casey.

"Blue eyes," said Monty.

"Aye, blue eyes. A big woman with blue eyes."

"She may have been a big woman when you knew her, she was a stick of a woman when I was growing up. But that might have been because she always fed herself second. I certainly never went hungry."

The bar hummed again.

"It's thirty years and more since she left Donegal. Not a word from her. Not one word. To me, or her dear dead father. Nor the husband she upped and left. God rest their souls. Why did you come here to find me? Here? In this bar? And now? What's your business—if you are who you say you are, and I don't believe it for a minute..." And he turned to the bar and there were shouts of "That's right Mick," and "Who are ya?"

"She left because of—as you say—her 'dear father' and her husband. She didn't say much except once she did say that her father, her husband and her brothers Michael and Patrick used to drink in the Olde Glen Bar until the money was gone. And when he got home that 'terrible man O'Malley' would take his fists to her."

Monty knew more of the beatings his mother had taken. How she'd suffered in what was to all intents and purposes an arranged marriage. How she'd secretly got herself a job in service in England through an agency in Dublin. How one night she'd slipped away from the drunken O'Malley and the following year, thanks to the new law in England, once she'd taken up her job as a scullery maid at Sandringham House, had quickly divorced her Irish past.

But that was powder to be kept dry. Monty needed to persuade this man of who he was. Not alienate him. Not embarrass him in front of his bar friends.

Mick Casey looked at the worn wooden edge of his stool. He looked at Monty.

"He was not a good man in drink," he said.

The bar hummed again.

"And he was in drink often," said Mick Casey. "Mind you, our Kathleen was known to like a dram or two. Our old Pappy working at the Crolly Distillery and all," and he laughed and turned to the press at the bar, who joined in the laughter, nodding to each other in memory of a fellow drinker long departed.

"I never knew my mother take a drink in her life," said Monty.

And the bar fell silent.

"Aye, that is true. Hated the drink she did. And who could blame her to be fair." And the Irishman paused.

"Monty Casey, you say?" said Mick Casey, "Monty *Casey*, I hear you call yourself? Now, how might that be?"

"Never knew my father," said Monty honestly. "Just me and my mother. The only family we knew."

And here he paused.

"Until now?" asked Monty.

"Well, we'll see about that," said his uncle. "We'll see about that. First, you'll take a drink with me? What'll it be?"

"I'll have a half of Guinness," said Monty.

"And maybe a shot of old Crolly to honour my dear old Pappy—your grandpappy, if what you say is true?"

"Why not?" said Monty.

"Then let's not skulk over here in the shadows young Monty. Let's be among the men at the bar," and he stood up.

This could be a long night, thought Monty.

Chapter 28
Irish Free State, 1933

It was a long night.

Monty stood at the bar with the men of Donegal and matched them drink for drink. Well half a pint for him, a pint for the men at the bar. And a single measure for him, a double for them. But it was still a long night and when, every now and then, there was a question of detail about who he was and where he came from, he told the vaguest of truths and so he would always be able to say that he told no absolute lies.

The only thing he did was substitute Sandringham House for a place called Glemham Hall away in Suffolk. Glemham was big enough to have scullery maids like his mother, gamekeepers like himself and big enough to never have heard of him at all should any questions ever make it back across the sea.

He'd only been to Glemham once himself as a stuffer on a double gun shoot day, loading an empty gun while a guest from Sandringham used a second gun to give both barrels to the pheasants above. That one visit was years ago, but he could describe the house—at least the parts he'd been allowed in—and the estate in crystal clarity.

The inevitable question was asked again and again to which he answered again and again "Me and the boy want a new start and work."

"So what'll you be needing a new start for?" asked Declan.

"Oh, you know, sometimes it's time to move on," he'd reply with honest vagueness.

"You'll be leaving a wife behind then?"

"I've everything that's dear to me upstairs," again with honest vagueness.

"You have money then?" said a thick-set man with hands like shovels nursing a whiskey glass.

"I have enough for two nights here that's for sure."

"I said, you'll have money then?" he said again. The gaggle at the bar leaned closer.

The penny dropped.

"I've enough for a round of drinks at the bar if that's what you mean?" said Monty.

"That is precisely what I mean," said shovel hands and the cheer went up, the drinks were served and Monty felt as if the time might be right to ask the question.

"So, what might a man do for work in these parts?" he said.

It was as if he'd insulted every mother in Ireland.

"There'll be no work for you in these parts," said a weasel-faced man at a table between the bar and the door. The man had not been party to Monty's largesse at the bar. The bar crowd fell silent. This was a man of little stature but some standing, Monty felt.

"I'm willing to do an honest day's work for an honest day's pay," said Monty.

"Aye, and what do you call an honest day's work?" asked the man.

"I can labour as good as any man," said Monty. "I've done gamekeeping. I've driven tractors. I can dig a ditch alongside the best."

"That's as maybe. But you, Englishman, you will get no work here. That's because you, Englishman, have made sure there is no work here," the weasel-faced man said, with a finality that was hummed with approval at the bar.

Monty turned to Mick Casey.

"You see Son," said his uncle, "there's a terrible trade war going on. You English. You're not happy we won the war and we fucked off. Telling you to fuck off at the same time. You, the English, you, you see, you're not happy at all. Sore losers you might say."

Humming of approval in the Olde Glen Bar was by now universal.

"And so," continued Mick Casey realising he had both the floor and the undisputed support of every man at the bar, "having been told rightly and royally to fuck right off, you've gone all mardy and what you couldn't win with men and guns you are now trying to do with customs men and tax."

Monty had no idea where this was going.

"You'll have had to answer yourself a few questions at the customs crossing post?" asked Mick Casey.

Monty stayed silent.

"Oh, we'll be seeing, then, that you preferred not to be answering questions?" said Mick Casey. It wasn't a question. It was a statement. It was the understanding in the whole bar that Monty had slipped into the Irish Free State unofficially. It did not make him suspect in the Olde Glen Bar. Most of the men in the bar went back and forth across the border unannounced and unnoticed. It didn't make them suspect him of anything in particular. If anything, it made Monty closer to them not farther apart.

"Well," continued Mick Casey, "you need to know that the English have slapped every duty on Ireland they can, to try to make us bow down. Pigs, cream, milk, lamb, beef, cheese. You name it, they've taxed it. And what do we do in Donegal? Well, pigs, cream, milk, lamb, beef, cheese and all of that. Luckily enough there are hundreds of roads between here and there and the English and their bastard cousins over the border can't stand on every street."

"Aye," murmured Declan.

"The bastards," said another man.

"And," said Mick, "it's lucky you English, you're all as fucking corrupt as we are!" And he raised his glass and the bar cheered.

When the cheering died down, Jim McLaughlin suggested it might be nearing closing time. The suggestion was howled down and majority rule prevailed over legal licensing hours. Mick Casey continued.

"So, my dear nephew Monty Casey, if that's who you say you are,"

"English spy more like," said the weasel.

"Now, now Colonel," said Mick Casey, with firmness but clear deference, "now Colonel. I wouldn't know even the English to send a spy across the border, into the Olde Glen Bar, and bring his boy with him. Eh?"

"That's right," said the landlord, serving drinks "the boy's upstairs as we speak. And he's paid for tomorrow night as well."

"There," said Mick Casey, "now that's not much of a spy, is it?" he said looking at the weasel.

"It's on you then, Mick Casey," said the weasel. "Just remember if no good comes of this, it's on you. You've no brother watching your back any more." The weasel stood, smacked his glass down on the table and left.

And the hush in the bar was tangible.

After more than a moment, Mick Casey turned back to the bar.

"Have no mind Monty lad, have no mind. It's still too fresh here. Too much trouble. Still a lot of trouble. And your trouble is you're English so there's no work. And there's no work because of the English. You'll get no work here because there is no work. Not farm work. Not gamekeeping. Not labouring. An Englishman won't find work here in Donegal. You may as well go home Son, wherever you say that might be."

Then a voice said, "There's always Captain Bastard."

Chapter 29
Irish Free State, 1933

Captain John Bashford inherited Leghowney House from a largely unknown bachelor godfather just after the Great War. It was both a blessing and a curse.

A blessing as in 1919 he had no idea what to do with his life come de-mob, no qualifications, certainly not for civilian life, no skills except minute taking and memo writing and no means of support either visible or unseen. At least, Leghowney House was somewhere to go.

A curse because it was vast. Truly vast. A huge pile in constant need of propping up, with barely a thousand acres of farmland to rent out, only four cottages the same, fishing rights on the Eske barely worth the paper the day tickets were written on and a view of the Blue Stack mountains to die for but, in revenue terms, pointless.

It was, in many ways, a perfect reflection of a house for Captain Bashford. Mostly non-descript, past its best, if there ever had been a best, and facing what could only be hazarded at as certain and terminal decline.

The young John Bashford had what many people would regard as an idyllic childhood and a privileged upbringing, but the captain never saw it as that.

The youngest of three brothers Bashford (very) minor started life in third place and never really accelerated out of it.

His mother died giving birth to him which left his father, if not resentful, then certainly distant. His father may not have been an emotional man, Derbyshire gentlemen farmers rarely were, but the young John noted at least his passing interest in the older brothers. Towards him there was tolerance. Distance.

His brothers were encouraged to take an active part in the farm, several thousand acres of sheep on the Peak above Matlock, and several thousand more of mixed arable crops below the town. John was not.

One thing the young John Bashford did enjoy on the farm was the shooting and the fishing. There were still plenty of brown trout to be had on the Derwent which snaked in and out of White Hill Farm and as a boy he found greater enjoyment in following the farm's gamekeeper round than following the farm manager round.

His older brothers were both taller and wider than him and were sent in turn to Eton College, the eldest by their paternal grandfather, the next by the maternal grandfather.

When it came to John, the obvious lack of both academic ability and prowess on the sporting field meant the decision was taken by his father to despatch him to Trent College twenty or so miles away as a boarder at the age of 13. Trent College was also refreshingly kinder on the farm finances than Eton College would have been.

His time at Trent College was neither a success nor a failure although one notably peevish Latin teacher did once write in his annual report that "after much examination of his character I have come to the inevitable conclusion that Bashford has what can only be described as hidden shallows."

At the end of school and with no clear vision of where to go and what to do, he had returned to White Hill Farm in the hope that his father might find something for him. He didn't. So it was with some relief that in August 1914 war was declared and the Bashford boys lined up to sign up.

His eldest brother was denied military service. He was by then running the farm and the nation and the war machine needed feeding.

His middle brother was sent to the infantry and after passing through officer training was despatched to the front line where he had a brief but thrilling six weeks culminating at the Battle of Neuve Chappelle in early 1915 when a lump of mortar casing sliced off most of his right kneecap.

Sent home, patched up and invalided out of the Great Conflict he returned to White Hill Farm a hero and while he would never bowl medium fast for Matlock Cricket Club ever again, he could still stand, shoot and fish and the limp he was left with seemed to make him strangely attractive to the eager population of Derbyshire farmers' daughters.

For John, the Great Conflict was much less successful. For the tens and hundreds of thousands of men and women who saw at first hand the full horror of the great slaughter Captain John Bashford saw mostly brown files on brown desks in small brown offices in the less fashionable parts of London in Woolwich and Pimlico and, for six months, Kent.

The army, it seemed, took his minor public-school education, a smattering of Latin and Ancient Greek and a less than robust physical presence to make him ideally qualified to join the Royal Army Ordnance Corps and to help organise the efficient running of the British war effort in general and, more specifically, to aid the sourcing, supply and transport of spare parts for military vehicles.

While men across the length and breadth of Britain returned in 1918, damaged physically and mentally, and for the rest of their lives stoically refusing to discuss what they had seen and, more tragically, what they had done, Captain John Bashford did not discuss his war because, frankly, there wasn't much to tell.

He rose to the rank of Captain within a year in the army when he took on the secretary's role for a range of various sub-committees. At the front, the officer class was being wiped out on an increasingly regular basis and men of his age were hurtling up through the officer ranks, Captain John Bashford attained the rank of captain and for three more years remained resolutely fixed there.

No, Captain Bashford never discussed "his war." Tales of committee agendas, minutes, recommendations, reports and conclusions would not hold an audience hoping for, at least, derring-do.

He wasn't even certain he'd actually made any difference. Reports and recommendations were sent off but he never actually saw orders fulfilled or despatched, never saw shipments arrive and never saw grateful men bring the machines of war back into play thanks to the work of Captain John Bashford, secretary to the working party directing the supply of spare parts.

He did, occasionally, visit factories. He spoke to industrialists in the Black Country about labour difficulties, skill shortages, and machine tool wear and tear but he never followed the trail from the factory floor to the theatre of war so who could say he had actually made a difference?

At the annual services of remembrance he attended each November, if he was ever asked, he would simply say "I played my part," which was, he thought, fair enough. He had played his part. He had played the part asked of him by the army and he played it to the best of his ability.

When de-mob came, he had returned briefly to White Hill Farm and told his father and brothers that he was only going to stay a while to 'consider his options' but in the end he'd hung around for a year helping out with the shoot, casting a hopeful fly on the River Derwent and turning out for Matlock Second XI at cricket, bowling a modest medium pace which, while never really attacking the batsmen, was skilful enough to be miserly in terms of conceding runs. Despite the Great Conflict taking most of the club's better players, Captain John Basford never made the Matlock Cricket Club's first XI.

Then, out of nowhere, a letter arrived, a meeting was had in a solicitor's office in London and he became the owner and, within two weeks, the occupier of Leghowney House. There was no farewell party as such, although on the night before his departure, his father produced a bottle of his finest port after dinner and his brothers presented him with a fine matching gun slip and cartridge bag with Capt. J Bashford etched on them.

So Captain John Bashford arrived in Ireland in the autumn of 1919 to take up residence, to take stock and to take the opportunity to start a new life.

Leghowney House was never going to be a gravy train to ride into old age. It creaked, it moaned and it was showing signs of both age and original poor craftsmanship. If Leghowney House could be said to have a mood, then the prevailing mood at Leghowney House could be described as "downcast."

To add insult to injury three years after inheriting the pile the seemingly endless war waged with the Irish was finally lost. At the subsequent division of the island of Ireland, the border was drawn and Captain Bashford was stuck 15 miles on the wrong side of the line in the Irish Free State, in enemy territory as such and he was condemned to a lifetime of being known as Captain Bastard.

He didn't care that much save for the near impossibility of getting anyone to do even the most basic labour for him. Even his plumber had to come over the border from Strabane. By 1933, Leghowney House survived thanks to the irregular quarterly rent from the farms on the estate, half a dozen or so driven game shoots in the winter, small change from fishing parties and the diminishing returns of four in-house paying spinster residents.

Miss Jocelyn Johnson was by 1933 in her late seventies and came with the house, so she'd lived at Leghowney House far longer than the captain and frequently told him how magnificent life in the house had once been. She used to have the big room upstairs but two years ago she failed to make the second part of the returning staircase and moved downstairs into what was the formal dining room with French windows out onto the lawns. A downstairs bathroom was installed in the vast space under the staircase.

The captain had no idea if she had ever been married. There was no talk of children. There were no photographs of family. She did, however, play the baby grand in the drawing room quite beautifully and demanded that it be tuned at least twice a year.

Her playing was much admired by the Wilson 'sisters' who looked entirely dissimilar and shared one room and one double bed to 'keep costs manageable'. Freda and Ada. The captain couldn't have made it up but when they replied to the small advertisement in The Lady magazine, he needed the money and, by 1933, they'd been residents of Leghowney House for some ten years.

Muriel De Courcey Villiers was his fourth resident. The captain had no idea who or what she was. She walked most days and kept part of the garden for herself, with her own arbour, cushions, honeysuckle, antirrhinums, painting easel and more. Her rent was by a standing order from the Mayfair branch of Coutts. She ate separately in her own room.

Meals at Leghowney House were rustic and hearty and with a southern Mediterranean twist, made as they were by Paloma, the female half of Carlos and Paloma, the Spanish general factotum cum chauffeur and housekeeper couple who breezed up via the London recruitment agency which specialised in Communist refugees from an increasingly dangerous Spain. Quite why you'd run away from one civil war zone to another was known only to them. Anyway, the captain was happy. No papers meant slave wages.

And no papers was exactly what Monty had.

The Olde Glen Bar had furnished him with a few details.

The address of Leghowney House.

The fact that no Irish man worth his name would ever work for Captain Bastard.

The fact that the captain was desperate for a gamekeeper as the last two had quit within the year for the sake of a plague of poachers and, well, because the captain was a bastard.

This served Monty well.

After a good morning's walk with Alfie and a round trip to look at the lie of the land, Monty knocked at the butler's entrance at the back of the house.

Paloma answered.

"Hello," he said, "I believe I might be the new gamekeeper," said Monty.

"Is you?" she said with such a heavy accent that it sounded more like a single word 'shew'.

"If I could speak to Captain Bashford?" he said, putting an arm out to stop Alfie from stepping in front of him and inside the house.

"Does Captain know you here?" she said.

"No," said Monty, "but I come recommended by Michael Casey of Donegal. I believe the captain knows Mr Casey."

The Spanish housekeeper knew a lost soul when she saw one, and she was looking at one right then.

"You wait," she said.

And it was a wait. Twenty minutes passed with Monty saying 'shhh' to Alfie at regular intervals and, briefly, 'good morning' to Miss Villiers as she passed through the house to attend to her private patch of garden.

Eventually, Captain Bashford appeared with Paloma who vaguely wafted a hand in Monty's direction and then slipped back into the kitchen.

"Who are you, what do you want?" said the captain.

"I understand you are in need of a keeper, sir," said Monty.

"Who told you that?" said the captain.

"The clientele of the Olde Glen Bar," said Monty.

"What do they know, eh? Scoundrels. If not worse. To a man."

"Well, it's the back end of June now. If you'll be wanting to make money from shooting, this coming season you are sorely running out of time. There are no shooting cover strips to speak of save the scruffy remains of last year, looks like what rearing pens you have are empty and I'd be amazed if you didn't have a dozen or more fox earths and that's just what I spied on the walk over here."

"Who are you?" said the captain. "Just who do you think you are? Telling me my own business."

"My name is Monty Casey. I'm Mick Casey's nephew. I've been a keeper these past ten years. This here is my son, Alfie. I'll be needing a cottage, free range of the land, four pounds a week, as many cartridges as I need and a horse and cart. Any old cart will do."

"You'll have references?" said the captain.

"Of course not," said Monty.

"Then it's three pounds a week," said the captain. "And your cottage is there," he said pointing to a little house behind a duck pond. "Come and see me at eight o'clock tomorrow morning. Don't be late or your first day will be your last."

Ah, thought Monty. Captain Bastard for sure.

With that Alfie and Monty set off back to the Olde Glen Bar for one last night before starting their new life on the Leghowney House estate.

145

Chapter 30
Irish Free State, 1933

Monty and Alfie ate their mutton stew supper in silence although they were aware of being, once again, the centre of attention at the Olde Glen Bar.

When they'd finished Monty nodded to Alfie and the boy made his way upstairs to bed as arranged for a wash and to lay out a clean set of clothes as his father had told him to.

Monty went to the bar, ordered half a Guinness and waited for the questions.

"So, you'll be working for Captain Bastard then?"

"I will. And I thank you all here at the Olde Glen Bar for pointing me in his direction."

"You're thanking us!" and laughter spread right round the dozen or so men in the bar.

"I do. And as word travels fast around these parts, I may as well tell you everything. I'm taking up a post as gamekeeper. Me and the boy get a cottage and a modest living and so again, I thank you. Now to show my thanks I propose to stand myself a round and then I'm away to bed. Me and Alfie have got a long day ahead."

In due course when the banter had mostly died down and the drinks had been drunk, Monty said goodbye to the crowd and went to go upstairs to bed. As he was leaving one voice shouted out "You'll be turning a blind eye to a spot of the occasional poaching, will you?" And laughter broke out again.

It was a glorious sunny day as Monty and Alfie arrived at Leghowney House with all their worldly possessions in a suitcase and two knapsacks.

Monty made himself known to Paloma at the butler's entrance and as he made his way to the cottage that was to be his and Alfie's home, he noticed Carlos working on an old but study-looking cart.

"Is for you?" said Carlos, and Monty nodded.

The cottage was in something of a terrible state both inside and out but its location couldn't have been more perfect sitting as it did by the pond. Monty would start leaving grain out for the mallards to tempt them to set up home and to see if he could coax a few ducklings out of them.

Inside there was just one main room with a very old-fashioned cast iron stove. That would take some cleaning but inside the pantry, Monty found a wire brush, a bucket, a mop, a stiff yard brush and some carbolic soap.

"Here you go Alfie, that's your job. I want to be able to see my face in that stove when you've finished. No rush," he said, "but there'll be no hot food until it sparkles."

Alfie sighed but didn't complain. He was used to chores.

Father and Son set about the house. There were two bedrooms upstairs, both with a little grate, the grubby curtains were taken down and shoved into a bucket full of water.

Outside there was an overgrown vegetable patch with the tops of a few of last year's carrots and parsnips visible and the remains of a fruit cage which had raspberry canes in full flower and what looked like very serviceable strawberry plants. Good old strawberry plants, he thought. Virtually indestructible.

There was also a small outbuilding which contained a copper with a fire pit under and a pretty healthy stack of wood.

Monty had already spotted a couple of dead trees which could be brought down to see him and the boy warm through the winter.

The housework didn't all get done very quickly, Monty had his job to do and house chores had to be fitted in and around that, but within a fortnight Keeper's Cottage looked clean enough to be comfortable and Alfie even put a jar of wild flowers on the kitchen table.

By day, Monty set about making an inventory of the estate and introducing himself to the three families who rented and farmed the land wrapped as a square around Leghowney House.

First of all he left them in no doubt that the traps he had already spotted on Leghowney House land were to be removed. Poaching was to stop. I don't mind the odd rabbit here and there he conceded, but no partridges, no pheasants and no ducks.

"Those birds are my living," he said. "You'll not be stealing from the captain, you'll be stealing from me, and I'll not be robbed," was the line he used for each of them.

Second thing, he told them, he'd need some shooting strips planting around the margins of the following fields. He'd seen their tenancy agreements and they were bound to plant them at their own expense.

Monty needed strips of kale so that he could persuade his birds to make their homes there. The grain that he'd be putting out would tempt them in and then come shoot days the beaters would drive them out.

Thirdly he addressed the fishing. They'll be no selling tickets to your friends in Donegal he told them. You have no rights on the river. I'll be watching over the river too he said, and he patted his shotgun which he was carrying, broken, over his shoulder, which was his way of making a point.

When he'd done his rounds, he knew that the families would have their heads together thinking of ways around everything he'd laid down. Monty was unconcerned. Locals taking liberties was the same at Sandringham as it would be here and he always kept one step ahead of the game. He would be here too.

His dealings with the captain needed to set off on the right foot too.

"I'll be needing some timber," he said reading from a piece of paper, "I've got the list here. The rearing pens need fixing. Some basic tools, hammers, saws, axes and more. Some wire. Who do you have an account with?"

The captain just laughed.

"An account? An account? I'm not sure you quite realise the lay of the land here," said the captain. "We're English. We don't get accounts. Sometimes even hard cash isn't enough, but given the trade war, times are hard and cash is at least starting to talk again."

"And we'll be needing poults," said Monty. "And grain. I can make the feeding trays myself. Where's the nearest game farmer?"

"How many birds do you want to get?" said the captain. "I've only sold five days so far this season. And one for me."

"If you are selling days at £250 for you and your guests to shoot birds then the men will expect to shoot plenty of birds," said Monty. "Eight thousand."

"Eight thousand! Eight thousand Mr Casey?" exploded the captain.

"I want to keep back ten per cent of the hens," said Monty, "let's say we keep eight hundred back and a hundred cocks and next year we'll breed some, maybe even most, of our own. Cheaper in the long run."

The captain saw the logic of this and he liked Mr Casey's attitude but the captain was already adding up the costs in his head. Monty called the captain

'Captain' and the captain called Monty 'Mr Casey'. It was formal and respectful and it suited both men.

"I think the last thieving Irish keeper got some from down Knock way but I really have no idea," said the captain.

"Then I'll be needing to go to Knock," said Monty. "There'll be a gunsmiths there I've no doubt. They'll know where to buy birds. And it's getting late. If they've got any still going for sale then, they'll be keen to get shut of them in late June."

So the next day with Carlos driving and Monty alongside him in the front and the captain sitting royally in the back, they went to Knock, found a gunsmith, found a farmer with birds for sale and the captain was impressed as Monty clearly knew what he was doing and drove a sensationally hard bargain.

The birds arrived the following week and Monty, with Alfie's help, had just about got the pens ready for them.

There was one more thing Monty needed to clear with the captain.

Picking his day he presented himself at the butler's door and Paloma went to find the master of Leghowney House.

"What is it, Mr Casey? Are we due to do an inspection walk? I thought that was tomorrow?"

"It is Captain. Nine-thirty. No, I was wondering something?"

"What is it, Mr Casey, what is it? I'm a busy man you know."

Monty knew that was the last thing the captain was.

"I was wondering, Captain; I was wondering whether you would let your three tenants have a little of the shooting?"

"Good God no!" said Captain Bashford. "Bloody Irish hooligans. They give me rent and that's the only arrangement I require to have with them."

Monty paused and looked at his boots to give the captain time to settle down.

"I really do think you should offer them a day at the end of the season," said Monty, "cock birds only. I need the hens for breeding next year. One cock'll keep half a dozen or more hens happy. The men, they can beat for themselves."

"Not a chance in hell," said the captain, "you don't know these people. They hate the English. They'd as soon do you harm than a favour."

Monty gave another little pause to let the captain huff and puff a bit longer.

"If I can go to them and say if they come along on your sold days, walk the beating line with me, bring their dogs for picking up the dead birds behind the guns, and get a little bit of cash on the side…and, and here's the bit they'll like, a free day's shooting at the captain's expense, then I think the poaching will be kept down and I get a team of beaters and dog-men. It'll make life a lot easier for us all."

The captain said nothing but looked at his gamekeeper.

"I'll think about it," said the captain. "Anything else?"

"Yes," said Monty. "I'll need a dog. One of the tenants has got a good-looking black Labrador and she looks like she's due to pup any day now."

"I'm not paying for it," said the captain. "Do what you like with your own money."

"Oh, he'll give me a bitch," said Monty, "in exchange for the pick of the first litter I get off her." Monty paused for emphasis "if he thinks I can get him and his band of brothers a clean-up day shooting at the end of the season."

The captain afforded himself a smile.

"You are a canny man, Mr Casey," said the captain and Monty walked back to his cottage. A successful day.

The house, the garden and the fruit cage were coming along nicely, carrots, cabbage, potatoes, onions and more in neat lines in the vegetable patch, the curtains washed and dried and rehung, bedding aired and repaired, mattresses beaten, carpets equally and later that evening the first hot meal of a freshly shot rabbit cooked into a delicious stew on Alfie's impressively shiny stove.

"This'll do Alfie boy," said his father. "This'll do."

Chapter 31
Irish Free State, 1933

The pattern of life at Keeper's Cottage at Leghowney House was quickly established.

The local school was a ten minute walk away and by the end of his first week, Alfie had worked out who the bullies were, felt the full force of childhood rage and civil war hatred and found a friend in Bridget O'Reilly.

There was quite an English contingent. While the war for independence and the civil war with the IRA meant most of the English had either gone back to the motherland or at least to its outpost in Northern Ireland, many remained.

For a start, there was the Reverend John Mitchell and his wife Judith who presided over the Donegal Town Church of Ireland Anglican church and who lived in a small vicarage midway between Leghowney and Donegal itself.

The couple were in their mid-fifties, childless and devoted to their small flock.

Monty and Alfie attended every Sunday with Alfie going to Sunday school for the first half of the service with a handful of other Protestant children and then joining Monty and the rest of the congregation for the final couple of—usually jolly—hymns and final prayers.

Monty explained his Protestant faith to the Olde Glen Bar simply by saying his mother had preached "God was God, Jesus was Jesus and the local church to the big house was half a mile away while the nearest Catholic church was ten miles away."

"She was both a God fearing and a practical woman," Monty told his Uncle Mick and the matter was never raised again.

The Reverend and his wife took a liking to Alfie and it wasn't long before Monty was able to call into the Olde Glen Bar after Sunday service while Alfie went back to the vicarage to play in the garden or do complicated jigsaws with Mrs Mitchell or to play them both at his new passion, cribbage.

There were a couple of English traders still in business in Donegal.

The Clark family ran a haberdasher and ladies' clothes shop on the main street. The fashions were always up to date and reasonably priced and half the ladies of Donegal and the surrounding villages had an item of clothing from Clark's in their wardrobe.

Mr Preston was a woodsman and in almost everyone's opinion, a fine woodsman and Monty may well be in need of him to clear away some scruffy tree branches hanging over the pond. He needed the ducks to be able to see the water and they were coming in to land in increasing numbers. It's amazing what free food will do for a duck.

There were other English families scattered about but they were not all big church people and a few also practiced their faith at the small Methodist chapel.

Monty became a regular in the Olde Glen Bar on a Sunday lunchtime. It was his only alcohol of the week and he looked forward to the banter at the bar. He took plenty of stick early on but he wasn't the only Englishman in the bar. He took care not to defend Captain Bastard too much but he did draw the line at the poaching at Leghowney House and he issued a general warning to the men to spread the word that poaching would no longer be tolerated.

But poachers are by their very nature sly creatures and only a couple of days later Monty was tracking along the edge of the river, walking his territory, defending his turf, when he saw a thin leader line tied to an overhanging branch. He knew there'd be a net in the water and that the poachers would return under cover of darkness to see what they'd caught.

He presented himself at the rear door of Leghowney House and asked Paloma to fetch the captain.

"What is it Mr Casey?" said the captain.

"Poachers," said Monty. "Found a net tied to a branch about 500 yards from the five-bar gate on the north side of the ten-acre field."

"Have you hoicked it out?" asked the captain.

"No," said Monty.

"Why the devil not?" asked the captain, irritated.

"We need to catch them at it," said Monty.

"Tell the police?" asked the captain.

"I think not," said Monty. "You might as well put a notice in the newspaper. We need to do this ourselves."

"Well, get on with it," said the captain, about to turn and go back inside.

"Not just me," said Monty. "For a start, there might be more than one of them and I don't fancy a good hiding. For another thing, we'll need witnesses. My word against theirs isn't going to stand up."

"What are you suggesting, Mr Casey?"

And so Monty laid out his plan.

At 9 o'clock that night, just as the last light of the day was going, Monty, the captain, Carlos and Paloma got into the car and drove it as close to the site of the net as they could without it being seen from the road or the five-bar gate. Monty was surprised that Paloma was with them. He wasn't to know that this was one of the least dangerous missions she'd ever been on.

Then they got out and laid down in the barley crop in the field, out of sight and silent.

Within the hour, in watery moonlight, they saw a flashlight and two men climbed over the gate and made their way down towards where they'd laid their net. Monty held up a hand to keep the other three lying down in the crop and then standing up he shouted out.

"I see you men. You are trespassing and poaching. I have my gun here. You will stand still," he commanded.

The two men froze, briefly, and then the one at the front said "We were only taking a shortcut, so we were. We don't know anything about no poachers," and he turned to his comrade and said, "Have you seen any poachers, Paddy?"

"None at all, none at all, Donal," said the second man and the two of them started laughing. The man at the front turned to Monty who could just about make out the younger brother of Declan from the Olde Glen Bar.

"So, if there's nothing more…and if you're objecting to us taking a shortcut, then we'll just get ourselves back to the road," he said and the men made to leave.

Captain Bashford heard the exchange and was incensed. He stood up and pulled his service revolver from its holster on his hip.

"Stand still you thieving bastards," he shouted. "Stand still or I shoot!"

"I don't think you'll be doing that," said the lead man and then added with menace, "Captain Bastard."

Years of resentment at everything Irish around him swirled into his head, he cocked his revolver, raised it high and was just about to shoot the lead man in the chest when Monty swung the barrels of his shotgun up knocking the captain's arm to the sky and the gun cracked and the shot rang out in the night.

The poachers froze.

Carlos and Paloma stood up.

Quick as a flash Monty said "Right, you've had your warning shot from the captain. As you say, Captain Bastard. You won't be wanting a second shot, will you?"

The two men realised that Monty had saved one of them from near certain death. They also realised they were seriously outnumbered. They surrendered.

Word of Monty's action spread. His standing at the Olde Glen Bar and among the farmer families on the estate rose dramatically. Captain Bashford knew he'd been saved from himself and from a great deal of trouble. A great deal of trouble indeed.

The men had been squeezed into the car, the net and the salmon caught in it were retrieved from the river as evidence and the whole party went to the local police station where even they couldn't help but make the formal charges.

A couple of weeks later when he was in the Olde Glen Bar there'd been a frosty silence but he toughed it out and eventually one of the locals said "Aw come on now Declan, Donal and Paddy were fair warned and they'll be fools to be caught."

"From what I hear Paddy's lucky to be alive," said Jim behind the bar. "Lucky to be alive and I think we all know it's thanks to Mr Casey here," he added nodding to Monty.

Another said, "he'll only be fined ten bob."

And a third said "fucking expensive salmon though," and a laugh around the bar drew a line under the matter.

Poaching on the Leghowney House estate stopped.

Uncle Mick was rarely in the Olde Glen Bar at any lunchtime from late Spring through to early October unless there was heavy rain. Farm labouring was long hours while the sun shone. But on one particular Sunday, pouring as it was, and Mick was in, Monty took him to one side, outside, as there was something he needed to sort out.

"Now Mick, that'll be something I'll need you to keep to yourself," said Monty.

"Right you are," said his uncle, sensing something juicy coming his way, and something he would have no hesitation in passing on to the bar at some future date. "What is it, lad?"

"I need papers," he said.

"Now, what sort of papers might they be?" said his uncle.

"I need a passport for me, probably one for Alfie, but more importantly for Alfie a birth certificate. I need to make him—well—legal."

"You mean," said his uncle, "illegally legal."

"I suppose that's exactly what I mean," conceded Monty.

"You'll not be wanting British passports then?" asked his uncle.

"I think, on balance, it's time to become citizens of the Irish Free State."

"A convert to the cause, would you believe it?" chuckled his uncle. And then a serious face. "This is not to be taken lightly, Monty lad."

"I know," said Monty.

"Not sure you do, boy. First, it is illegal, and while there are many men floating around free Ireland with false papers, not many of them sleep well at night. Your uncle Paddy for a start, wherever he may be, may he be alive and well. Then," he said, "second—it'll not be cheap."

"How 'not cheap' is 'not cheap'?" asked Monty.

"Well, I've no fucking idea but you being English doesn't make this enterprise easier—or cheaper."

"No," said Monty.

"And third—and you need to think about this—it'll not stay secret. If—and I mean if—we can get you passports and birth certificates people will know who you are, where you live, where you work and where Alfie goes to school. There may come a day when they need, shall we say, a 'favour'."

"What sort of favour?"

"How the fuck do I know?"

"I'll take the chance. There's no future for Alfie without a genuine identity."

"Well, genuine is the one thing it fucking won't be, will it?"

"It'll be good enough. He can't spend his life living at Leghowney not able to get a job or cross the border or even go back to England one day if he wants."

"You'll not be going back I take it," asked Uncle Mick, searching for a glimpse into the past.

"I like it here very much," smiled Monty. "Can you help?"

"Aye probably," said his uncle. "I'll see you next Sunday. The weather's set to be awful for a week. Bring the boy. Bring plenty of money."

The following week Monty and Alfie went to church as usual and then both went to the Olde Glen Bar 'for family business' Monty explained to the Reverend and Mrs Mitchell.

Monty had no idea how much this venture was going to cost so he put all the money still left in the tin, plus the little extra he'd managed to save from his meagre wages, and distributed it around various pockets so he didn't reveal his stash all in one handful.

There'd be time to top up the tin this winter with tips from the shoot days and the trading of a few rabbits and hares off the estate during the long, cold winter months.

Mick was outside the bar standing next to an old van and a man wearing truly filthy dungarees.

"This is John. He'll be driving. He'll need paying," said his uncle.

"Okay," said Monty "Where we off to?"

"Sligo Town."

"Really?"

"Further away the better, frankly. And this man is good. Half the IRA are carrying his passports," and he and John chuckled. Monty had never seen him before and doubted very much that John was his name.

And so they went to Sligo, rang a doorbell behind a photographer's shop, sat down, talked to the man with glasses and a magnifying glass, gave over the dates of birth, which were true, and then a whole lot of other details which were not.

Money changed hands.

John drove them back to the Olde Glen Bar. Monty never saw him again.

Two weeks later Uncle Mick handed over two birth certificates and two passports.

"Welcome to the Irish Free State," said his uncle. "And it's five quid for my trouble."

And he meant it.

Chapter 32
Norfolk, Present Day

It was mid-September before Mark once again opened himself a bottle of Corona beer, pushed a wedge of lime in its neck, took a satisfying slug and clicked open the computer desktop file marked "Find Alfie Sidebottom."

He opened his cardboard file too and pulled out the various printouts of birth certificates and wedding certificates and notes he'd jotted down.

Within an hour, he was back up to speed with what he knew.

Which was not much.

Monty Sidebottom and his son Alfie went away one day in 1933 and when they went away, they left literally not a trace. So where did they go? Mark had gone back a few generations on Monty's side of the family and they were pretty much all, to a man, agricultural workers from north Norfolk. And pretty much all dead, so no one to run to there and even if there was, they would be no further away from the scene of the crime than a tuppenny bus trip.

Let's go the other way then, he thought, and see if we can find out about your mother, the interesting Irish divorcee. Now what's that about?

"So, Kathleen O'Malley," he said out loud to the computer in front of him, "let's see just who you are."

The wedding certificate mentioned her father Declan Casey and her husband, of course, Patrick O'Malley.

"Let's hit the websites," he said, snapping the cap off another beer.

The British Census applied in Ireland until 1922 and independence and it was carried out every 10 years from 1831. He found the 1901 census and put in a search for Patrick O'Malley and Kathleen O'Malley in Donegal.

"Bingo," he said when the result flew back. "Patrick O'Malley, blah blah blah. Damn. No Kathleen O'Malley. She must have been on her way to England."

Find their marriage certificate he wrote on his recycled half of A4.

But then he thought it through. If Kathleen O'Malley was divorced, pregnant and married again in 1904, in England, then in 1901 she must be already here.

Definitely not bingo.

He went back to 1891 and put in a search for her father Declan Casey and her maiden name Kathleen Casey. Bloody hell. No results.

He hit the search engines and found out that all the census results for 1891 for Ireland had been destroyed in a fire at the records office in 1922.

The act of a vengeful Irish army wiping out the colonial past perhaps?

The trouble with his mission of Find Alfie Sidebottom was that it kept throwing up interesting sidelines. Mark spent half an hour reading all about the fire which happened two days into the Irish civil war.

It turned out probably not to be a fire *per se* but a massive explosion which destroyed not only the Public Records Office but severely damaged the main Dublin court complex.

Census records for the whole of the 19th century were wiped out along with hundreds of years of documented history including Church of Ireland parish records and details of records of Crown lands going back to the 14th century.

"This search is pointless enough without this," he said. It was definitely time for another beer.

He returned to his computer, returned in time to 1901 and typed in the names again. Well, there was Declan Casey, living on the Glebe. Distillery Labourer was listed as his profession. Also, the fact he could read but, oddly, not write. There was no Kathleen living in the household but there was a Mrs Aisling Kilpatrick who was listed as housekeeper and she could read and write. She was also a good 20 years younger than Declan.

You dirty old dog Declan Casey thought Mark. Could that explain why Kathleen was out of the house? You couldn't have two ladies in the house, could you? Your daughter and your "housekeeper".

Then there were Patrick and Michael Casey both in the house, both listed as farm labourers even though Michael was barely 15. The baby of the family thought Mark.

But where is your big sister? She was not with her husband of the time in 1901. She almost certainly wouldn't leave the family home until she was married so by 1901, she must, absolutely must, have already upped and left the marriage and made her way to England.

The rest of the information on the census form was largely irrelevant. The family was Roman Catholic. Both boys could read and write. But boys they were.

"Uncle Patrick and Uncle Michael. Well, well, Monty Sidebottom. Did you run for help to your uncles? Let's see if we can find out..."

He looked first, as he now always did, for a grave. Let's start with a time and place of death and work backwards he thought.

He typed in 'Montgomery Sidebottom' in an Irish version of the British graveyard site.

Nothing. Not one single Montgomery Sidebottom dead in the whole of Ireland, ever.

So he tried Alfred Sidebottom. There were a few Alfred Sidebottoms to check out. There seemed to be a Sidebottom cluster in the port of Howth near Dublin, chandlers, sailors, fishermen. Men of the sea all of them but none was the right age.

"Am I chasing the world's only two known immortals?" he mused out loud, to himself, to the laptop and then to the fridge and a fourth beer. He'd run out of lime. He added 'limes' to the shopping list on his desk.

Okay, one last shot and we'll call it a night.

He typed in Montgomery Casey, hit the return button and...nothing. It seemed hopeless.

"What if Monty changed his name to, ooh let's say Mick Jagger and took Alfie—or rather Ringo Starr as he was known by then—off on a return banana boat to Brazil, or wherever banana boats go to. And from. The West Indies more likely," again, out loud.

"Right come on my beauty, one last try. Alfred Casey, Donegal." And he hit the return button.

"Yay," he said when three Alfred Caseys came up dead in Donegal. "Boo," he said when not one of them was, could have been or was even remotely anything to do with his Alfie Sidebottom.

He had run into enough brick walls for one night. He closed his computer down. Picked up his strangely bland, lime-less bottle of beer and idly picked up *Your Local Paper* the weekly freebie that he occasionally advertised in.

The front page was something about King's Lynn war memorial getting a grant from the War Memorials Trust to have a complete facelift and all the names of the dead from two world wars picked out once again in gilt.

Flicking through what was clearly a thin week for news something buried on page five caught his eye.

St Margaret's Doctor
Death: Trial Date Set

Your Local Paper was a weekly, and so it was rare that the conclusion of a trial coincided with the actual publication deadline. Anyway, it was mostly ads and they almost certainly wouldn't have a reporter to spare to sit through a trial. But it contained the allowable trial details.

Mark knew a bit about court cases. He'd covered a few for the *EDP* newspaper and, during the heyday, if it could be called that, of his London freelance career, he'd done the usual hanging outside court to snap a naughty footballer being banned for drink driving or some even naughtier minor rock star being given community service order for the 'my heroin hell' story he'd sell to the *Sun* the next day. Imagine if you were the retired librarian assigned his community service. Some long-haired rock God weeding your garden for a week. That would have made a better picture.

But this caught his eye because it was the crash outside the shop. It read simply:

King's Lynn magistrates heard that Emma McMillan, 36, of Church Street, Dersingham pleaded not guilty to causing the death by dangerous driving of St Margaret's doctor Simon Jones of Stanhoe. She pleaded guilty to driving while under the influence of drugs. The court heard that Ms McMillan admitted to smoking a joint before driving. She was banned from driving for a year, fined £300 and ordered to pay £50 court costs. The magistrates decided to hear the dangerous driving case themselves and set a trial date for October 14th.

Mark pulled his diary over to him and looked three weeks ahead. He had nothing on that day that couldn't be moved, cancelled or just handed over to Trish.

He wrote 'trial' in his diary and 0930.

Chapter 33
Irish Free State, 1933

Eight weeks later on a fine late summer's afternoon, Alfie ran home from school and burst into the Keeper's Cottage with its new hand-painted wooden nameplate fixed to the side of the front door.

"You call it what you like Mr Casey," the captain had said, "makes no odds to me." He was pleased that such ownership of the name of his cottage possibly meant Mr Casey might be planning on staying a while at least. That suited the captain.

In burst Alfie.

"Where is she? Where is she?" he said and he was literally jumping up and down with excitement. "Have you got her?"

"Aye, she's out back in her pen. Go and see," said his father and as Alfie ran out Monty followed.

"Hello, hello you," said Alfie picking up the tiny black Labrador puppy. "Welcome to Keeper's Cottage. My name's Alfie. What's yours?"

He turned to his father.

"Well, that's one to discuss over dinner. Now that we've got her, we can take a good look at her and see what name suits her."

"Can she come in the house?"

"No. Only at night and only until she's about six months old. I've told you, she's not a pet, boy. She's a working dog and she'll earn her keep. She'll be living outside. We'll make her a fine kennel. She'll know her place and she'll be fine with it. It'll suit her better when she comes to have her own puppies."

"Ok, but until then can she sleep in my room at night?" asked Alfie.

His father was not the tough man he made out.

"Aye ok, but not on the bed," he said.

That was a rule which didn't last a single night. From that first night, the dog followed Alfie everywhere.

Over dinner, chicken from the yard and more fine vegetables from the Keeper's Cottage patch, they turned to the matter of names.

Alfie wanted Bouncy.

Monty argued that the name would be ridiculous when she was a retired old girl struggling with dodgy hips. Alfie didn't want to think about that. Also, Monty needed a name he could shout and not inspire ridicule among his team of beaters on shoot days. Or for that matter ridicule from boys in the Olde Glen Bar.

So Monty had wanted Bouncer but Alfie thought that sounded too much like a dog's name, not a name for a beautiful young girl puppy.

They settled simply on Bounce.

Twice a week at nine-thirty in the morning Monty would present himself at the butler's door of the big house. The door, he noticed, needed a new frame and at least two coats of paint. The rain causing the first to rot, and the sun causing the second to crack and peel off. He doubted either job would be done this year.

"Now then, Mr Casey," said the captain that morning, "I understand there's an addition to the estate. Mrs Villiers spotted young Alfie with a pup."

"That's right, Captain. We've called her Bounce."

"So can I assume you went ahead and told my thieving, poaching, robbing, in arrears tenants that they'd be getting a day's shooting at the end of the season?"

"I did, Captain."

"Before I actually gave you permission to do it?"

"I did, Captain."

Both men knew it had to be done this way otherwise Monty could never have raised the 25 men and boys and the dogs he'd need to run a successful day's shoot. Beaters, men with dogs retrieving dead birds and chasing down injured ones and a couple of carts with horses and drivers would not have been easy to find. It was all getting a little easier as the trade war between free Ireland and protectionist England was taking money out of everyone's pockets except the smugglers and the corrupt excise men. Pay for a day's beating or picking up dead birds was a welcome addition to family funds, But Captain Bastard remained an unpopular man.

"And what have you promised to pay this gang on the day?"

"Three shillings a man, one and sixpence a boy. In cash, on the day, plus some broth and bread in the field after four drives."

"Anything else?"

"A crate of beer after a successful day and a brace of birds per family."

"Have you now? My last keeper promised me I'd only have to pay two shillings a man."

"Well, where are those men, Captain?"

"To be fair, Mr Casey, he couldn't produce them," said the captain.

"Then to be fair, Captain," said Monty, "when I can't produce them, my men are only two shillings a day."

Monty kept a straight face.

The captain smiled. His respect for Mr Casey grew with each day, especially after the incident of the night of the poachers. It should grow too. Little did he know he had a Royal Sandringham House gamekeeper working his estate. But he still had a point to make.

"To my thinking then," said the captain, "in many ways, Mr Casey, you have gained a dog at my expense."

"In a small way, perhaps, Captain. Yet I have also gained the wherewithal to run the shoot."

"Nevertheless I shall have the pick of her first litter as a repayment," said the captain. "My old boy Blackie probably only has a couple of shoot seasons left in him. A new dog could learn some old tricks from him before he goes."

"I can't do that, Captain," said Monty. "First pick has gone to old man Delaney as part of the deal. I can't go back on my word. You can have second pick, Captain."

"So be it," said the captain and with that they'd reached a compromise which suited both men and they'd also reached a tight-knit cluster of trees at the top of a small rise.

"What's been put in there, Mr Casey?" said the captain pointing at a narrow strip about ten yards wide of a crop he didn't recognise.

"Mustard," said Monty. "We're playing catch-up this year. We had to put mustard in this year even though it's more expensive than kale. I was glad to see it go in as quick as it did, it grows like wildfire and with food and some coaxing I should be able to get the birds thinking of it as home."

"I assume the fact they've planted it at all is wrapped up in your deal, the beaters' wages of sin and the free shoot at the end of the season?"

"As you know, Captain, they have to do it. It's in their *tenancies*. But shall we say it's not in their *tendencies*? Easier to lead a cow to water, I think, than to push it," said Monty.

"You are probably right," said the captain, "although it sticks in the craw a bit. A man's signature on a piece of paper should be his word. In fact, a man's word should be his word."

"Well, I have their word on what we've agreed. Now, let me show you the pheasant pens in the woods."

"Why pheasant? Meant to ask you in Knock when you were buying. This has been known as a partridge shoot. Pheasant are fat little buggers. Eat you out of house and home."

"But look back, Captain," and they turned at the top of the rise, on the edge of the copse. "I saw this view, this copse of trees and this beautiful even downward slope the first day I came to see you. This, Captain, is a pheasant drive and it's a classic." Monty turned and the captain turned with him, "the birds are penned up in the trees there. No poaching at all so far as I can see..." Monty paused for approval that his firm but friendly, softly-softly tactics with the tenants were paying off.

It didn't come.

"Yes, yes," said the captain, "And—"

"Well, we keep the pheasants nice and warm and fed up here in the woods and then in the mustard when it gets up, then come a shoot day we run the beating line through the trees, gather them all into the mustard so they're packed nice and tight, push 'em through to the end. The birds won't rise until the very end of the mustard cover. They'll just keep walking through the crop until they absolutely have to fly."

"And the guns are down there at the bottom of the hill?"

"Yes. In front of that hedge. When we've pushed them as far as we can through the mustard the pheasants will fly pretty much all at once, they fly higher than partridge, faster than partridge, especially with a wind up their behinds, and they'll keep rising to get over the hedge there and then aim for that line of birch about half a mile down there."

"How many of the greedy buggers have you put in there then?"

"Five hundred."

"Five hundred? Is that all?" The captain was incredulous. "I've sold six days now, all good chaps over from England on shooting trips—apart from one bunch of Ulstermen from the Strabane Sporting Club. Plus my day. Plus your free one to the gravy train riders. And you've put down just 500 pheasants? And we bought 8,000 birds?"

Monty paused to let the captain's mood calm a little.

"I promise you, Captain," he said evenly, "those birds will come out so thick and fast and fly so high that your guns down there will get both barrels at them and be lucky to hit one. Lucky to hit one. What a sight it'll be for them. They'll have a go at them, mostly miss, but they'll all go to their beds dreaming of the fast, high-flying birds at the Leghowney House Shoot. They can get their fill of shooting birds on the other drives. But it'll be this drive, this drive…where they'll be lucky to get one each, this drive which will stick in their memories for the rest of their lives…"

"So long as it lasts in the memory until next year and they come back for more," smiled the captain.

"And tell their friends," said Monty, and the men both smiled and continued their inspection of the estate.

Chapter 34
Norfolk, Present Day

Mark was up a little earlier than usual on the day of the start of the trial. He wanted a decent breakfast first and a quick chat with Trish on the phone about what needed doing that day, which was not much.

He'd decided he'd get the bus into King's Lynn.

The bus stop was practically outside the Visionary shop door and would drop him off five minutes' walk from the magistrates court. It meant he didn't have to faff around with the multi-storey car park, which he hated, and it also meant if it turned out to be a quite boring affair, he could pack it in and go and have a few beers in the old-fashioned pubs around the Tuesday Market Place, something he rarely got to do.

For some reason, he'd decided to wear a suit, possibly because it felt like a formal occasion.

He had a few suits. Quite liked wearing them in fact. Almost never with a tie, a fashion accessory almost exclusively reserved these days he thought for MPs and television newsreaders. The only ties he still owned were an old school tie for sentimental reasons, a black tie for less sentimental reasons and a green tie with a pheasant embroidered on it which he wore when in his tweeds out photographing the coffee table glossy keepsakes on shoot days. You had to look the part.

None of those ties actually went with the navy blue Paul Smith suit he selected from his wardrobe and the non-iron white Marks and Spencer shirt he married it with. It was, in fact, a suit he had first worn at a wedding some years ago. It still fitted and looked, well, smart he thought.

The bus took less than 40 minutes, he arrived at the court about half past nine got himself a surprisingly drinkable coffee from a vending machine and sat down to read a couple of pages of the *Daily Telegraph* he'd picked up from an old-fashioned newsagent, sweetshop and tobacconist on the walk through the back streets of the town. Tobacconist shops. A dying breed for obvious reasons.

He saw Emma McMillan arrive.

She was a little 'less' than he remembered. Quite petite in fact. Had she been wearing a big coat that day? He remembered she seemed bigger somehow, sitting dazed on the pavement, while he reeled off his shots. Or maybe just the stress of the past months had shrunk her somehow.

She looked smart though. Quite a fitted dress with a black jacket nipped in at the waist.

Her face was serious. Well, it would be, he thought, but if you replaced that frown with a smile then you'd have quite an attractive woman. What was the phrase Trish used with the younger kids when they were dragged in front of the school photo set? "Turn that frown upside down!" she'd say, smiling like a gibbon to grab a shot mummy and daddy would want to buy by the truckload.

She was with an overweight, slightly unimpressive man, in a not quite big enough and far too heavy navy chalk-striped suit. It would once have been quite a thing, thick wool suit, big white stripes, navy and white polka dot tie. The look, thought Mark, of a once ambitious man.

The unimpressive man was on home ground though. Mark watched as he found the clerk's window and chatted through the grille, waving hello to the court police officer passing through the modern reception area. He then put his hand in the small of the back of his client and ushered her towards the entrance door to the courtroom.

A young woman in her late twenties, crisply dressed, briskly walked through and caught up with the solicitor and client just as they passed into the court.

Mark went over to the notice boards on the far wall, found the list of the day's court proceedings and saw that Emma McMillan was first up. The trial was listed for two days. He dumped his coffee cup in the recycling area of the twin holder bin and walked into the courtroom. The court usher by the door pointed him towards the three rows of benches which made up the public viewing area.

Two women sat on the benches. One, the older one, at the far end of the first row. Blonde of a sort. Possibly grey, possibly 40. Looked a little 'tightly wrapped' he thought. Wonder what her interest is? And the same for you, he thought, as he passed a much younger, much blonder woman at the end of the back bench, next to the door. Mark made his way down the middle bench and sat in the middle of it.

The court usher came over to them and asked them if they'd all turned off their mobile phones. None of them had.

A second team of solicitors arrived, two women and a much younger man. They walked down the centre aisle and occupied the seats to the left with the prosecuting solicitor team nodding to the defence solicitor as they took up their seats. The younger man sat behind the two women who were clearly senior in both age and status.

The only other person in court right then was a man in his late fifties, notepad and pencil poised. The classic local reporter thought Mark, although not likely to be working for anyone in particular.

There was a time when a local newspaper, every local newspaper, would have a dedicated court reporter, sometimes more if it covered a big enough patch, like *The Yorkshire Post* or the mighty *Northern Echo*. In those days Chief Court Reporter was a prestigious job and one with status, even within police and lawyerly circles. It required patience. The ability to sit for days through the boring legalese. It also needed someone with the fastest and most legible shorthand. It required someone who loved grubbing through the low life and the misery that was the usual court parade. A good living it was too as when some terrible murder happened on your patch you could sell your soul and the contents of your contacts book to the highest bidding national tabloid hack from the pack that swarmed up from Fleet Street.

Those days were long gone. This man, thought Mark, was probably a long redundant journo hanging around the Magistrates Court, the County Court and the cop shop picking up titbits to sell to the newsrooms of the *Lynn News, Your Local Paper* where Mark had seen the story himself, the *EDP* if it was of county-wide interest and maybe even BBC Radio Norfolk. If he could sell the story to all of those, thought Mark, he might make £150. Poor bugger.

At that point, a side door opened and a bookish man walked into court with, in fact, some books, and sat at the desk in front of the raised bench at the very back of the courtroom under the Royal emblem.

At precisely ten o'clock, the usher moved to the same side door at the back of the court. The door opened and in walked a woman, another woman and a man in that order.

"All rise," demanded the usher.

The magistrates filed in and took their seats. The meagre population of the courtroom sat down.

This is real life theatre, thought Mark Elwin.
This is it, thought Emma McMillan.

Chapter 35
Irish Free State, 1933

The summer of 1933 at Leghowney House passed quickly into autumn.

Alfie spent increasing amounts of time at the vicarage where his repertoire of card games learned from the Reverend and Mrs Mitchell now included rummy and poker as well as cribbage.

"Poker?" asked his father.

"We play for matches," explained Alfie, "We each get 50 matches at the start and we play until someone has them all."

Nevertheless, thought Monty, poker? With the Reverend and Mrs Mitchell? He let it pass. Alfie was happy there in the vicarage and garden and his stories of vicarage afternoon cream teas with cucumber sandwiches, scones and lashings of sweet tea made him deeply envious.

Bounce would join Alfie on his days at the vicarage. At first, she was carried in a wicker basket given to him by Mrs Mitchell. Then on a long slim leather slip leash also given to him by Mrs Mitchell. Gun dogs, according to his father, never wore collars. She is not, his father would repeat, a pet. That's what Monty said. She clearly was a pet as far as Alfie was concerned. She clearly was a pet as far as Bounce was concerned.

Occasionally, Alfie would help his father as he took the old heavy horse and tumbril cart around the fields filling up the feeding hoppers and water troughs. The now fully-grown partridges and pheasants always scattered when they arrived but rushed back to peck away at the feed trays once they'd gone.

The growing duck population on the pond in front of Keeper's Cottage, however, knew no such shyness and gathered around quacking and climbing over each other to get at the free food. Occasionally his father would grab one for the pot and break its neck there and then. The rest of the ducks just carried on feeding.

Early in September Alfie went back to school but not before he'd joined his father, the captain and half a dozen men from the farms walking through all the strips of mustard crops where the game birds had made their homes. Waving flags and banging their sticks against trees and hedgerows they spent all day scaring the birds into taking to the air.

These birds were walkers by nature. Monty needed to get them used to flying. He also needed to know where they would fly to and to make sure that over the next 24 hours, they all came back to the mustard for their free food and where he could find them next time when the guns would be waiting for them.

Sunday lunchtimes at the Olde Glen Bar were pleasant, sitting on the benches outside in the early autumn sunshine, but there were noticeably fewer locals and mostly it was just the old men, too old for the fields, or in a couple of cases, retired teachers or bank clerks, who joined Monty. Declan was a fixture. Monty never knew what Declan did. He assumed at first that it would come up in conversation, but it never did and Monty knew better than to ask. He was suspected of smuggling across the border to Ulster. Or back again. But he never did ask and, indeed, never found out.

Father Clary the local priest came in from time to time. He shared his bonhomie among all of Donegal's licenced premises though he'd never been known to buy a drink.

Mr Clark the shopkeeper joined now and then and the mood was usually one of light-hearted banter, local gossip and enquiries of Monty about life working for Captain Bastard.

One Sunday in early September the mood darkened though as they discussed the recent big Nazi rally at Nuremberg and there was talk in every Donegal bar of another war with Germany. The captain was full of it too on his twice-weekly tours of inspection of the estate. The captain was sure war was coming. He seemed quite keen on it in fact. "Unfinished business, Mr Casey. Unfinished business."

The Olde Glen Bar was no different in the sense that the possibility of another conflict after the war to end all wars was certainly discussed, at length, in detail and, as the drink flowed, with rising decibels. The political discussion group at the bar on a rare rainy Sunday was, however, certain that whatever the events in Europe, the Irish Free State would not be involved.

"We're sick of fighting," said Declan and looking straight at Monty he said "We've been fighting the English forever. De Valera will not be wanting to send Irishmen to fight an English war."

Sensing rising tension from behind the bar the landlord said "Aye, and we've been fighting ourselves for too long too."

That was a view shared by all. It seemed to settle the mood. Monty stayed out of this discussion and only rejoined when the talk shifted back to the state of the county's fields.

The first shoot of the season was in the second week of October and it was a nervous time for both Monty and the captain.

Carlos had retrieved two old covered carts from one of the barns, one for the men who'd paid to shoot and a larger but less comfortable one for the men who would be paid to beat. It took him a week of hammer, grease and sweat to get them fit to be pulled around the estate by the horses.

The first shoot party arrived in three cars late on a Thursday evening. They'd been shooting that day over the border near Enniskillen and assured the captain on arrival that it had been a splendid day with nearly 800 birds shot. The captain was quick to remind them that they had only paid for a 500 bag of birds the following day.

Their guns and various cartridge bags, sticks and shooting paraphernalia were unloaded by Carlos and stored in the gun room.

Paloma had prepared cold meats, pickles, crusty bread, boiled potatoes and some crisp late salad from the kitchen garden followed by cakes, biscuits and cheese.

There were two cases of claret, four bottles of port on a side table and two jugs of lemonade. The meal was presided over at first by the captain but he was soon outranked by the retired Colonel whose shooting party this was. By the end of the meal, only the lemonade remained.

Eight of the bedrooms which were not too shabby had been allocated to the men. There were dogs everywhere. The spinsters were confined to barracks when shooting parties were in residence.

The next day Monty rose at six o'clock and walked the estate. Everything, especially the birds, was exactly where he wanted. By eight o'clock, the men and boys started arriving from the farms. There were a few he didn't recognise, substitutes for those needed elsewhere, but there were, crucially, enough of them. Men with dogs were despatched one way to wait for the birds to fall out of the sky, Carlos in the driving seat on one of the carts took the beaters to another place. Carlos was then to return to the house.

Monty was in charge of shoot days. Even in charge of the captain and the old Colonel and his men. They gathered in front of Leghowney House, had bacon rolls and sloe gin for breakfast, loaded themselves into their gun cart and headed off for a day of sport.

By four o'clock, it was all over.

The beaters, men and boys and the dog-men had been paid and two crates of beer had been carried off.

The birds shot were counted and numbered 412 partridge, 24 pheasant, 18 pigeons, 12 ducks, 8 teal, 4 jays, 3 magpies and a very unlucky vixen. Game cards were recorded and handed to each of the guns.

Sandwiches and cake were served with a jug of tea amongst the cars after they'd loaded up their guns, and their dogs and swapped boots for brogues.

Before they left the birds and the fox were laid out on the ground, the group assembled and with the captain on one end and Monty on the other end of the group Carlos took a souvenir photograph with the Colonel's camera.

When they'd gone, the captain was brimming with rare bonhomie.

"Excellent food, Paloma, and well done, Carlos, for getting those old carts moving. Well done, well done. Help yourselves to a bottle of claret from the cellar. Not the stuff at the back, mind!" he laughed. The Spanish couple left.

"Dougall's are coming for this lot tomorrow," said Monty referring to the game dealer in Donegal. Shot birds for the tables of Donegal didn't fetch much but it was worth having.

"481 birds shot on a 500-bird day, eh Mr Casey?"

"Yes, Captain. And only 436 of them at our expense. The good Lord provided the rest. And," as Monty was very pleased with the result, "only a handful of pheasant shot on what we might call High Drive?"

"They absolutely loved it! Did you hear them? I was standing with the Colonel. Roaring with laughter by the end. Ragging his chums. Couldn't hit a cow's arse with a banjo he said to his next-door man. Quite so. Excellent economy and an excellent day. You are a very talented man, Mr Casey. Keep the teal back for the house," he said. "That'll feed the ladies for a couple of days. As I say, a great day Mr Casey. Good afternoon," and with that the captain turned and went inside his grand front door.

The captain did not offer Monty a bottle of claret. Monty didn't mind. As the men of the shooting party had made to leave each of the guns had shaken his hand and congratulated him on presenting the birds so well for them. They'd mutter 'a grand day' and "well done Mr Casey, an excellent day's work," or something similar. In each handshake, they pressed into his palm a crisp English pound note which Monty then seamlessly slipped into the pocket of his shooting breeks. It was an unseen ritual. Neither the giver nor the receiver viewed the money as it changed hands. That would be too vulgar indeed.

Eight crisp English one pound notes were therefore placed in the money tin which was in turn put to the back of the dresser drawer. Eight pounds. Nearly three weeks' wages. Monty went to bed a tired, happy man.

Chapter 36
Norfolk, Present Day

Mark didn't bother with a beer in the Tuesday Market Place pubs after all. He went straight home on the bus and decided to have an evening with the 'Find Alfie Sidebottom' file.

He thought he probably wouldn't go back to court the next day. It very much looked like a foregone conclusion.

As he cracked the cap off a cold Corona and shoved in the wedge of lime he did, however, retrieve the memory card of his shots from the morning of the crash.

Yes, there it all was. Just as he'd heard in court. A clear road. A Range Rover and a VW three-quarters face on. Cars parked along the High Street. A white van over there. Why are vans always white, he thought? Except Post Office vans of course.

The man in the brown jacket was there. Emma McMillan being pulled out of the car. Then her sitting on the pavement.

Yes, she did look a little bit bigger and it wasn't just the coat. That's what months of worry will do to you, he thought.

Then it was police and ambulances and more police and cars edging by them, desperate to get out of the way before the police cones trapped them on the High Street.

Then exactly 50 minutes later he'd taken his last shot, all time coded, all filed away. He kept everything. Who knew—the man in the brown coat might go on to be a serial killer? Or win Britain's Got Talent. In either event, Mark would have a very nice photo story to sell.

He'd done his civic duty too. When the 'Accident Here' boards went up, he'd phoned the police.

"Did you see the accident, sir?"

"No..." he'd replied.

"Then why are you calling?"

"I have photographs."

"We have our own photographs, sir. If you did not witness the incident, thank you for your call."

Click. Whrrrr.

Mark returned to Sidebottom Senior and Son.

"Right, where shall we start?" he said, opening files both electronic and paper.

"You boys are immortal," he told himself out loud, "you have unknown names, you are possibly in Donegal, possibly on a banana boat to a destination unknown. And if you are in Donegal, you're not dead and buried there and you are on no known census records. In fact, if you are there, how on earth did you get there? Let's consult the Great God Google."

He knew they were not in Ireland in 1931 when there was an Irish Census and there was no census in 1941 because of the war but there was one in 1951.

He typed in both Montgomery and Monty and Alfred and Alfie and gave them both surnames, Sidebottom and Casey. Eight named searches. Off you go my beauties.

Nothing. Nothing at all.

Mark was getting used to it by now.

He searched by 'gamekeeper' and 'Donegal' of which there were a few but none remotely or possibly his human quarry.

It was clear that census searches and graveyards were not going to find either of them in Ireland. He could, of course, be searching in entirely the wrong place but a fox pursued goes to ground in a familiar den Mark reckoned.

School. Alfie must have gone to school. He looked online and hope rose. There they were—Donegal school registers online. Then hope faded. Only until 1922 when the Irish Free State took over. After that, they were available only as paper documents deep in some archive and Mark really wasn't going to go to Donegal to search through the school registers of what looked like three dozen Donegal schools in 1933.

This was going to be a four beer night, he knew it.

Mark turned by instinct to local newspapers. It was a world he knew but it was a dying world and while every newspaper used to have a librarian who carefully made micro-fiche copies of every story in every edition, and made detailed cross-references, it was unlikely either the newspapers or the records had survived from the 1930s.

He was wrong.

The Donegal People's Press was founded in 1931 and it had survived, in various forms, through various mergers and ultimate name changes but there was at least a continuous line of publication through to that very morning.

He prayed to the Great God Google.

His prayer was answered.

There it was. A free online searchable database for *The Donegal People's Press*.

Mark typed in 'Monty Sidebottom' and 'gamekeeper' and the spinning circle of 'computer thinking about it' came up on the screen. He went and cracked himself another "Mark thinking about it," beer.

When he eased himself back into his chair, the computer came up with 'Monty' and 'gamekeeper' highlighted. Sidebottom had a line through it.

He clicked the link.

Was he finally close?

"Come on, come on, come on!" he shouted at his computer and the on-screen circle of 'computer thinking about it' spun on and on.

And then there it was.

Leghowney House Gamekeeper
Traps Poacher

Mark scrolled quickly down until he saw this phrase:

Giving evidence to the Justices of the District Court, Monty Casey, gamekeeper at the Leghowney House estate, said he had, with others, confronted Donal McCabe of attempting to take a salmon in a net from the River Eske on the night of…

'Monty' and 'gamekeeper' were highlighted.

"Bloody hell," he said out loud. "Bloody hell!" and he got up and bounced up and down, up and down, punching the air, a bit of beer sloshing onto his face, but bouncing, bouncing, bouncing. It was a good job he lived in a flat above his own shop…there'd have been phone calls to the police otherwise.

"Monty Casey. You runaway from justice. Here you are wanted for murder and you're having a go at the man for nicking a salmon! Oi you," he said pointing at his screen, "leave the poor feller alone." And he laughed out loud.

He read the eight paragraphs again and again and again. It was nothing really. Local chap, Donal McCabe, caught poaching, with a young lad unnamed, evidence from Monty Casey, plea of guilty, ten-shilling fine.

But there again it was everything. Everything. Monty Casey, gamekeeper, it had to be Monty Sidebottom. It just had to be.

He wanted more. The door had opened just a crack. Now Mark wanted to kick it open.

Now he had more than a name. He had an address. Leghowney House.

He opened up another Google search for the *Donegal People's Press* for Monty Casey.

Nothing.

"Oh come on. Come on. You surely can't just pop up once." Mark realised that if he searched his own name, even in these days of information overload, you got little more than a couple of references to the shop and a Companies House listing.

He found a bigger site.

The Irish Newspaper Archive. He typed in the words 'Monty' 'Casey' 'Leghowney' and hit search. To be fair, he thought, he was searching every newspaper, in Ireland, ever.

Within five seconds, there it was. One result. But that's all he needed. From the *Tyrone and Donegal Advertiser* October 14th 1933.

Colonel Jamieson Party Enjoy
Fine Day's Shooting

It was a picture story. There in front of a grand country house and in front of several rows of shot game was a shooting party, moustachioed men in tweeds, named in order of rank, Colonel Jamieson first, with Captain Bashford of Leghowney House to the right, and Mr Monty Casey, gamekeeper to the left. Least in rank, the last man named, but for Mark Elwin, at that point in time, the most important man in the world.

There he was. He zoomed in on Monty's face. It went grainy but searching through his paper file, just to be absolutely certain, he got the printouts of the

EDP stories of the murder at Keeper's Cottage and of the police hunt for murder suspect Monty Sidebottom.

There, yes, was Monty Sidebottom, and there, yes, on the screen, was Monty Casey.

The same man.

"Got you!" he said.

Chapter 37
Norfolk, Present Day

It turned out to be a five-beer night, and a small whisky, and another slightly larger whisky as, like all hounds after a fox, Mark could scent his quarry and through the Great God Google, he went at full tally-ho after him.

He gave up at one in the morning.

Nothing else. Not a thing more of Monty Casey.

He had found plenty on Captain Bashford. There were galas and charity dinners. There was another shoot picture but no Monty Casey which made Mark think he may have moved on and disappeared once again into the mist. Then he thought a father couldn't possibly keep dragging a child from one job to another. But there again there was no evidence of a child.

He found newspaper articles on the sale by auction of Leghowney House after the war and, indeed, its demolition for a new housing estate in the 1970s.

He searched again for the deaths of father and son and again drew a complete blank.

He retired to bed a little light-headed and whisky-breathed, elated at finding Monty and disappointed at losing him again at the same time.

When he closed the file down on his laptop, he noted that the file was still called 'Find Alfie Sidebottom' and not "Catch a Glimpse of Alfie Sidebottom's father."

He had found nothing of the boy.

He woke in the morning a little later than he wanted to, looked at his diary, saw he'd written 'trial' in it and decided that—as he had little better to do—he may as well go. Trish could mind the shop.

It was too late to catch the bus so he drove into King's Lynn decided against the multi-storey and opted for the more expensive Tuesday Market Place car park opposite the Corn Exchange Theatre.

He made the court building with just enough time for a few bites of a newsagent cheese sandwich and a couple of swigs of vending machine coffee before he took up his seat in the middle of the middle bench once again, probable wife down and in front, probable assignation younger woman left and behind.

"All rise," said the usher and the magisterial parade entered.

The clerk spoke a few words, the Presiding Justice in the middle of the top table said 'Mr O'Grady' and Eric O'Grady rose from his seat and called his client to the witness stand.

Emma McMillan looked neither nervous nor confident. If it was possible to be a professional defendant, as opposed to a serial defendant, then that's how she looked.

She read the oath in a clear voice, Mark put his elbows on his knees and propped his chin up in his hands.

"Turn that frown upside down," he thought. The more at ease she looked the better she would appear to the magistrates. Easier said than done.

Eric O'Grady took his client very carefully through her medical history, her mild multiple sclerosis, the symptoms and her use of cannabis or 'grass' as she insisted on calling it.

"There's a difference between the grass that I smoke, for medical reasons, and skunk that people smoke to get out of their heads," she said.

Mark was very much looking at the bench. Two ladies of a certain age, he thought, for whom drugs were drugs no matter how many Ministry of Justice awareness courses they went on and the older man who may well have been a retired major with nothing else to do but stick it to the low life of King's Lynn.

Good luck with that subtle difference Ms Defendant, he thought.

The suggestion that smoking her morning joint made her a better driver as it eased her tension and her occasional twitchy legs was really going too far.

The prosecution will have a field day with that.

Then she told of her journey that day, dropping her daughter Daisy off at school, how she was a single mother, no she didn't know what she'd do for Daisy if she had to go to prison. This is better thought Mark. She's a good mum. Make sure the bench knows it.

She was off to work, excellent. A grafter too. Making her way in the world. Always had a job. Make sure the bench knows it.

Then the actual crash. She never saw his car coming.

"It came out of nowhere. His car. Out of nowhere. I looked left and right. There was nothing coming, then bang. The next thing I know I'm being pulled out of my car and sitting on the kerb of the road," she said.

With that and a couple of other little personal details Mr O'Grady sat down and Ms Rose, rose.

"Did you smoke cannabis every morning?"

"Yes," said Emma McMillan.

"For how many years?"

"Five or six," she replied.

Oh dear, this was not going well.

"So for five or six years, you have been driving around the streets of Norfolk under the influence of drugs?"

"I'm not 'under the influence'. I'm not some junky. I'm a very careful driver. I'm a very responsible person. Do you think I'd put my own daughter in a car and drive it if I was off my head?"

"I'll ask the questions, Ms McMillan," said the prosecutor.

Ouch thought Mark.

"If you weren't—to use your words—off your head, why did you pull out in front of a Range Rover?"

"I don't know. It happened so fast. He just came out of nowhere. Maybe he was driving too quickly. We know he was late for an appointment."

"Ms McMillan, you have testified in this court and in your statement at the time that you had a clear view of the road…then why, I ask again, why did you pull out?"

"He came out of nowhere," she repeated. "I was not driving dangerously. I am not a dangerous driver."

"Well, you admit to driving every day under the influence of drugs. And you were on the wrong side of the road."

"I was just on the wrong side of the road. Don't say it like I was driving down his side of the road," Emma said, just the right side of not getting cross.

"Nevertheless on a clear dry day with vision left and right, you pulled out over the other side of the road straight into the path of an oncoming vehicle."

Silence.

"Isn't that true Ms McMillan?"

Silence.

"No more questions," said Ms Rose, considering it job done and a job well done at that.

Emma McMillan returned to her place next to her defence lawyer.

Mark watched her and saw the look of resignation on her face.

Then something came to mind.

Out of a mental mist. Something from last night.

What was it? He was rifling through the memory of his evening.

What *was* it?

And then it came to him.

No.

Actually no, his brain was computing. Really no. That's really *not* right. That just isn't true.

His brain finally twigged and his body moved at the same time.

He shuffled along the bench towards the door where the usher was standing and whispered to him.

"Go and ask the reporter over there for a sheet of his pad and a pencil, would you?"

"What?" whispered the usher.

"Oh, forget it," said Mark. "I'm just going for a quick word with the reporter over there. Ok?"

Before the usher could say anything, Mark walked over, gave a cursory half nod, half bow to the magistrates' bench and shuffled in next to the bemused reporter.

"Alright mate?" whispered the reporter.

Mark indicated pencil and paper.

The reporter tore out a sheet and handed him a chewed pencil from his inside pocket.

Mark leaned in and whispered "Cheers mate. Great story. Honest. We'll both make something out of this. Stick with me," and gave him his pencil back.

The journalist stared at his back. A great story? That'll be the first in a very long time, he thought.

Mark went back to the usher and gave an even less convincing nod to the bench.

On the witness stand was a doctor of some kind, a medical expert brought in to testify to the possible benefits of 'medicinal cannabis'. Eric O'Grady hadn't begun to coax his witness to support his client.

"Here," said Mark to the usher, "give this to the defendant. Please."

"I can't do that sir," he whispered back.

"Then give it to Mr O'Grady or his sidekick," said Mark in a slightly louder whisper.

"What on earth is going on at the back there, usher?" said the Presiding Justice.

The whole court, Emma McMillan, Mr O'Grady, and the backup prosecution team all looked at Mark.

"Man here says he's got a message for Mr O'Grady ma'am."

"And?" said the Presiding Justice. "What of it? Is it relevant to the case?"

"I think so," said the usher and Mark stood nodding next to him.

"Then give Mr O'Grady the message and let's get on. It's nearly lunchtime. Mr O'Grady, have you any more witnesses to come?"

"Yes ma'am. After the good doctor, two more. Character witnesses."

"Then we will resume after lunch," she said and stood up, as did the rest of the court.

The usher took the torn piece of paper to Eric O'Grady who read the scribbled note. He handed it to his client. She read it and turned to look at Mark at the back of the court.

She looked back at the note.

It read "Your client was not driving dangerously. I can prove it."

Chapter 38
Norfolk, Present Day

Mark was back in his car and driving home shouting 'get out of my way idiot' and 'go, go, go' to various cars whose drivers were behaving, mostly, only judiciously and legally, waiting at traffic lights and at junctions.

"Tell them I'll be back after lunch. Just need to nip home for something. Back as soon as I can," he'd garbled to the usher on his way out of court.

And on his way home he was. Quickly parking in the backyard and tearing up the stairs at Visionary to the flat shouting 'I'm not here' to Trish as he went, then 'See you later' to Trish as he ran out again having loaded a memory card and printed off four large 10 x 8 colour prints.

Then a repeat trip back to his car parking spot in Tuesday Market Place, not bad he thought, just under an hour and only a couple of speed limits broken. His parking spot was taken and he had to drive round and round the bloody one-way car park system until the woman in the ancient 4 x 4 SUV pulled out and as she did, he eased into the space behind her.

By the time he made it back to court, it was already in session. The doctor had been in the witness stand and out and Mr O'Grady was now taking Emma McMillan's employer through a rehearsed series of questions which showed his client to be reliable, honest, decent, hardworking and all the rest and finally, and most importantly, never remotely 'off her head' on drugs in any way.

Emma McMillan looked to the back of the court. Mark couldn't know it but she'd been looking back at the court every thirty seconds since proceedings had resumed.

"He said he'd be back after lunch," the usher had told her.

Then where was he? And who was he, this man? Her actual life did not depend on it. But it felt like it.

As soon as she spotted Mark, she nudged her lawyer and the defence team looked back.

The right-hand magistrate saw what was going on.

"Mr O'Grady, what on earth is it with you today? Are you with us or not?"

"Ma'am. Might I request a short adjournment?"

"Whatever for?"

"I believe there may be some new evidence, unknown to me until this point in time, which may have significant importance…and which the court may wish to consider."

"But we're nearly done, Mr O'Grady?" said the Presiding Justice and her two colleagues were nodding to her and both whispering unheard words.

"Twenty minutes ma'am?" asked the man for the defence.

"Ms Rose?" the Presiding Justice asked of the prosecution.

The woman for the Crown stood up. "In the interests of justice…" she said.

Eric O'Grady looked at the Crown's side with eyes which he hoped they understood as "thank you."

"Oh, very well Mr O'Grady. This had better be of value to the court," and the Presiding Justice stood up.

"All rise," said the usher.

The journalist nipped across from his bench as Mark was making his way out of court.

"What is it? What you got?" he said to Mark, tailing him past the usher.

"Wait and see but I'll give you an interview to go with the story if it all works out as I hope it does and," he tapped the envelope in his hand, "there's a picture to go with it."

Mark gave him his card.

"Mind you," said Mark, "I want 50% of what you sell it for. And, trust me, this should make all your usual stuff and possibly a couple of the nationals."

The use of the phrase 'the nationals' was music to both their ears. Neither had got a story into the nationals for years. And one of them had been really trying.

Eric O'Grady, his assistant and his client were onto him and they went out into the reception area.

Mark took control. He thought it would be easier that way. He spotted the young man, the prosecution junior, work experience, bag carrier, whatever he was looking over towards them and so Mark said "Let's just go over here a minute."

Emma McMillan could wait no longer.

"Look Mr ..." she started.

"Elwin," he said. "Mark Elwin. Just... Mark."

"Please..." she said and looked straight at him. At close range, he could see her eyes were almost black.

"Yes, right," he said. "Look, you won't remember, but when that guy was pulling you out of your car, I was standing on the pavement outside my shop and was taking photographs of everything."

He realised that made him sound bad. One man helping. Another watching and taking pictures.

"I'm a photographer," he said.

He realised that had not redeemed him.

"Anyway," he pressed on, "look at these," he said taking two prints out of the envelope. He handed them to Emma McMillan who fanned them out, looked at them and then gave them to her lawyer to her right.

"I don't get it," she said. "The police have pictures just like these. What's your point, Mr Elwin?"

"Look," said Mark. "This one here, this one was taken seconds after the crash. I heard the crash, picked up a camera and took this photograph. Look. You're still in your car."

"So?" said Eric O'Grady.

"So look at this one..." said Mark, tapping a print.

"So? What am I looking for?" asked the man for the defence.

"Yes, Mr Elwin," said Emma.

"Mark, please..." he said.

"This one, this one here..." he said pulling out a second print, "This one was taken just fifteen seconds later. Look there are the automatically recorded time codes there on the prints. Here is our good Samaritan arriving to help Ms McMillan, here, out of her car. The next two show the police turning up and that PC who gave evidence, the first one."

"Adams," said Eric O'Grady.

"Yes, that's him arriving and then that's him looking at the scene. All time coded over six minutes later."

"Mr Elwin please, please tell me how this helps me?" said Emma McMillan. "Please?"

Mark Elwin paused.

"Here, look at this one. Taken within seconds of the crash. At the junction. A Yodel white delivery van parked illegally on double yellow lines. Right there."

They all looked carefully.

The defendant and lawyer looked at Mark. He turned to the petite woman looking up at him.

"You couldn't see clearly left and right," he said. "Couldn't possibly have. There was an illegally parked delivery van right there. You might have been able to see left and right eventually…but only by edging out and possibly edging slightly across the white line in the middle of the road. A man coming the other way, possibly speeding, would have had his view of you, Miss, Ms McMillan, completely obscured by the illegally parked van."

"But the police photographs…" she said.

"He'd gone fifteen seconds later," said Mark. "Here, look at this. 15 seconds later. Van—gone! All timecoded. No mistake at all."

"But I don't remember the van?" she said.

"Doesn't really matter," said Mark. "As you say, it all happened so quickly."

"But I don't remember," she said.

"It doesn't matter," Mark said again, and he put his hand on the arm that was holding the photographs. "You've now got the photographs," he said. "You could only have been edging out around an illegally parked delivery van. Carefully edging out. A man driving too fast the other way…boom," said Mark, clapping his hands together and then regretting both the hand clap and the use of the word 'boom'.

"I'm not a lawyer, Mr O'Grady," he said trying to recover solemnity, "but, in your view, could a woman edging out past an illegally parked delivery van and being hit by a speeding car…could that be regarded as 'dangerous driving'?"

"Not in my view, Mr Elwin, not in my view. Unfortunately, it's not my view that counts."

Chapter 39
Norfolk, Present Day

Proceedings in court were over within fifteen minutes. Both sets of lawyers approached the bench with the clerk listening in and offering advice. The photographs were shown. There were occasional looks back to where Mark was sitting.

The lawyers returned to their seats. Eric O'Grady had a big smile on his face and he nodded up to Mark. Emma McMillan turned and gave him a big smile too. The journalist was scribbling shorthand down at 120 words a minute and hoping he could decipher it later.

The Presiding Justice said, "For the sake of the record Ms Rose."

And the prosecutor stood up.

"In the light of new photographic evidence, it is clear that the defendant did not have a clear view of the road as her view to her left was obscured by an illegally parked delivery van. This would necessitate her edging out into the road to gain both a view and to execute her turn. The deceased would have had his view of the defendant's car also obscured by the illegally parked vehicle. This plus the very real possibility that the deceased was speeding means that the Crown now proposes to withdraw the charge of causing death by dangerous driving."

"Nooooooooooo," came the wail to his front and right. Ellen Jones rose noisily and banged out of court.

"She killed my husband," she screamed as she turned by the court door. "You," and she pointed to Emma McMillan. "You…" but before she could say any more the usher arrived and expertly and firmly gripped her by the elbow and steered her out of the courtroom.

Mark turned and looked over his shoulder to his left. The probable assignation woman had already gone.

The journalist caught his eye and thumbed towards the door.

Mark met him in the lobby.

"The pub?" asked the journalist.

"Where else?" said Mark.

They retreated to the Maid's Head pub on the Tuesday Market Place and over two decent pints of Woodforde's Wherry real ale Dave Stilgoe got his interview, his story and his two photographs.

"Before and after," said the journalist. "You couldn't email me them electronically, could you?" and he handed him his card.

"Of course," said Mark.

"I should think the *Daily Mail* might be interested in this, written in a certain way, maybe the *Telegraph* too," said the happy journalist. "They both like a naughty doctor story. And," said the happy reporter, "an amateur sleuth."

"You might be right. Anyway, thanks for the use of the pencil. Don't forget my 50%," said Mark with a laugh as he left the pub. It was just the tiniest taste of a photojournalistic career he nearly had. He loved it. He mentally wrote off any chance of seeing his 50%.

The next day Mark walked the few steps from his shop to the newsagent where he collected copies of the *Eastern Daily Press* and there it was, front page lead story, by-lined 'By David Stilgoe, Special Court Correspondent'.

"Wow, a lead story and a new title for you. Not a bad day's work," said Mark out loud and gave himself a mental pat on the back as he read about his own near-heroic part in making sure justice was done.

He tuned into BBC Radio Norfolk and heard his name and his story being told by the newsreader and then a couple of minutes of himself being interviewed that they had recorded on the phone the night before.

There he was again in the *Daily Mail*, but only in the *Daily Mail*, as Dave had called him the night before to tell him they'd paid for an exclusive as long as they could have an interview with the "photographer sleuth."

"All publicity is good publicity," he said to Trish when she arrived for work, shoving the *EDP* under her nose.

"I've already heard. Everyone and their mum has been phoning me." "Isn't that who you work with?" she mimicked, in a broad Norfolk accent.

"More to come on Sunday," he said. "*The Mail on Sunday* want an exclusive interview with the 'sleuth' photographer." He stood no chance of wiping the smile from his face.

"Ah well, I need an 'interview' with my 'assistant photographer' for this Saturday's wedding," said Trish doing the inverted commas gesture with her hands both times.

That brought him down to earth. From hero to zero in ten seconds flat he thought.

On Saturday, the wedding came and went, lenses were changed, shutters opened and closed, the drone flew and the happy couple left for their reception. Trish's organisation was once again faultless.

On Sunday morning, he slobbed around the flat in tracksuit bottoms and settled down with marmite on toast and a fancy frothy coffee and read his story in the *Mail on Sunday*.

David Stilgoe had got himself an 'additional reporting by' writing credit, Mark's interview done on Friday afternoon woven into an intrepid tale of opportunism and eagle-eyed near caped crusader stuff.

They'd also interviewed Emma McMillan who said "she never had time to thank him. He just disappeared."

"Ah well," he said to himself, "that's a super-hero for you!"

He thought about diving into the 'Find Alfie Sidebottom' file but decided that the month-end invoices wouldn't do themselves and that he'd have to write off the day to earning the pounds.

On the Monday morning Trish breezed in at quarter past ten, turned the cheery cod 1950s sign to "Yes, we are open!" and shouted "I'm here. Batman… Robin's here."

Mark appeared and he knew it was going to be a dreary day of wedding photograph proofs and editing drone footage. He hated it. But the juicy fee of £4000 plus VAT for a day's work was not to be sniffed at. He'd started a new cash pile marked "House number 4" in his mind.

They were both at the back of the shop in the office dealing with the harvest of images from Saturday's wedding when the bell above the door clanged to announce a rare passing customer.

Trish could see the shop from her seat.

"Are you going?" asked Mark.

"No," said Trish. "You can get this one."

Mark looked at her. Trish jerked her head to the right, towards the shop. Mark leaned forward and looked down towards the shop counter.

And there she was. Emma McMillan. She was wearing a blue printed tea dress and her hair was pulled back into a ponytail. She looked years younger, almost girlish.

Trish stared at him and mouthed "Go on."

Mark walked out of the office and towards her and said, smiling, but almost too breezily, "Hello, and what can I do for you?"

She looked at him for a second.

"Nice interview in the paper," she said.

Was she cross? Mark studied her face. No, she was teasing him. She was teasing him and that's good he thought.

"Ah well, when you're a guardian of justice, naturally the newspapers all want a piece of you."

Don't go too far Mark, he warned himself.

"Of course they do," she smiled and paused. Looked down at the small white handbag she'd placed on the counter. "I've come to say thank you, Mr Elwin."

"Mark," he said.

"Mark," she said.

"I've come to say thank you, Mark. When, actually, I don't know how to thank you."

Before she launched into her speech about how terrible the worry about going to prison had been, about how much it meant to her, and to Daisy, and her own mother Mark simply said "You could have dinner with me?"

"What?" she said.

"To thank me," he said. "You could have dinner with me."

In the back office, Trish theatrically crossed her fingers.

"Oh," said Emma McMillan. "Okay."

Chapter 40
Ireland, 1954 Onwards

The sign said simply 'Casey' and had been put in place over the window of a former cobbler and shoe shop on Main Street in Donegal Town in 1954.

1954 was a big year for Alfie Casey. He'd just returned from Dublin after four years in law school and four more as an articled clerk and junior solicitor with Sexton and Sexton, a big city law firm, where he'd finally specialised in contract law.

Alfie had seen himself rising through the ranks of the legal profession in the capital, brokering big corporate deals, featuring in the newspapers alongside the great and the good just as old man John Sexton did. Soon he saw himself buying one of those big fancy houses in Malahide, just along the coast, overlooking the sea and the castle.

That's how Alfie saw his future, in 1954.

Bridget O'Reilly saw things entirely differently.

She had watched Alfie grow from a schoolboy to a man. She had, with the Reverend and Mrs Mitchell, waved him off to Trinity College just after the war and had happily waited for him to come home at the end of every term.

She had also happily trekked backwards and forwards from Donegal to Dublin while Alfie learned his trade and the two of them had a high old time in the dance halls on a Saturday night and recovering in his rooms on a Sunday.

But enough was enough. She was nearly thirty and by anyone's standards, she should have been married with a clutch of babies by now. So, one day, she had said to him, are you coming home to your bride or not?

He went home.

It was a tough call in 1954, a Catholic bride and a Protestant groom. So they slipped away and had a brief civil wedding with a friend each as witness and then attended mass as husband and wife one week and then stood before Reverend Mitchell as husband and wife the next.

Alfie brushed up on criminal law, conveyancing and probate put a sign over the shop and opened for business as a one-man band solicitor.

Alfie treated both sides of the political and religious divide with an even hand even during the brutal years and as a result, the Casey law firm grew in both reputation and size.

By the time Mark had tracked him down Casey's had grown to include no fewer than 14 partners and a small army of support staff which were now based in a smart new office development just out of Donegal Town.

The original office with Alfie's first desk and chair remained with a couple of administration people just so Casey's and Donegal Town were together forever.

After looking for so long into the past for Alfie Sidebottom, it was when Mark looked at the present that he had finally found his man.

If there are no death certificates then maybe they're not dead, he'd reasoned. Well, Monty had to be, somewhere. But Alfie, like his own grandmother, could be alive even though there had been nothing of him between 1933 and the census of 1951.

There were going to be lots of Caseys in Ireland, to put it mildly so he limited himself to Donegal in the hope that young Alfie had stayed close. There were lots of Caseys in the Donegal area too but, in the end, there were, over the decades, only a few Alfred Caseys and, in the end, just the one Alfred Casey he was looking for.

His man had barely left a footprint. Alfie had happily retired to the Old Vicarage 30 years previously, years before the Great God Google, search engines and the whole internet era had a chance to smear his identity across the virtual world in order to help the real world find him.

Yet he'd left a trace. A mention in the 'About' page of the 'Casey: Law For All' website, a photograph of the lawyer as a young man and a biography of his son John Casey, now managing partner. Alfred Casey pictured as guest of honour at the opening of the new headquarters out of town. He looked a lot like his mother in the wedding photograph in the EDP story.

Once located, Mark filled in a few details of the empty years but there remained nothing of Monty. Alfie may have left a light footprint over the years. In Ireland, Monty had left just the two newspaper cuttings—the single court report and the shooting photograph.

What was Mark to do now that he had finally found Alfie Sidebottom?

He had no sense of success.

No feeling that the months spent toying with the 'Find Alfie Sidebottom' file had reached a conclusion. They hadn't. Monty was still AWOL. How had the pair made it to Ireland in the first place? How had the son of a refugee from justice managed to end up the cornerstone of provincial law in Ireland?

It came down to a simple choice. Did Mark try to contact Alfie Sidebottom or not? Did he visit upon a very old man events from another lifetime? Or, having found his man, did he let sleeping dogs lie?

"Well, for one thing, he doesn't know he had a brother," said Emma.

It was their third date and Mark had waited until this third date, another gastropub dinner, to tell her of his—what was it?—hobby?

"I don't know what happened to the half-brother," he said. "Anyway, I'm sick of chasing Sidebottoms."

"No, you're not," she said. "You are dying to know where Monty went to for a start."

"I'm dying to know where Alfie was until 1954. There's no trace of him anywhere."

"You'll have to call," she said. "Or you'll not rest."

"And say what? Excuse me, Mr Respectable. Wasn't your father a fugitive murderer?"

"Maybe he wasn't."

"Wasn't what?"

"A fugitive murderer."

Chapter 41
Norfolk, Present Day

For two weeks and three more dates, Mark veered between deciding he was imminently calling Ireland and launching into the big 'ha ha found you!' speech and, more often, gently closing down the 'Find Alfie Sidebottom' file and keeping his mouth shut.

For dates four, five and six Emma found this entertaining and, at times, even endearing. By date seven, her heart had decided that Mark Elwin was actually a big 'yes' in terms of boyfriend material and she was beginning to be sick and tired of the whole Sidebottom saga.

"Right," she said over a coffee and free chocolate mint wafers after Sunday lunch at the Rose and Crown, "this could go on forever. Call Ireland. Sort yourself out. Get it off your chest. See it through. Whatever you want to call it, get on with it."

"Ah, yes," he said about to tread the same careworn weary path he had a dozen times and more "but this man is 95 years old and has a perfectly respectable life. Am I the person, I mean do I actually have the right, as it were, to throw an emotional hand grenade into that life? I'm not sure I do," he said.

"Then shut up and never mention it again," said Emma. She wasn't teasing this time.

"But," he said.

"I mean it, Mark..."

"But," he pressed on holding up the palm of his hand, "what if I was to call up and give him every chance of telling me to bugger off without ever risking, without ever compromising, without...what's the word I'm looking for, look what I mean is if I give him every get out clause possible?"

"How do you mean? And make this brief and to the point. Brief. And. To the point," she said. "Brief," she said again.

"Ok," he said. "How about this? I call the office. I speak to his son."

"Who says he'll take the call?"

"No one," he brushed her aside. This was a plan two weeks in the making and he was finally unfurling it for approval, not for scrutiny.

"I say to John Casey, 'I'm enquiring on behalf of my grandmother. She's trying to trace old classmates. It is VERY unlikely that your father is the boy we are looking for. It really is VERY unlikely that your father is an old classmate of hers but…would you ask him if he knew a Lauretta Harrison at school?'"

"Harrison?"

"Maiden name, silly billy," he said.

"Of course."

"If he asks which school then I'll say Sandringham. Sandringham in Norfolk."

"Which will be a shock. Why would his dad have been at school in England?"

"Exactly."

"Yes, exactly," she said.

"Well, I can't lie. I'll just say, 'Yes, that's why I think we have probably got the wrong boy.' I'll have to keep saying 'boy' as, of course, my grandmother doesn't remember an Alfie Casey but an Alfie Sidebottom. However," Mark said, holding up his hand again, to stay any possible doubt, "I reckon if I just keep saying 'boy' it'll pass John Casey by. He'll just assume I mean Alfie Casey. So, when, if, maybe, whatever, son John says to his dad 'you'll never believe this but…' then Alfie can then decide whether or not to say 'never heard of her' and his secret stays safe or 'actually son, there's something you should know'."

"Right," she said, hovering over the word. "So you plan to call Ireland but in such a way as to almost make sure nothing happens?"

"No," he said. "It's to call Ireland and to give Ireland the chance to come clean. I can't flush out a 95-year-old man after all this time. Not in my gift. But just in case he fancies telling all…"

"Do it tomorrow," she said.

"What?"

"Do it tomorrow. Stop messing about. I've had enough. There are things to do," she said.

"What things?" he said.

"Try not to be too thick Mark Elwin," she said. "There might be a life to be had once you get this off your chest," and she smiled. She was teasing him again. He hadn't got used to it just yet. He liked it nevertheless.

At half past nine, the following morning she called him.

"Well?"

"Not done it yet," he said.

At a quarter past one on her lunch break, she called again.

"Things to do. On it. On it," he said.

At half past three on her way to pick up Daisy from school she called again.

"I'll do it, I'll do it," he said.

"Do it now," she said and hung up. She'd never hung up on him before.

"Do it now," he said out loud to himself.

"Do what now?" asked Trish from the shop.

"Nothing," he said. "Just going up to the flat," he said.

Upstairs he sat at his desk and took out the paper 'Find Alfie Sidebottom' file for absolutely no reason whatsoever. It just seemed the right thing to do. To have all the paperwork on hand.

He called the number off the Casey website and an efficient young female voice answered.

"I'd like to speak to John Casey if I could. I'm calling from England. It is in regard to his father Alfred Casey."

In regard to? In regard to? what on earth had made him use such an archaic phrase?

"I'll put you through to his PA."

Click. Brief whirr.

"John Casey's office," said an equally efficient young female voice.

"Ah hello," said Mark and he launched into his much-rehearsed spiel. "My name is Mark Elwin. My grandmother is Lauretta Harrison. She is 95 years old and is trying to track down old school friends and I am helping her. It is remotely possible that Alfred Casey was a school friend of hers. Could I possibly have two minutes of John Casey's time? Please?"

"Please hold, Mister…"

"Elwin," he said. "Mark Elwin."

The line went to bingy bongy holding music. It seemed like an age.

"Putting you through Mr Elwin," said the voice.

"John Casey," said the next voice. "This all sounds very exciting. How can I help?"

"Well," said Mark and even though rehearsals for this part of the exchange had been going on in his head for some time the words did not come easily, "I believe your father and my grandmother may have been at school together. She's mentioned him. I'm trying to track down people for her."

"Well, quite a task Mr Elwin, quite a task. Which school might that have been then? Leghowney?"

"Er, no. Sandringham."

"Sandringham?"

"Yes. Sandringham primary school."

"Sandringham as in the King? As in England?"

"That's right," said Mark. "I realise that it is extremely unlikely that your father is the boy my grandmother remembers. I mean, genuinely unlikely."

"She says she remembers an Alfie Casey?"

Mark now had a choice. Strategic simple lie. Or tell the whole story. He chose a strategic simple lie.

"Yes," he said "she remembers an Alfie Casey and your father is an Alfie Casey. And according to all my searches, there aren't many around."

"But Mr Elwin," said the voice on the phone, "my father has never even been to England. I'm afraid you will have to look elsewhere. And good luck tracking down all the ninety plus Alfred Caseys in the world," he chuckled down the line.

"No I agree it was a long shot," said Mark. "Nevertheless, worth a try. And, he said, actually in the British Isles, only one who is 95. Could I just give your PA my mobile number…just in case?"

"Ah, sure you can," said John Casey, "I'll put you back. And good luck again Mr Elwin."

It was a deftly arranged conceit that Mark was proud of. It let John Casey close the door on the eccentric Englishman, while the eccentric Englishman put his foot in the door with his phone number.

It was five past nine the next morning when his mobile phone rang.

"Hello?"

"Mr Elwin. It's John Casey here. We spoke yesterday."

Chapter 42
Donegal Town, Present Day

"Yes, yes. He wants me to go to Ireland," Mark said to Emma as she stood in his shop with Daisy after school that day.

"Who does? The son or the father?"

"Mum, I'm going to look at the cameras, okay?"

"Yes sweetheart," said Emma. This wasn't how she'd imagined her daughter meeting Mark for the first time, but she'd been living with this saga for a month now and Mark was bursting with news.

"Well, the son said so but his father is the one asking."

"What has he said to the son?"

"Well, that's the thing. Nothing. John Casey phones up this morning and says he told his father about this Englishman, grandmother story and so on expecting his father to laugh it off as a weird phone call. But no. Apparently, Alfie said to his son "Thank God. At last." And that's it. Apart from asking me to go over to see him."

"What, he said nothing?"

"Apparently not. His son, his wife, and their kids are all gathered around him pestering him and going on at him but apparently, he just smiled and said 'I've waited this long, I can wait a little longer' and refused to say any more."

"And you said to his son?"

"I said if he can wait then so can I. I mean, I don't really know what happened. Only Alfie Casey does. I could tell him this and that but it's only newspaper reports and a few birth, death and marriage certificates. No, only one person has the story and I'm just as keen as his son is to hear it."

"So are you going?"

"Good God yes."

"When?"

"Tomorrow."

"Tomorrow?"

"Of course," he said with a broad smile. "What is there to wait for?"

"Well, nothing I suppose."

"East Midlands to Knock airport. Fiat 500 booked and waiting. Two nights B&B in a place called the Olde Glen Bar in Donegal Town. Hey hey! At last. Found Alfie Sidebottom!" and in his excitement, Mark went to kiss her, but she swerved away and put her hand up all in one movement and turned and pointed towards Daisy.

Too late. Daisy had seen the whole swerve. Anyway, she was 12. She knew what was going on.

Less than 24 hours later Mark was sitting at a table in the Olde Glen Bar and was nursing a cup of coffee when John Casey came in, thrust out a hand and introduced himself.

"Mr Elwin," he said.

"Mark."

"Mark. You can have no idea the excitement you have caused."

"Well," and all Mark could think of was 'murder'.

"Excitement is usually a good thing," said Mark.

"It certainly is and I cannot begin to tell you what excitement this has caused in the whole family. Thank you for coming over so promptly. I think we all would have exploded if the tension went on for another day."

"Ah," said Mark. Maybe this was the worst idea he'd ever had. "What has been said?"

"Nothing," said John Casey, "infuriating man. Nothing at all. He's told us to wait for you. And I'm to ask you nothing either. He wants to be the first for everything. So, it'll be ten minutes to the Old Vicarage and you'll be having something of an audience. Just about the whole family is there…" And he carried on talking as they left the Olde Glen Bar and got into the Jaguar parked outside "…everyone bar my sister Aisling and her tribe as they're all down in New Zealand these past ten years. But they've been told, don't you worry, they've set up some kind of internet conference link thing but, to be honest, I'm not certain I have any idea how to make that work. It seems the kids have!"

They were driving now.

"Wow. Okay. I wasn't expecting anything like this," said Mark. "I hope I haven't caused too much of a fuss."

"A fuss? A fuss? A fuss doesn't even begin to come close Mr Elwin," and he laughed out loud.

Oh, good lord. I'm about to tell you that your grandfather was a murderer and you don't think 'fuss' is adequate. You may well be right thought Mark.

"I wasn't expecting an audience," said Mark.

"Well, to be fair, the whole town will know of it soon enough Mr Elwin. Welcome to Ireland."

"Mark, please," he said.

I'm not sure you'll be wanting the whole town to know this, he thought.

Ten minutes later they pulled into the drive of the fine Old Vicarage.

"Beautiful house," said Mark.

"Isn't it," said John Casey. "My dad mostly grew up here after Grandad went to war. The Reverend and Auntie Judith were very good. Like their own."

"Went to war you say?"

"Ah, listen to me," said John Casey. "I'm to tell you nothing so I am. Don't tell the old man, for goodness sake. Here we are."

As they pulled up outside the front porch with its fine stained glass side panels, a surge of children from toddlers to surly teenagers spilled out of the house followed by a trio of mothers trying to shoo them back inside.

"Ah, there's a welcoming committee all right. The old man will have been enjoying this. Keeping us all waiting. Always enjoys a sense of drama he does."

You have no idea, thought Mark. Again.

"Come on in now. Out of the way you brats," he said, leading Mark, randomly shouting out names "My sister Kathleen there, sister-in-law Josie, Declan, Jimmy, big lad at the back that's John junior."

And so Mark was ushered through the Casey clan and into the fine Victorian front sitting room.

There was a theatrical hush as mothers shushed their own children and big children shushed all the little children.

In a wingback chair, with its back to the large side window but in a prime spot pointing at the fireplace, sat Alfred Casey. Grey flannel trousers, turnups, smart, shiny black Oxford shoes, a sharp collared white shirt, a striped tie and a double-breasted navy-blue blazer. A crisper ninety-five-year-old you could not possibly have hoped to meet.

He stood up, effortlessly and stood ramrod straight.

He took a step towards Mark, thrust out his right hand and said "I have often wondered how this moment might arrive. Mr Elwin, Alfred Casey."

"I am pleased to meet you… Mr Sidebottom," said Mark and the theatrical hush in the room became an eerie silence.

Chapter 43
Donegal Town, Present Day

"Mr Sidebottom?" said one of the women and maybe a dozen pairs of eyes swivelled to look at the old man as he settled back into his chair and indicated its twin brother opposite also pointing towards the fireplace.

"Oh, I wouldn't be getting excited about a name, eh Mr Elwin? If you'll be getting excited about little things like that, you'll be liable to explode in the next half an hour, eh Mr Elwin?" he said.

"Mark, please."

"Mr Elwin, why don't you tell me your story and I'll chip in with mine and we'll see where we get to. How's that for a plan? Let's start with quiet from you lot," he said and he swept an arm around the room in front of three sets of parents and half a dozen children or maybe even more.

Alfie was still clearly the patriarch in charge, thought Mark.

"And let Mr Elwin begin. Now your grandmother is little Lauretta you say? How is she?"

"Mark, please…"

Alfie gestured a little come on sign to him with his hand.

"Okay…my grandmother is Lauretta Carey, Lauretta Harrison as a child and she is currently in a care home in Norfolk. She is, I think, the kindest thing to say is, she's physically quite well, in a wheelchair, but quite well but not, shall we say, entirely with us."

"Now, I am sorry to hear that Mr Elwin."

Mark mentally gave up on informality.

"Yes, well that's as maybe but one evening—I go over most Friday evenings, although she hasn't a clue who I am—but one evening she turned to me and recalled with absolute clarity a scene from her school days. She said the teacher…"

"Mrs Cartwright," said Alfie.

The family looked at each other and then to Alfie who smiled broadly and held up his hand like a traffic policeman halting advancing traffic.

"Mrs Cartwright," said Alfie again "Ooh she was quick with that ruler she was. A real dragon," he chuckled as he transported himself back to the sun-dappled Sandringham classroom of more than 85 years ago.

"I'm so sorry Mr Elwin. Please allow an old man a little indulgence. Do go on…"

"Well, my grandmother said the teacher… Mrs Cartwright…was having real trouble getting the class to calm down and keep quiet and that one young man at the time, one Alfie Sidebottom was nattering with his mate…"

"Edward Charlton," said Alfie. "Ed Charlton. Now he was a character," said Alfie.

"She never mentioned him. Just you, Sir," said Mark wondering if that had taken formality too far. He wiped away the thought.

"So, then my grandmother tries telling this man here," and he half turned to the family audience and then indicated Alfie, "to keep quiet only for the teacher to turn back to the class, catch my grandmother talking and the upshot was my grandmother got three slaps on the palm of her hand from the teacher's ruler."

"It is too little, too late but I will happily apologise to you now, profusely and unreservedly Mr Elwin for the trouble I caused your grandmother," and Alfie chuckled.

He's enjoying every minute of this thought Mark.

"Well, you see that was remarkable enough. My grandmother doesn't even remember me, practically her last remaining relative and only visitor, but she remembered that school story with 20/20 hindsight. Crystal clear."

"But that wouldn't have set you off looking for me would it now Mr Elwin?" said Alfie, again with a smile in his eyes.

"Er no. That'd be what she said next."

"And what might that have been, Mr Elwin?"

The old boy really was enjoying this! Well, if the old boy is ok with it, he thought…

"She said the next day your uncle was found shot dead and that you and your father went missing and were never heard of again."

"Oh my goodness," said one of the women.

"Grandpa?" said one of the boys.

"Grandpa, did your daddy kill someone?" said one of the little ones.

"Now hold your tongues you lot," said Alfie, revelling in the awe and surprise among his clan. "You know what I said. A fantastic tale but you have to be quiet. All of you. I want to listen to what Mr Elwin has to say and to how he's found himself right here in this sitting room after all this time. Mr Elwin, the floor, as they say, is yours."

"But you know what happened? I don't," said Mark.

"No, but I want to hear your detective story. I want to know how you found us here. In Donegal Town."

And so Mark began the story of his online search, the newspaper reports, of the police, of murder, long nights drawing a blank, no death certificates, no graves, the police trail going cold, his own trail growing cold until he switched his search to the Irish Free State, a search hampered by the war for independence, the civil war, incomplete records, destroyed records and finally just his two newspaper articles.

"The truth is Mr …" Mark hesitated, "Casey…that I never found you in the past at all. I found a couple of traces of your father, a couple of newspaper cuttings, but that was it. And then he disappeared. It was only when I gave up, I suppose in 1951 when there was again no trace of you or your father in the census. I gave up trying to find your trail out of Norfolk and just looked, well, at Donegal. And there, hiding all this time in plain sight, there you were."

"Well, find me you have," said Alfie. "I suppose now you'll be wanting to hear what really happened?"

"Yes!" shouted two of the children.

"Shhhh," said a mother.

"Well, I've waited a long time to tell this story. There were times at my age I thought I never would. There were times I thought I really couldn't. There were times when, like you Mr Elwin, when the internet and the like started, I went online and read and read again the newspaper stories from the time and wondered if anyone, anywhere, was still trying to get at the truth. But no one was. I did check from time to time so I did see that my mother had died."

"You have brother," said Mark, perhaps too bluntly.

"Do I now?" said Alfie, utterly unfazed. "well, I pretty much thought there might be something like that. Is he still alive?"

"I don't know," said Mark. "I can't say he's dead. I can't say he's alive. I never looked really. He wasn't part of the story. For me."

"Oh, but he is in many ways. Anyway, he paused and gathered the many, many," thoughts in his head. "As I say. I've been waiting a long time to tell this story," he said, and the family audience collectively sat up or stood up straight and tuned in.

"And I can wait a little longer," he said, to the utter disbelief of the Casey clan. You could even hear the collective 'Oh noes' from an iPad screen beaming the drama to the New Zealand audience.

"Kathleen, that buffet in the dining room will not eat itself. I suggest we get some food down us first. There's a lot to get through."

There was a collective groan from children and an adolescent boy's voice muttered "he's gone for 100% theatre," although Mark couldn't tell which one it was.

Alfie stood up and took Mark by the elbow.

"You'll join me in a glass of wine, Mr Elwin? I'll not see you thirsty and you'll not be going home to England to tell them that Alfie Sidebottom turned out to be a mean host."

Chapter 44
Donegal Town, Present Day

The spread was enormous, covering a dining room table that could easily seat sixteen people. Mark and Alfie headed the line to fill up plates with cold meats and buttered new potatoes and salads.

Alfie settled himself into another high wingback chair in the bay window overlooking the vast lawns of the Old Vicarage running down to the orchard.

He's like a prince on his throne watching over his realm, thought Mark.

The Casey family ate like there was no tomorrow. It wasn't hunger that drove them. In fact, they hardly filled their plates. They just wanted this interlude to be over and to get back to the sitting room for part two of the great story.

Alfie chatted to Mark about his work as a photographer, about Norfolk in general and more about his schoolgirl friend Lauretta Harrison, what she had done in life, marriage and children.

Eventually, Alfie stood up.

"Recharge your glass, Mr Elwin," said Alfie. "Let's put this lot out of their misery."

Back in the sitting room and settled back into his chair Alfie said "Right-ho Mr Elwin, where shall we begin?"

"Well," said Mark. "Why did you run? Why did your father run and take you? I never really understood why a man running from a murder hunt would take a child with him?"

"Well, for one thing, there's no certainty that there was ever a murder, Mr Elwin. No certainty at all," and again he raised his traffic policeman's hand against the growing noise of mumblings.

"I saw nothing that morning so I can't say for certain what happened. My mother Nika," again he raised his hand against the family mumbles, "Yes, my mother was called Nika. It's an unusual Norfolk name," he said to his family. "My mother was arguing with my Uncle Clem. I was hiding by the back door to my home, Keeper's Cottage at Sandringham. That's right," he said to the children in particular, "the King of England's Sandringham Estate. What do you think of that eh?"

He'd paused until the hum in the room stopped.

"Now, Sandringham School had closed early and unexpectedly for the day. Mrs Cartwright was poorly. So I'm home practically first thing in the morning really when my mother would not have been expecting me. No mobiles in those days! Oh, do stop mumbling for goodness sake children! There'll be time for questions later," and he smiled.

"I heard an almighty argument," he continued, his audience once again quiet, "There was talk of a child. There was a single gunshot and then I heard my mother wailing and crying out Uncle Clem's name. I did not see how Uncle Clem was shot or how it happened."

Mark raised a hand like a child in class.

"Mr Elwin…" said Alfie giving up the floor and taking a sip of wine.

"That's not fair," said a child.

"Shhhh," said a mother.

"So if your father was nowhere near the shooting, why did he run?" asked Mark.

"Good question. Good question. First, you are right; Mr Elwin, my father, had nothing to do with the shooting. He was and remains wholly innocent of any crime, well, save a little fraud and falsifying later," said Alfie and chuckled again. "I ran like the wind that morning up to Hanging Wood and fetched him. When we got back, it was as if he knew exactly what to do. I was sent up and downstairs half a dozen times fetching clothes and packing food and water. I heard various bits of my mother and father rowing. He said 'you'll hang' to my mother, he said something about her keeping her 'bastard child' and he said he'd be ruined by 'scandal'."

Mark raised a hand again.

Alfie nodded.

"Why did he bring all that suspicion and trouble down on himself and you?"

"Oh, Mr Elwin, I think he was doing what he could to avoid, yes avoid, all that suspicion and trouble. Imagine if we had stayed? Police investigation, court case, scandal in the papers, the very real prospect in those days of my mother, an adulteress don't forget, with her hands on a loaded weapon beside the body of her lover—her husband's brother no less... No, she'd have hanged for certain in those days. And my father knew that."

Mark put his hand up again. Another nod from Alfie.

"But to actually put himself up as a prime candidate for murder?"

The word murder triggered more almost theatrical oooohs including tinny computer speaker ooohs from the New Zealand audience.

"Not really Mr Elwin. Had we been caught by the police both of us would simply have told the truth. My father was in no danger of being charged with anything. But the scandal you see...he'd never work again. Never. Scandal you see. Not good for a man who could only really work for the grandest families in England. And protecting me. He was concerned that I'd always be known as the boy whose mother was hanged for the murder of her lover. What did he have to stay for?"

Mark didn't raise his hand this time. The precedent had been set and the pattern emerged of a question-and-answer session with the story getting increasingly close to the lives of the family audience.

"One thing I never could quite work out was where you ran to and how you ended up here. I only looked here as I thought here might be your only family. I did think that there was no hiding place for you in Norfolk. Too well known, too many police..."

"Well, Mr Elwin, I have no idea if my father was heading straight for Donegal but he was certainly heading straight out of Norfolk as you say. We were away from Norfolk within 24 hours. Well, we set sail in less than 12 hours."

"Set sail?"

"Set sail, Mr Elwin."

"Okay let's just go back... So what time did you start running?"

"Before noon."

"But the shooting wasn't reported until gone five in the evening?"

"Exactly so Mr Elwin. My father was drawing suspicion away from my mother, my mother was giving us every chance to get away. And we did. With the help of a man called Jethro Springer. A fisherman and father's best friend for 25 years and more."

"But why would he help?"

"And another good question Mr Elwin. Have you never considered a career in newspapers?"

Something for another time thought Mark.

"It was something that as a boy growing up, I always thought that was the big risk my father took but as I gained a bit more knowledge of life and friendship and the way of the world, there was no risk at all. None at all. Firstly, they'd been best friends for nearly 25 years, all their lives. Why wouldn't Jethro help? Secondly, I reckon Father had already discussed with Jethro my mother's, shall we say, playing around with Uncle Clem. He was his best friend, so there'd be no surprise there. Also number three, the Springer family—you might say—were no big fans of authority, certainly not the police or the customs men. They probably made as much money from occasional night running over to Holland and back with various bits of contraband as they did from crabs and mackerel. And having taken us to Boston, when he was back, he'd hardly be wanting to admit to helping a runaway murder suspect would he?"

"Boston?"

"Oh yes, Mr Elwin. Brancaster Staithe to Boston—Lincolnshire—It's no distance at all. By boat."

"So by the time, the police search was in full swing the next morning..."

"We were on a train to Nottingham."

"Nottingham?" said Mark. This tale was becoming like something out of a John Buchan novel.

"Oh yes, Mr Elwin. I think Father's first thought was to get out of Norfolk. I think at some point either on the boat or overnight tied up in harbour, he'd decided we were going to Donegal."

"But Nottingham?"

"He was laying a false trail, he was. It was obvious looking back. You see, if anyone recognised us from Boston station, well, Mr Policeman, they'd say, they bought tickets to Nottingham. If they looked there, then yes, we got off and went into the city where we bought new clothes. If they did go back to Nottingham station, they'd only track us to Manchester. And if they managed that, and I very much doubt they even got to Boston, but then even if they tracked us to Manchester, they'd only get us to Liverpool, then they'd only get us on a boat to Belfast, from there to Enniskillen by train and then we slipped over the border on foot into the Irish Free State."

And as the pace of the story increased so did the tension in the family audience until they could no longer contain themselves and they gasped and looked at each other in comic book astonishment, and then slowly a little round of applause broke out.

"Go on, Father, go on," said Kathleen, excitedly.

Alfie deliberately and slowly looked at his watch.

"Too much for this night," he said to a crescendo of disappointment.

He chuckled.

A round of 'no' and 'please' swept through the family but Alfie was on his feet and the story telling was clearly over for the day.

"John," he said, "you'll return Mr Elwin to the Olde Glen Bar where he'll no doubt be wanting time for a glass of something tasty and some supper. Mr Elwin will you join us after lunch tomorrow when we will keep this disreputable lot further entertained."

"I will," said Mark.

I can't wait, he thought.

Chapter 45
Donegal Town, Present day

Mark spent a very pleasant morning mooching around Donegal Town, window shopping, investigating churches both Catholic and Protestant and strolling in the grounds of Donegal Castle. What an agreeable town this is, he thought. There were worse places to run to.

Over lunch at the Olde Glen Bar he jotted down a few questions for Alfie and was ready and waiting for John Casey to give him a lift back to the Old Vicarage where Alfie was already in position and the family audience poised for more excitement.

"Mr Elwin, welcome back. Is the Olde Glen Bar looking after you?"

"They are, they are," said Mark.

"Then you'll be keen to be asking more questions."

"I am. So, you walked into the Irish Free State. How did you know where to go?"

"Another great question Mr Elwin. My father's mother, my grandmother, was apparently a keen supporter of the Temperance Movement in her time. Never touched a drop of the demon drink. According to father she told tales of her 'Irish husband' as she called him, and her father, and her brothers all drinking their money away in, of all places for you to choose to stay Mr Elwin, the Olde Glen Bar. By the way, which room are you in Mr Elwin?"

"The one at the front overlooking the road."

"Heavens be. The same room father and I stayed in while waiting to speak to Uncle Mick."

"Michael and Patrick Casey. Uncles. Yes, I found those on a census. 1901. No mention of Kathleen."

"No, no, my grandmother, she'd have gone to England by then. But you know that part of the story from your wedding certificates. Well Uncle Mick pointed us towards Captain Bashford at Leghowney House and that's where you found my father as a gamekeeper in your two newspaper cuttings."

"Yes," said Mark. "But that's all. No census during the war of course and in the 1951 census he's disappeared again and still no sign of you. I just don't get it."

"Ah, you were looking in the wrong places, Mr Elwin, and you've just mentioned the reason. The war. As soon as England declared war on Germany, Mr Elwin, my father felt it was his duty to answer the call. We may have been passport carrying Irishmen by then but father was an Englishman and had been in service to the old King. He got on the train to Belfast and joined the 1st Irish Fusiliers."

"I see. Hang on, … passports? How did you get Irish passports?"

"Easy enough, Mr Elwin. First you get forged Irish Free State passports and then when the Republic comes in, you send them off and you get real Irish passports back! Suddenly you're legitimate!" and Alfie chuckled.

"Forged passports?" said son John, astonished that his father had been on a forged passport.

"Now, now John. Needs must. Anyway, what they going to do about it now? An old man like me. Pillar of the community. Defender of justice," and he chuckled again.

"Didn't anyone check?" asked Mark.

"In the Irish Free State before the war, Mr Elwin? Really? It's not like today. No-one held records on very much at all. I had a passable passport you might say, the new Government issued me with a replacement. Simple."

"Fair enough," said Mark. "Nevertheless in 1939 when your father left to go to war, what about you? You'd be what, 13, 14?"

"Yes indeed, just 14. Well, I came here. To this very house. Reverend John Mitchell and his wife Judith took me in as their own. We'd known them ever since we arrived really. I spent a lot of time here in school holidays. A second home for me. John here is named after the Reverend," and he pointed to his son.

"This is my home Mr Elwin and apart from a couple of years after they retired back to England in 1959 and before I could buy it, it has been home for nearly 80 years. A home for myself and my beloved Bridget, may she rest in peace, and all of these people behind you, they have loved it as a home at some time during those 80 years. John and Aisling back there and the three monsters have it now and let very kindly have me as their lodger."

Groans from the younger Casey generation. They'd heard the 'I'm just the lodger' line many, many times before.

"Anyway, back to my father," he continued "You've found no trace of him you say?"

"None outside the two newspaper cuttings."

"Ah, but if you had checked with the Commonwealth War Graves Commission you'd have seen that Fusilier Montgomery Casey of the 1st Irish Fusiliers died on the beach at Dunkirk. He's buried in Dunkirk Town Cemetery."

"Of course! The war. It never occurred to me. It never, ever occurred to me." Mark was cross with himself. "Ireland neutral. I imagined that fact, plus him still being on the run as it were, would mean he'd stick here."

"You didn't know my father," said Alfie.

"But then you. Where were you?"

"I was here right through the war and after that with the help of John and Judith I took up a place at Trinity College Dublin and read law. As did John here after me," he said extending his arm towards his son again.

"But the census. You don't exist," Mark joked. "I checked the 1951 census. You don't exist."

"Ah, well, in 1951 I was in student digs with Mrs O'Hare. Aye, along with five other lads. Cash rent you understand Mr Elwin. Cash rent! Quite how the widow O'Hare managed to live the life of luxury she did all alone in that vast mansion no-one will ever know," chuckled Alfie.

Mark didn't get it and it translated onto his face.

"She lived alone, Mr Elwin. No lodgers, no rent, no cheques, no tax."

"And no record in the census! I feel a bit stupid," admitted Mark.

"Not at all Mr Elwin, not at all. You got from a one-off remark by your grandmother all the way to here. I think that's pretty remarkable. And thanks to you it has finally allowed me to get all of this off my mind before I'm called upstairs."

"Well, it's an incredible story. Truly remarkable," said Mark.

Alfie held up his traffic policeman hand again.

"Time for questions from the back in good time," said Alfie fearing a full-on interrogation from his clan. "I've a couple of questions for you now, Mr Elwin if I may."

"Certainly," said Mark, uncertainly.

"My mother's grave you say?"

"Yes, Dersingham Church yard. St Nicholas's. Pretty place, for a graveyard."

"Have you been to see it?"

"No," said Mark. For some reason he felt ashamed he hadn't.

"I would like to see it," said Alfie and there was another audible and collective 'ooh' from the Casey clan.

"I would like to see it." He repeated.

"And I would like to go to look at Keeper's Cottage at Sandringham too. Is it still there? Of course it is. And I should like to visit your grandmother if I may?"

"Of course. I doubt she'll recognise you. Doesn't know me anymore and apart from that one time…"

"Nevertheless, Mr Elwin. It is probably my last chance to just put a hand back through time and touch my childhood. I had to abandon that childhood. I had to deny its existence. Now it has been returned to me by you, Mr Elwin. I thank you for it."

"It was, and is, my pleasure," he said.

"And just one more thing before John here gives to a lift back to the dear Olde Glen."

"What's that?"

"I'd like to clear my father's name."

"Really? Does it matter? Won't you get in trouble? False passports and the like?"

"I'm 95 years old Mr Elwin. Do you think I care?"

"Well I suppose we could go to the police. Someone in the police must be interested. You must have contacts with the police here. Do you want to set up a meeting here first and let them liaise with England?"

"Oh, no, no, no Mr Elwin. That'll take far too long and no-one will want to be either responsible for such a cold, cold case or be keen to take on the paperwork. If your police are anything like ours, and I'm pretty sure they are, it'll be at best a long and bureaucratic waste of everyone's time. No, I was thinking more of completing the Eastern Daily Press file on the case. Could you help with that, Mr Elwin?"

"Oh I can do better than that," said Mark. "As it happens I have recently acquired a very good contact at the Mail on Sunday newspaper."

"Do you think they'd be interested in our story Mr Elwin?"

"I think they'd be so interested that there'd likely be a decent payment for the exclusive! Royalty, murder—possibly not murder but you know what I mean—an eighty-year-old mystery. They'll take your arm off," and he laughed out loud at the thought.

"Our arms, Mr Elwin. This is as much about the story of your search as it is of my life's story. And as for any fee, well, I think you can have that for all your trouble."

"Well, it'll be no trouble getting them interested I can promise you that."

"Excellent," said Alfie. "Well, well. Going home to England. No, not home. Home is here. Going back to England. Who'd have thought it?"

Chapter 46
Norfolk, Present Day

Mark had been keeping Emma up to date with long phone calls from his room at the Olde Glen Bar but he kept news of Alfie Casey's planned trip to Norfolk a surprise until he got home.

"When's he coming then?" she asked as they tucked into fish and chips sitting in the wall of the quayside at Wells-next-the-Sea. It was a lovely autumn day and they'd decided on the full tourist seaside experience, a beach walk, fish and chips for lunch and a pint in The Edinburgh pub to close the trip.

"Next weekend. He and John booked into the Rose and Crown Friday and Saturday night. Friday night to meet Lauretta, Saturday at Keeper's Cottage and then his mother's grave and of course the interview with the *Mail on Sunday*. And," he said triumphantly, "not only are we getting fifteen hundred quid for the story, I'm getting another five hundred and a picture credit for taking the photos. A return to the pages of the national press!"

"Well done you," she said and gave him a peck on the cheek.

The week drifted by. Mark and Trish prepared for another shoot party coffee table book but they were over the madness of the summer now and life at Visionary proceeded at a much more leisurely pace.

One evening, before it was dark, Mark found himself driving through Dersingham after going to his favourite butcher for his favourite sausages for breakfast the next day and realised he was driving past St Nicholas church. He pulled his car over and parked in front of the huge medieval tithe barn that in its day, and at this time of year, would have been stacked high with ten per cent of all the farm produce produced by the parish farmers—great and good and, indeed, the not so great and good.

He didn't know why he hadn't been before. He opened the church gate and went through the archway into the graveyard. It took him twenty minutes but in the end he found what he was looking for. A simple stone. "Here lies Nika Sidebottom," it said.

"What a life. What a tragic life," Mark said out loud. He couldn't begin to understand a mother's life never knowing what happened to her firstborn. Whether he was even alive? Where he was? Whether or not he was happy? Married? Mark thought she must have turned those questions over in her mind every single day. Did she punish herself at all, wondered Mark?

"You don't know me, Nika Sidebottom," said Mark to the grave, "but I've found Alfie and I'm going to bring him to see you."

Mark had called the journalist at the *Mail on Sunday* as soon as he got back to Norfolk. The journalist was more than delighted to be gifted the story.

He went away and dug around in the archives, got the background to the *Sandringham Murder Mystery* all written up and checked with Mark once or twice a day to make sure everything was in order. His colleague the crime correspondent confirmed with his police contacts that the file was indeed still open, but only in the sense that there had been no conclusion. It hadn't been looked at for more than sixty years.

All that was needed were the pictures of the reunion with Lauretta, some poignant shots at Keeper's Cottage and Nika Sidebottom's grave and the story was all but written save for a few quotes from Alfie to be extracted after the visit to his mother's grave.

Mark drove to East Midlands Airport to meet the Ryanair flight from Knock.

"Not arrested then?" he joked as Father and Son walked towards him through the arrivals hall.

"Not at all Mr Elwin," said John, smiling. "Two highly respectable Irish lawyers? Both with perfectly good passports. Now who'd be interested in them?"

In the car Mark filled them in on the dealings with the newspaper and the schedule for the trip, they chatted about the weather and generally filled the time with idle chatter but as soon as the 'Welcome to Norfolk. Nelson's County' sign was passed Alfie was in a world of his own. The world as it was in 1933.

He briefly came out of his reverie.

"I should also like to go Brancaster Staithe," he said. "I want to go to the little harbour there. Yes, to the little harbour Mr Elwin. Are there any fishing boats still there?"

"Two or three," said Mark.

"And the sailors' cottages?"

"Second homes or holiday lets but yes, they're still there."

"Wonderful," said Alfie and he drifted back to 1933.

"Don't expect too much," Mark said as they parked up at Lower Farm Care Home and walked towards reception.

"That's her room there," he said, pointing from the car park but there was no one inside. "She must be just finishing her dinner. I'll go and get her and bring her to her room. Then I'll come and get you."

"Whatever you think best Mr Elwin," said John as they arrived in reception.

Lower Farm Care Home had been told in advance of the extra visitors and Mrs Jenkins the senior nurse fussed over them and produced cups of tea for the two Irish men.

Mark found his grandmother at the dining table and caught her slipping some sachets of Coleman's English Mustard into her handbag. For one week only, she could keep them.

"Hello Lauretta," he said.

"Hello young man," she said.

"I'm going to push you back to your room, ok?"

"Yes," she said. "I'm finished here."

"And you've got two more visitors today."

"Two more?" she said.

"Yes, two more than me Lauretta. Two more than me." It was clear she thought Mark was just another member of the care home staff wheeling her about the place whenever she needed to be somewhere.

"Well, that'll be lovely," she said. "Who are they?"

"Why don't we just wait and see?"

"Alright," she said. And then "What's that you're carrying?"

"That's my camera, Lauretta," said Mark.

"What have you got a camera for?" she asked.

"Oh," he said, "I've got a camera because I'm a photographer."

"Are you now," she said and then her brief spark of interest died.

Back in her room, he positioned her with her back to the window so she wouldn't fall into staring out at the car park and he went to retrieve Alfie and John from reception.

"Are we ready?" he said.

"Does she know who we are, Mr Elwin?" asked Alfie.

"Not at all. Not at all. No point telling her anyway Mr Casey. She'd have forgotten what I'd said by the time I got here to reception," said Mark.

"Aye, it's a terrible thing," said the old man, "the one thing I've still got is all my marbles…before you say anything at all John!"

Mark went first and led the way.

"Lauretta," he said from the doorway.

She looked up.

"Yes," she said.

"I've got someone here to see you," said Mark.

"Who is it? Is it the doctor? I've told him there's nothing wrong with me. Tell him to go away and bother someone else."

"No, it's not the doctor," said Mark and he stepped inside her room and then to one side, by the bed. He lifted his camera to his eye.

The old man walked in.

His grandmother looked at him.

She looked hard at him and then frowned, raised her right hand and pointed a finger straight at him.

"Alfie Sidebottom," she said. "You are a very naughty boy!"

Chapter 47
Norfolk, Present Day

The next day Mark collected his guests from the pub where they also met up with the journalist from the *Mail on Sunday*.

The deal was Father and Son were left alone at each of the four destinations they'd planned on visiting, Keeper's Cottage, the old school house, the little harbour at Brancaster Staithe and finally his mother's grave at Dersingham Churchyard.

When the father had talked through his memories with his son then Mark and the *Mail on Sunday* man would join them, Mark to get pictures of the old man and the journalist to capture a few words on his smartphone.

It was a subdued day.

When they finally reached the church, even John Casey stood back and left his father alone. Mark opted for a long-distance shot from behind. When Alfie rejoined the rest of them there were tears in his eyes.

"I need to thank you again, Mr Elwin," he said. "This is a day I never thought I'd have, and I thank you for it."

Then he said "Enough. Enough for one day. I think it's back to the Rose and Crown now. I'm going to have a lie down before supper."

Father and Son did not want company that evening and so it was the following morning, Sunday, when Mark collected the men and took them to the airport to go home. There was a brief farewell at the drop-off zone.

"Thank you for what you did Mr Elwin," said John Casey, "This has meant so much to my father. So much to the whole family," and he added with a smile and a raised eye, "now that we've all got over the shock of it."

The story appeared in the *Mail on Sunday* the following week.

Mark got up early, walked half a dozen shops down from Visionary, bought three copies of the paper and went back to the flat where Emma was up and making a pot of coffee and sausage sandwiches.

They settled at the kitchen table where the file 'Find Alfie Sidebottom' had also been put.

"Why three copies?" asked Emma.

"One for us," he said handing it across the table, "one to send to Ireland," he said pulling his chair in a little, "and one to keep in as near pristine condition as we can, for the file."

The main story was some political scandal involving a backbench MP and forged expenses but above the headline was printed "Sandringham Royal Murder Mystery Solved After 80 Years." Then under that "*Mail on Sunday* Exclusive pages 12—13."

They opened the newspaper together and there it was spread over two pages, the same headline but with the by-line "Exclusive Photographs by Mark Elwin."

And then, under a picture of Mark himself, it was captioned "The sleuth photographer solves another case."

"Sleuth photographer, eh?" said Emma.

"That's me," smiled Mark.

"I hope you're not going to make a habit of this Mark Elwin," she said.

Chapter 48
Morecambe, Lancashire, Present Day

There was always entertainment at The Bay Independent Living development on a Saturday evening and the showing of the *Sound of Music* had been well received by the twenty or so residents who turned up.

The insistence on nostalgia at these Saturday screenings wasn't always to his taste, mind. He might be getting on but he wasn't brain dead and the sign at the gate to the complex did say Independent Living and not Slowly Dying from the Neck Up.

Nevertheless, he'd been at The Bay for the seven years since he gave up the farm and it still suited him.

He'd recently found companionship—'nothing more than that' he'd say if there was a cheeky eyebrow raised—with the widow Mrs Rosenbloom who'd moved into a first-floor apartment directly above him.

Together, they took in whatever cultural delights the Lancashire coast threw up and they made a ferociously competitive pair at weekly whist. They'd promised to treat themselves to one of those Beginners Bridge weekends advertised in the *Daily Telegraph,* separate rooms of course.

He'd moved to The Bay after turning 80 and the farm had become just too much for him to manage, especially since his beloved Mary had passed away so unexpectedly the year before.

As a couple, they hadn't been blessed with children but they had been blessed with many friends and the community of All Saints church where they had been the beating heart of the congregation for over 50 years.

The farm itself was rented from the Church of England and while it was just 300 acres it had provided them with a comfortable, if not a handsome, living over the years. The C of E benefitted not just from the rent always being paid on time but from a lifetime dedicated to the maintenance of All Saints, hedge trimming, door mending, and grass cutting.

Breakfast at The Bay was always a little later on a Sunday morning, an 8 o'clock start rather than seven-thirty, and he was there on the stroke of opening time at the on-site Bay View brasserie and bar. It was a little luxury of his not to make his own breakfast on Sundays.

Mrs Rosenbloom would not be joining him. Every other Sunday she was taken out for brunch by her daughter and her son-in-law, a successful dentist in nearby upmarket St Anne's.

Today was such a Sunday.

He was always first into breakfast as he had Churchwarden duties to perform at All Saints, opening up, firing up the ancient overhead electric heaters and laying out the trestle table for post-service cups of tea. Mrs Kendall would surely bring homemade biscuits as she had done every Sunday since what must have been the beginning of time.

Settling at his breakfast table a pretty waitress came over and he ordered his usual eggs and bacon, toast and tea.

He decided to treat himself after church, as he sometimes did, with a visit to that white monument to Art Deco beauty which was The Midland Hotel. He would have an early afternoon cocktail in the magnificent sweeping bar with views over the Irish Sea. If it was warm enough, he'd sit on the terrace and take in the awesomeness of nature before him, the huge and dangerous Morecambe Bay to the front and the rise of the hills and mountains of the Lake District to his right.

While he was waiting for his breakfast to arrive, he wandered over to the table where the complementary Bay View brasserie and bar Sunday newspapers were on offer.

Normally he'd take the news section and the sports section of the increasingly bulky *Sunday Times*, catch up on whatever was going on in the world and then turn to the football pages. This morning he was keen to read all about his beloved Norwich City who'd scored an unlikely away win at Manchester City the day before.

On this particular Sunday, for no real reason, he'd decided on something lighter and he scooped up the *Mail on Sunday* and took it back to his table just in time for the tray of eggs, bacon, tea and toast to be laid out before him.

He pushed his plate a little to his right to make room for the paper and after pouring his tea and adding a little milk, he turned to the front page. That's when he saw the banner above the headline for the lead story. "Sandringham Royal Murder Mystery Solved After 80 Years."

Slowly, he turned to the inside pages.

Twenty minutes later, the pretty waitress returned. Eggs, bacon, tea and toast were in place and untouched.

"Is everything alright, my lovely?" she asked in her slow Lancashire burr.

He looked up at her and then back to his newspaper which he then picked up, closed and folded in half exactly as it had been laid out on the complementary newspaper table. He put it down and placed the fingertips of eight fingers lightly on top of it as if to hold it gently in place.

"Is everything alright?" she asked again.

He looked out of the window at the sea.

"Is everything alright, Mr Sidebottom?" she asked again.

Looking out across the Irish Sea, he said simply, "I think so."

Printed in Great Britain
by Amazon